MASTERSON

Richard S. Wheeler

A TOM DOHERTY ASSOCIATES BOOK
NEW YORK

This is a work of fiction. All the characters and events portrayed in this book are either products of the author's imagination or are used fictitiously.

MASTERSON

Copyright © 1999 by Richard S. Wheeler

A Forge Book
Published by Tom Doherty Associates, LLC
175 Fifth Avenue
New York, NY 10010

www.tor.com

Forge® is a registered trademark of Tom Doherty Associates, LLC.

ISBN 0-812-56856-7

First edition: October 1999
First mass market edition: June 2000

Printed in the United States of America

0 9 8 7 6 5 4 3 2 1

Praise for Richard S. Wheeler

"Wheeler is among the two or three top living writers of Western historicals—if not the best. . . . Strong on character, and as factual as possible, of course, as it moves smartly along."   —*Kirkus Reviews* on *Masterson*

"All of the details and characters ring true. . . . The pacing of the novel is impeccable. He blends the various white and Indian cultures together into a believable world with never a false beat. *Dark Passage* is well worth reading."   —*The Missoulian*

"Wheeler is the author of some thirty works of fiction set in the American West. Yet it is in his books about the hard-rock mines when he is clearly in his element. *Sun Mountain* is no exception. . . . The historically accurate picture of Virginia City at its zenith makes *Sun Mountain* an excellent read."   —*The Denver Post*

"Richard Wheeler evokes a nightmare as he writes about the San Francisco earthquake of 1906 and its aftermath. . . . As one expects of Wheeler, his female characters are strong and complex. . . . His deft touch with both dialogue and narrative bring 1906 San Francisco and its inhabitants to vibrant life."
      —*Amarillo Globe-News* on *Aftershocks*

"Wheeler creates characters who never react or behave like clichés."   —*Booklist*

"Wheeler is a genius of structure and form."
      —*El Paso Herald-Post*

"Wheeler continues to be one of the best of the Western novelists/historians."   —*Salt Lake City Observer*

By Richard S. Wheeler
from Tom Doherty Associates

For Tim Cahill
with admiration

CHAPTER 1

Well, hell, I guess it all started this way. Louella wanted to meet me for dinner at Shanley's Grill after work. Shanley's was an odd choice, given her purposes, but maybe not so odd. Maybe she figured she would get a better story that way.

I could hardly land in my usual banquette before half the sports in New York joined me. I haven't eaten alone in a decade. If Louella wanted a private interview, she wasn't going to get it there. Maybe that would come later. This time she would probably just collect stories. She was a good mean reporter with the soul of a born gossip and the heart of a snake. I liked her.

I set out from the *Morning Telegraph* about six-thirty, having wound up my column and turned it over to the copy editors, who would interrupt their nonstop penny-ante poker game long enough to eyeball it. They rarely changed a word, especially when the pot was fat. I stepped into a dank November chill that sent forebodings through me. The air smelled of winter and death. Maybe my own, which is why Louella was stalking me.

When I was younger, the hike from the paper, on Fiftieth Street and Eighth Avenue, down to Shanley's, on Broadway and Forty-third, was nothing. But time has slowed me and sometimes I felt the reproach of that ancient bullet wound in my leg, giving my stride the slightest halt.

Hell yes, death. That's what this was all about. There had been more than usual of it the last few years; the Great War had cut holes in the ranks of fathers and brothers and sons, and then the Spanish flu had massacred whole neighborhoods.

Death was not new to me. I could smell it and I could sense it and I could foretell it. Mine was around the corner, but I paid it no heed. I regretted nothing. But what Louella said made sense: it was time to put my yarns down on paper. Little did I imagine, at that moment, what fate held in store or what her request would do to me.

I wrestled with the idea at first. But what finally persuaded me was the chance to set the record straight and cut through all the hokum that the dime novelists and assorted jackasses had piled over the real man like a heap of manure. Buntline was long dead, but his invention lived on. In truth, I thrived on that crap, and maybe it had even saved my life a few times, which was why I rarely set out the facts. But maybe I would now.

I was of two minds about it. Some cynical part of me whispered that even if I gave her the straight of it, she would sensationalize it like all the rest. Well, hell, I'd go find out.

I walked slowly over to Broadway and then down to Shanley's in the twilight, feeling my heart labor. The city's lights abolished weather and night, and its crowded sidewalks abolished memories, especially of the lonely prairies. I wondered whether I could dredge up one true thing, one plain and unadorned fact for my very junior associate at the *Telegraph,* Miss Louella Parsons, editor of the motion picture news and stalker of the notorious. My memory had shrunk even

as my waistline had expanded, my neck and face along
with it, and I considered both battles lost.

For a man of five feet and eight, that extra fifty
pounds looked like pure bloat, and I had to haul every
ounce of it. I had always prided myself on being trim
and fit, and in the old days my life depended on it.
But now I despaired before every looking glass and
the weight on my legs and back did nothing to improve my comfort or my mood. The deeds ascribed to
me by yellow-jacket dime novelists had produced a
mental corpulence as puffy as my old carcass.

Hell, if Louella discovered the truth about my alleged bloodstained, body-strewn life as a lawman, she
might just put the cap on her Parker fountain pen and
smile that twisted smile of hers and find herself someone a bit more gaudy to gossip about.

I scorned coats, even though people kept telling me
I would catch pneumonia, but I always wore my
broad-brimmed light gray fedora, which served as umbrella, sun-shade, and skull-warmer. If Louella had
seen me in my earlier days, even as late as when I
was managing that emporium in Creede, she would
have marveled at my gaudy dress. I was wearing
lavender corduroy back then, which matched my
gaudy mind; not the somber dark suit they would
probably bury me in now.

That Masterson and this Masterson were still the
same man; only the times had changed. That Masterson was always armed. This one hadn't kept a revolver
on his person since he had gotten into trouble for pack-
ing one.

I use another weapon these days: my pen. Words
make better bullets. There's an Underwood on my
desk, and I can hammer it with my two trigger fingers,

but I prefer to scribble my columns. I shoot words now and hit whatever I want to hit, without aiming. I am better with words than I ever was with a revolver.

I have no use for the West, hate the damn place, and that goes double for that two-bit city of Denver. New York is my city and my home, and has been for many years. The youthful Bartholomew—that's how I was christened and how Bat got hung on me—might have bridled at it, but an old man revels in it. I like all those people who pass me by, the gals painted up and unafraid of anything on earth, with skirts up to their knees, the gents slick and sharp. I like the street-cars, with their acrid odors and the trolleys that pull down electricity from the overhead wires. Every time they scrape across some junction overhead those wands arc and pop like a revolver, and I dive for the nearest doorway.

Hell, I even like the rancid steam that boils up from the grilles in the streets, the busy cough of the motor-cars, and especially the electrical lights everywhere. They are magic. I never heard of an old man who didn't like electrical lights. Cities are light. The wilderness is dark. Just ask an old buffalo skinner who peeled hides for months on end where there were no lights and no heat. And in the cities are women. There sure as hell were no women out on the plains of Kansas.

That's my humor these days, you see. It is not anything Louella would understand. She's the youngest black widow spider in the gossip business. She will ask me about all that, and I'll tell her nothing. Gents don't talk about their women. And I can't remember the half of them anyway. Hell, if I started talking about my women, it'd take a week. She'll persist, and try to find out on the sly, and I'll just tell her to get the movie actors to blab, because I won't. It would hurt Emma. She's been my wife, sort of, for decades. When she came to Denver to play at the Palace, which I owned, she moved in permanently. For years before that she had been one of my temporaries. I am fond of her. We live separate lives, which is good, because we bicker.

I arrived at Shanley's a little winded, and was rewarded by a pearly glow of light from the milk-glass fixtures, the babble of voices, the redolent fog of tobacco, the fine musk of good flank-cut steak, the dark oiled wainscoting, and buxom Louella perched primly in my banquette, along with that kid, Runyon, who's all right even if he's got everything all wrong. I predict a bad end for him.

They were two martinis ahead of me, drinking their hearts out, well aware that the curtain was descending and soon not a one of us would be able to buy a damned drop of booze.

The theatergoers had filled the place and were sawing at beef, but Shanley's knew enough not to surrender Masterson's banquette to some pipefitter from Hoboken.

"Miss Parsons, Mr. Runyon," I said, sliding across brown leather to settle beside Louella. I separated my fedora from my balding head and felt naked.

"I brought Damon. He wants to hear all this stuff too."

"The real stuff, Bat," Damon said.

"The real stuff," I said, nodding to Gregorio, who hastened to provision me. "Before I cash in."

"You planning on it?"

"Hell yes," I replied. "You both going to write this up, or what?"

"He's along for the ride," she said.

"I don't talk before I eat," I said.

I usually saved my drinking until later, and invariably at the Metropole Hotel's bar, a block south. That was the only place on earth to do any serious drinking. But I never noticed the spirits; they had no effect on me except to relax me a little and drive a few aches into their gopher holes.

Miss Parsons and Mr. Runyon ordered a third round. Gregorio laid a Waldorf salad and seltzer lemonade before me, and I assuaged my belly, scarcely noticing my dinner companions. Food and drink and brag are the best entertainments left to old men.

I was too busy eating to talk, so Louella did. "Here's what I'm going to do. I'm going to take notes. Stuff for the column. Maybe a feature article or two. Maybe I'll write a book some day. But all I'll promise is a great obit."

I laughed. That doll had a quirky way that reminded me of the broads out West.

"Okay, kid," I said. "What do you want to know?"

"The stories. The stuff you tell the guys."

"You'll need to pump me full of booze for that. It takes three whiskey sours."

She puckered up. "Here, dammit," she said. She yanked a big manila envelope from an enormous handbag, and sprayed yellowed clippings across the linen. "I got most of this from our morgue. Damon got a bunch more. You've sure spilled a lot of ink, Bat."

There, on the table, lay a fat legend. I nodded.

"Is this stuff true?" she asked.

"Like what?"

"Have you killed twenty-six men? Have you been charged with first-degree murder four times? Did you shoot down seven cowboys and bring their heads in a sack back to Dodge City? Have you owned cathouses?"

I laughed. This was going to be choice.

CHAPTER 2

I studied those clippings for a moment. I was familiar with all of them. Some were reprints from various papers around the country. I spotted the old *New York Sun* story, with its headline: "A MILD-EYED MAN WHO HAS KILLED TWENTY-SIX PERSONS." And that other chestnut, published by the *Kansas City Journal*, bearing the title "BAT'S BULLETS." And that marvel that burped out of Leoti, Kansas, which proclaimed that I had killed a man on each of my birthdays. And some sort of typescript copied from Cy Warman's book, proclaiming that my hands were red with blood and I'd killed no less than twenty men.

"Fiction," I said.

Louella looked a bit disappointed.

The theater crowd ditched Shanley's for their orchestra seats and temporarily the grill turned quiet and serene, a weeknight intermezzo. Blue cigar smoke drifted past the milk-glass globes. I like the smell of cigars. I was getting itchy to repair to the Metropole Bar and do some drinking with old friends there, but I had promised Louella an interview, as many as she wanted, so I sat quietly, nursing a big dry patch on my throat. God only knows what I'll be feeling in a few months when the saloons close and the damn Eighteenth Amendment takes over.

I'll have to say this for Louella Parsons: she's a hell of a fine campaigner, and having started to collect all the dubious strands of William Barclay Masterson's life on paper, she wouldn't give up. Hell, she could find a nude girl in Fatty Arbuckle's closet just by asking around, and I knew she would find a few items in mine.

"All right, dammit," she said. "There's other leads for a Masterson story. Who's the greatest gunfighter of them all? You?"

I always bridled at that word, gunfighter, but I hid all that behind a stare. "I am not a gunfighter and never have been," I replied. "Why would I stand around being a target?"

She looked annoyed so I relented.

"Wyatt Earp," I said. "Hell, there's no one even remotely like him. He runs icewater in his plumbing. He is absolutely deadly, and calm under fire. He'll stand there and let suckers try to murder him. He knows a revolver's useless unless it's aimed carefully, so he aims it and doesn't worry about getting off the first shot. He's fearless and can think and act under pressures that turn other men to blubber. He puts the bullet where he wants it, from the waist, without aiming. He's cautious and realistic and his mind's one jump ahead of everyone else's. When he's on the warpath, his target is as good as dead. He's in a class by himself."

She scribbled something and then lobbed another. "Well, what about Doc Holliday?"

"A man who could use a short gun effectively. I never liked him, but he had his virtues. He could be affectionate, and had a dry wit, but he also had an evil temper. Hell, you never knew what would set him off."

"Sure, but who was the better gunman, you or him?"

I sighed. "I'm not a gunman. Holliday could draw and shoot a man between the eyeballs before anyone knew there was a quarrel. He was formidable. I felt sorry for him, in a way. He was living out a death sentence, you know. Consumption."

"Sure, but what about you?" Runyon broke in. "Cut the modesty, Bat."

I stared at him a moment too long. I wasn't sure I liked that brash young scribbler. "I have never been a gunfighter," I repeated.

"You're the greatest of them all," Louella said, seeing another of her leads sail into space.

"I am very good with short and long firearms," I said. "Is that enough?"

"No."

I sighed, thinking back over the years as a sheriff, undersheriff, deputy city marshal, United States marshal, and city marshal in places like Dodge City, Trinidad, Denver—and New York. "I don't like to kill, so I don't. I have spent my entire career as a lawman trying not to kill. I succeeded."

She pounced on the *New York Sun* story. I had read it many times and simply smiled when she thrust it at me. Then she whipped out the Kansas City *Journal* item. I was familiar with that one, too. It ended up,

Whether he has killed his twenty-six men as is popularly asserted, cannot be positively ascertained without careful and extensive research, for he is himself quite reticent on the subject. But

that many men have fallen by his deadly revolver
and rifle is an established fact, and he furnishes
a rare illustration of the fact that the thrilling stories of life on the frontier are not always over-
drawn.

"Are these true?" she asked.

"No, but it amuses me that people believe that
stuff."

Real consternation bloomed in Louella's sullen
face. "What the hell am I going to write about?"

"The true Masterson."

She grunted.

"Why the modesty, Bat?" Runyon asked.

I ignored my growing distaste for him. "So write a
novel," I said.

Louella wasn't giving up. "I read all this stuff that
says you're the best-known man between Chicago and
San Francisco. Why do they call you 'Colonel' Masterson? Why is it that you can walk into a saloon and
the hoods slip out the back door? Why are you a friend
of William Pinkerton? Why did Teddy Roosevelt and
you correspond? Why is it that I can talk to any Hollywood director, like John Ford, and he knows who
you are and talks in sort of hushed tones about you?
Or Harry Carey or William Hart or Tom Mix? Tell
me that, W. B."

I sort of liked the W. B. No one had called me that
before.

"I was good at enforcing the law," I said. "Good
enough so that I could never get reelected. I got to be
sheriff of Ford County—that's in Kansas—by three
votes. Next time around, I got half the votes of my
opponent, Hinkle. After a few of those I quit running."
I smiled.

"I don't get it," Runyon said.

"You wouldn't," I said.

They had asked the standard questions, the usual nonsense. I had dodged questions like these more times than I could remember. No one had ever asked me the right questions; no one had ever plumbed the real Bat Masterson. Hell, that was all right with me. The Masterson legend might survive, but I would rest in peace. I had told them what's what. Louella sighed, stared into the haze, and began to squirm. A good sign.

They shoved some scraps of beef around Shanley's blue-trimmed porcelain, pronounced their exit lines, and beat a retreat. They were looking for a complicated killer named Bat Masterson. I am a simple man. They were going to huddle somewhere and figure if old Masterson was simply tidying up his history before he croaked—in which case he was a purveyor of the horse apple—or whether there never was a story in the first place. If Louella came back for more, I'd tell her more about the real Masterson, but I didn't expect it.

I had done all this before. I told skinny reporters and fat editors and retired detectives from Carson City to San Diego the same thing: no bodies, not a gunfighter, and they just tucked away their lead pencils, quit buying me drinks, and vanished. Some day, some good reporter would ask the next question: Okay, Bat, tell me the real story.

Maybe Louella would. I'd give her a raise if she did. Officially, that wasn't my province, but the secretary and vice president of a newspaper can make things happen. I didn't own the *Morning Telegraph*, but my stamp was on it.

I would drift down the street in a moment. But I was enjoying the lull at Shanley's, and the medium-done steak rested comfortably in my belly, and if I walked into the Metropole Bar I wouldn't have the moment I wanted, which was to remember the old days—if I could. In the middle of a comfortable New York grill, with electrical lights and steam heat, and automobiles honking outside, and punk kids rambling from booth to booth hawking discount tickets for shows that had just started, how could I remember what it was like back then?

I could remember the blackness of the nights out there, when there was no electricity and no one had heard of electrical bulbs or stringing wires around. I could remember sleeping cold, so cold that no bedroll or dozen bedrolls would keep me from shaking. I could remember the stars. I hardly see stars in the city. Hell, in Manhattan you don't know stars exist. I could remember the wind and how it blew through the cracks in the plank buildings of those cow towns, and made the lamps flicker, and jammed crystals of snow under the door and through the windows and even on top of the blankets.

I knew I shouldn't be impatient with those kids. City slickers, just like me. How could they know anything, anyway? This was their world, comfortable and safe and happy. How could they know the other one? There wasn't any frontier now. No cow towns, either. No badmen, no randy and rowdy Texas cowboys half crazy for booze and women and music after months on a hard cold trail, men I enjoyed and drank with—except when they got crazy. It wasn't just that forty or fifty years had elapsed; it was that a curtain had fallen that separated those times from this one.

I signed the tab, left a generous tip for Gregorio, and lumbered to my feet. I was occupying a strange body, one I no longer liked much. I had always liked my body. They used to say it was perfectly formed, or they'd say it was compact, or they'd say it was hefty or blocky, stuff like that. Now my flesh was a stranger to me, sometimes alarming and always grudging. The diabetes made me nauseous and weak, and the damned diet, which I did my best to ignore, irritated me.

I clamped my fedora over my monkish bald spot and worked my way out and onto the restless street. Even now, after two decades in New York, I marveled at the unending crowds on the pavement. The Metropole was just a block away, at Forty-second, enough steps to settle my dinner, and I repaired there, just as I had done for years and decades. The place was run by the Considines, sons of a gambling friend of mine.

There, in its oddly gloomy confines, were my friends, and there I stopped every night to swill drinks and argue about Jack Dempsey and get tips on nags. The Metropole hosted fight promoters such as my pal Tex Rickard, cops like Val O'Farrell, sports and gamblers, men who remembered every swing in every bare-knuckle brawl ever fought.

The Metropole was home to assorted slugs without visible means of support, all of them with monickers like "The Two-by-Six Kid." I'd followed the fight for years, and refereed every time I could, and when I didn't do that, I'd seconded fighters, a long string of them out West. I settled into a booth with Tom O'Rourke and Bill Muldoon, and in moments one of the Considine boys—their pa had been a Seattle tinhorn—served up a sour.

I looked at that damned drink and thought, God, I won't be able to get one of these pretty soon. They're going to shut down the whole shebang. I lifted it and drank, as if it was communion wine, which it was, after a fashion.

.It was going to be a Manassa Mauler night again. O'Rourke was dilating on the prowess of Dempsey, who had become world heavyweight champ in July after decking Jess Willard in three rounds, at Toledo. No one had ever seen his like, and the man regularly excited several hundred thousand utterances in the Metropole every night. Dempsey was a westerner, so I understood him. It was said he got his start as a bouncer in a Nevada whorehouse, and I liked that, too. But best of all, he was pure brute, sailing right in, bobbing around, pounding his opponents into pulp with short rights so fast I could hardly see them. He was one mean son of a bitch, the kind we grew out there in the wild country, sort of like me, except that I'm meaner.

"So you're late," said Tom.

"I got a pair of reporters trying to tell lies about me," I replied. "I got grilled at the grill."

"Was it twenty-six you killed, or forty?"

"For you, Tom, I'll confess to a hundred seventy-one."

I drank my sour and beckoned the barkeep. "Bring me a double," I said.

That's how my life was. I couldn't escape the mythology even when I wanted to, and Miss Parsons wasn't going to help me.

CHAPTER 3

I quit the Metropole after midnight, as usual, and decided to catch a hack down to my apartment off Madison Square. I would probably beat Emma home. She was as much a night owl as I, and had her own circle of Broadway pals. She had been a song-and-dance gal when I met her, and now she spent evenings backstage with friends in the variety and vaudeville theaters, usually Florenz Ziegfeld's Follies, ending up with a midnight snack after each show.

The managements had accepted her as seamstress and mother confessor for the girls, and an unpaid and savvy stagehand who had more than once rescued a performance from calamity. She loved that life, and I loved my sporting life, and somehow everything had worked out, but not until some stormy times had faded.

There was always a hack waiting at the Metropole, and I clambered in. I used to walk home, afraid of nothing, but now my diabetes had weakened my pins and I was no longer a match for footpads. It had been inevitable that we would settle close to Madison Square Garden, where a boxing arena had been operating since 1890. I could walk a couple of blocks to any fight worth watching.

My sporting friends at the paper and the Metropole scarcely knew Emma, which suited me fine. She had kept her statuesque blond beauty, remained slim, and looked much younger than me, though she was only four years my junior. I never gazed at her but that I felt a wild rush of delight in her statuesque elegance.

She had learned to accept my long absences, when I followed the fights, my occasional disappearances, and—earlier—a little cheating. Her devotion had triumphed: she outlasted my temptations, and the flings with other women had vanished when I finally learned what a twenty-four-karat doll I had in my apartment. And even now, sometimes, we coupled more for the tender communion of our bond than for any sensations of the flesh. She had always been an avid lover and I don't recollect a single headache.

I paid the hack driver and climbed the two flights, puffing my way up, and found she had beaten me home this night and had readied our bedtime ritual, a snifter of brandy for a nightcap. I had laid in a couple extra bottles, dreading the passage of Prohibition, a reform that would destroy everything I stood for, every pleasure in my life. But it wouldn't do any good. It was enough to make a man want to ditch the country.

She kissed me and set my snifter before me at the kitchen table. It was during these moments that we shared the day.

"Florenz is gonna redo the show," she said. "Less vaudeville, more showgirls and tight costumes. You should see the outfits. The girls are gonna catch cold!"

"I guess I'd better come see," I said. "I'm a good judge of horseflesh."

She smiled.

I always had a pocketful of "Annie Oakleys"—free passes pressed on me by every troupe in town. But I wouldn't need any if she were at the stage door to let me in.

"They started writing my obituary tonight," I said.

"They've been doing that for thirty years," she retorted. "Who?"

"Couple of kids, Louella Parsons, our film editor, and that sportswriter for the *American,* Runyon."

"He's no kid, Bat. Thirties, somewhere."

"Well, you know what I mean."

"Why now?"

"Hell, I guess they figure I'm going to croak."

She smiled wryly. "You could take off some weight," she said.

That was a bone of contention. Harry Gross, my doctor, had been telling me to lose weight but I wasn't much for following a diet. I had hardening of the arteries as a result of the diabetes, and he had told me flatly that most of the sand had run through my hourglass. He was pretty solemn about it.

"Bat, if you have any loose ends to tie up, now's the time to tie them up," the sonofabitch had said.

I had ignored him.

"I told Louella I'm the product of a bunch of dime novelists. I told her I didn't shoot anyone if I could help it. I told her I wasn't a gunman and if she wanted to do stories about Wild West gunmen, she should go talk to Wyatt out in L.A., or write up Holliday. Hell, my entire peace officer career lasted a decade, except for a few special assignments. But I've lived a whole life since the mid-eighties, and yet the dime novelists never touch *that* William B. Masterson."

She sipped and shrugged. "I like the legend, Big Bad Bat."

"That's my Emma. I probably should have filled Louella full of bunk. Fess up to a dozen more corpses not in the official count. Deathbed confession."

I watched that wry smile lift the corners of her lovely lips.

"What are you gonna do?"

"Let it ride. I don't think Louella'll come back to the well again."

"You're not happy," she said, catching something in my face.

I sighed. She had a way of plumbing my depths. "Em, I like the legend. I remember when I was managing the Denver Exchange in Creede, in 'ninety-two, last of the big boomtowns, and I was no kid. That was a saloon and dance hall and gambling emporium, and all I had to do was stroll through there and things stayed quiet. The lid never blew off the way it always did in camps like that. I liked that. 'Here comes Masterson,' they'd say, and behaved themselves."

"It wasn't a legend, Bat," she said.

"That's where I have trouble with it. Part of it's real. I could always deal with troublemakers, even the human rattlers."

"No legend," she whispered.

"Those dead men, the notches in the gun, those are a legend. I told Louella they didn't happen."

She eyed me reproachfully and tossed off the brandy. I don't know how the hell she does that. I have to sip it.

"Well, love, you're a famous man—in some circles. Notorious in other circles. Everybody in the country knows Bat Masterson. If you're worried about how you'll be remembered, you still have a choice." She paused. "But that's the heart of it, isn't it? You don't know what you want. If you ask me, I think you should write down what you know is true—just because it's true. Getting it right is reason enough."

I nodded. In my mind I saw myself walking into a western saloon, just as I had done thousands of times, walking with a badge on my shirt, watching the place quiet, watching the braggarts down their drinks and slither out into the night.

And I had always liked the big halloo from the barkeeps, who hated trouble because it cost them money, and the crooked grins of a thousand Texas cowboys just off the trail, blowing off six months' wages and all the lust that had built in their young lean woman-starved bodies after months on the trail herding the longhorns north to the rails.

I liked those boys even if they were powderkegs when they arrived at Dodge. I liked them even when one ranny or another wanted to tree the town, shoot out the windows. Even when I had to approach one of those drink-crazed boys and lay the barrel of my Colt's over his skull to settle him down.

I laid that barrel over plenty of thick Texas craniums and there were plenty who hated me for it, including some steel-hard ranchers like Clay Allison. I wounded a few because I shot for the hand, the arm, the leg— never the head or gut or heart if I could help it. But I didn't always have a choice. Things happened fast. Funny where reputations come from. I never in my long life sought one, and yet one settled on my shoulders, light and ephemeral but real. There goes Masterson, and watch out!

Emma was right. Before Louella Parsons or Damon Runyon got hold of me, I had to make up my own mind. Did I want to leave behind me the dime-novel legend or the real man? Odd how that simple question made me squirm. Wild Bill Hickok, Wyatt and Virgil Earp, Buffalo Bill Cody, Billy the Kid, Doc Holliday, Pat Garrett . . . and someone called Masterson who wasn't me.

She plucked up our snifters and set them in the zinc sink, her gesture of surrender to Morpheus. She smiled, invitingly, because she had always been a flirt, and headed into the darkness of the hall. I thought I'd follow, but I didn't. Instead, I drifted into the darkened parlor and watched the night from the window, looking at the electrical street lamps at the intersections, looking at the white vapor eddying from a thousand chimneys and pipes. New York never slept.

My legs hurt again. The old-age diabetes made them cold. I pull wool stockings on my feet these days because I sleep better when my toes aren't so icy. Emma makes a joke of them. Don't you touch me with those bare feet, she'd say, and then hug me anyway while I ran bare feet up her calf just to be mean. She is some woman.

I was tired. I don't weather as well as I used to. I tried to remember Dodge, and Trinidad, and Pueblo, and Tombstone, and Creede, and I couldn't. I could remember Kansas City and Denver because they were big, warm, comfortable places like New York. But Dodge hadn't been comfortable ten days of the year, with the wind sailing through those thin plank walls, and black night in every direction, and empty spaces, unsettled and waiting for the plow, and no trees. And danger. I thrived on it. The frontier was dull; nothing ever made it entertaining except danger, which is maybe why so many of us hunted it down.

Had it been a good life? I tried to answer that one, and couldn't. I couldn't say for sure whether I had done anything of note, or had just existed the way most people do. I had no answers there in the dark but I did know suddenly that all this was important—the most important thing left for me to do, except maybe strangle everyone who enacted the Volstead Act.

Some people live unexamined lives. They simply exist and never wonder how they did, or what they still could do, or whether they had contributed anything. They live and die without taking a close look at themselves. I might have been like that once, but age changes a person.

And now this. Louella Parsons had started something far more important to me than she or I had realized. I knew, sitting there, that I wanted to examine my entire life. Time was running out. Before I died, I wanted to come to some conclusions about Masterson. Not until I did that could I die in peace. In all my life I had never felt a deeper need.

I quit and headed for bed. Even if Emma were sound asleep, she would throw an arm over me and nestle into my shoulder, and I liked that. There aren't many pleasures left to a man whose carcass is falling apart, but that was prime.

I'd stop by Miss Parsons's desk in the morning, the beggar with hat in hand, and I'd say something like this: "Louella, you can write up the damn legend if you want—dozens of articles and a few books to help you, and even some pieces I wrote. Or you can let me try to tell you how it was out there. I'm not sure you'll understand. You have to live the frontier to understand it. But if you want, I'll tell you the real story of Bat Masterson and you can write it up."

I halfway hoped that Louella Parsons would be more interested in writing up moving picture actors like Mabel Normand or Ben Turpin or Mary Pickford.

Hell, I didn't belong to these times.

CHAPTER 4

T he next forenoon, while I slumped over my desk trying to do a column when nothing came to mind, my gaze kept returning to Miss Parsons, over in the corner, the receiver of the Bell telephone cemented to her ear, making the *Morning Telegraph* the best purveyor of celebrity news in New York. That's what worried me. If I wanted to set the record straight, Louella Parsons was the last person I should be dealing with.

There has always been a part of me hidden from the world, a part that considers good and evil and reaches toward duty and rightness, no matter how I might be hurt by it. I knew I should correct the exaggerations, spike the nonsense, and give the world a much-diminished Masterson; a sportswriter soon forgotten. I liked truth.

I waited until my biographer finally clamped the receiver into its cradle and then I approached her desk.

"Louella, are you still thinking about doing my story?" I asked.

"Well," she said, "I might, after a while. But William Hart's coming East soon, and I've got Ethel Barrymore lined up for an interview, and—"

"That's fine," I said, relieved. "I might write up a few notes for posterity, just to put things right."

"No, don't do that. Give me the chance!"

"To do what?"

"The stuff about you. Not just for my column. I'm going to write some features."

"Which Masterson, Louella?"

"Huh?"

"The real one or the legend? I'm going to tell you about the real one and I'm going to tear that legend to pieces. Now, listen, doll. This is important. I'll tell you what this is all about. It's about a man wrestling with his own legend."

I saw doubt flare in her eyes. I had known the broad several years, and fathomed some things about her that I don't think she even knew about herself. She came alive in the company of any celebrity, and turned into a virtual wallflower alone. It was almost as if she had no self and had to find it in the success of others. Given a free rein, she would write of a Masterson more notorious than even the bloody-handed monster of the sensational press.

She surprised me. "Shanley's at six?"

I agreed. But I did not see much future in the arrangement.

I beat her there, ordered a seltzer lemonade and chased away a couple of pals, telling them that I was going to do some business.

She blew in out of the November rain, showered me with the drip from her umbrella, and settled in for some martinis. That was her ritual; I had mine. In a few minutes we would negotiate. If she did it my way, I'd cooperate; if not, she could rehash all the pulp fiction that mentioned Masterson, but not with my help.

"Here's the deal," she said. "I want to do a few pieces, and there's only one thing I want to cover. Dodge."

"Dodge!"

"Yeah, you told me that was where it all happened. That was just a few years in a long life. You're a gambler, you're a sportsman, you referee fights, you write columns. You've run variety theaters, dance halls, saloons, and gambling parlors. You've had a thousand women." She beamed at me, as if she had just scored some sort of coup. "But I want Dodge. That's what the whole country wants. Dodge."

I laughed. "Dodge. You're a dodge-drafter."

"Dodge. From about eighteen-seventy-five or 'six, until you left for the last time."

"Lawman stuff. Gunfighter stuff."

"You betcha."

"There will be terms and conditions to this deal. Are you willing?"

"Spill it."

"Truth."

She waited for more, sipped her booze and surrendered. "That's it?"

"Truth."

"A little garnish? A little praise? A little exaggeration?"

"I'm too old for that crap."

"Dodge and Truth." She hoisted her glass, and I hoisted mine, and we toasted the compact.

The uncanny Gregorio reprovisioned us, laid out the Waldorfs, and hovered just out of earshot.

She wasn't ready for her Waldorf. She wanted to down a few first. I admit my notions are eccentric. Normal people drink a few and then chow down. She was normal. Sort of. Lady gossip reporters who peek through cracks in the bedroom shades are a breed unto themselves.

"Who were your women in Dodge?" she asked.

I laughed. "Save it for the movie actors."

She shrugged. "Okay, William B. Masterson's in Dodge City, Kansas, about eighteen-seventy-six. I'll take notes."

"Make it eighteen-seventy-eight," I said. "That was the year everything happened."

"Like what?"

"I guess I'd better set the stage. You're a generation removed from even the last of the frontier. Here we are, off Times Square, in the heart of New York, and I somehow have to transport you back to a different world."

"Is it so hard, Bat?"

I wondered how to tell a city broad writing about motion picture actors how it was. A city gal surrounded by electrical lights, automobiles and trucks, streetcars, big hospitals, paved streets, telephones, ocean liners—what would a broad like her know?

"There was nothing there," I said. "*Nothing.* Empty prairies, mostly flat but plenty of hilly areas. Indians, cabins made of sod, not a tree anywhere. The whole town of Dodge was built of wood imported on the Atchison, Topeka, and Santa Fe. Where the hell was a tree? Every fire in Dodge was fueled by cordwood brought in by the railroad. The place started as a supply camp for buffalo hunters, the place to bring in the flint hides, sell them, spend the cash to reprovision, and blow the rest having a good time in the saloons."

"And cathouses."

I laughed. Louella was sharp, and I wasn't going to have to veil this story behind polite gauze.

"I was there then, working for the best of the buffalo hunters, Tom Nixon; dirty bloody filthy work, skinning those monsters, watching the bugs squirm, and cutting out buffalo tongues to ship east. Dangerous work. Indians didn't like it and wiped out hunting camps everywhere. Rivals murdered each other and stole the hides. Snakes, freeze-ups, starvation, thirst, sickness, exposure killed a bunch more. That was my apprenticeship."

"What were the hides good for?"

"Not much good for shoe leather, but plenty good for leather belts to run machinery; for carriage robes, army greatcoats. And the tongues are a delicacy. So rough old Dodge did its trade, mostly from board-and-batten shacks, tent saloons, earthen huts."

"It seems impossible that you did that. Look at you now."

"Hell yes, look at me. The mark's on me. Scars. Bullet hole in my leg. Eyes with the color bleached out by the harsh sun. That was something you've never seen, sun like that, glaring down on you until you couldn't stand to look at the world."

She scribbled a note or two, but mostly she just listened. She was waiting for the good stuff about guns and outlaws and keeping the lid on Dodge City, but I wasn't in any hurry to tell her all that.

I knew it wouldn't do much good. She'd begin her articles with some lead or other about the town that had a man for breakfast. She'd write what she had to write, and I'd tell my story the way I wanted to tell it, and that's how history ends up.

"I'll tell you something else, Louella. Any man who's hunted buffalo knows all about death. Fast death, slow death, vital organs, carcass eaters, bugs, worms, stink, puke."

Her gaze was wandering. She was taking in the guests at Shanley's preparing to table-hop and pick up a quick story if someone like Lionel Barrymore wandered in.

I sliced my medallions of beef into wafers so I could

talk and eat at the same time, and doggedly returned to my story. No one ever accused Bat Masterson of a lack of determination.

"In eighteen-seventy-eight I was the Ford County sheriff. My brother Ed was the city marshal—until April. Wyatt Earp came in and became an assistant city marshal. Luke Short, the gambler, was dealing at the Long Branch. Doc Holliday—whose reputation has been slimed up by the yellowback novelists— came in to practice dentistry and ended up dealing faro.

"We were all there. People whose names you know, and whose reputations you think you know, but not a one of us resembled what we were made out to be by packs of scribblers who traffic in lies."

She stared, blankly, a smile pasted on her face.

To hell with her, I thought.

CHAPTER 5

For several days Miss Parsons busied herself with interviews and gossip, and I supposed the project was decently buried. All she would talk about was the new John Gilbert, Mary Pickford film, *Heart o' the Hills.* That suited me fine. I'd had misgivings all along, and I was glad things had come to a halt before we were one reel into my picture.

But then, on a Friday afternoon, she braced me.

"How about you and me have dinner at Shanley's?" she asked.

"I'm married."

"You know what I mean, my features."

"Forget the damned features. I'm heading for the Metropole tonight. Good beef there, too, and all the sports in town."

"How about dealing me in?"

I smiled. The Metropole Bar was a male stronghold, but women weren't excluded so long as they were escorted. The Considine boys threw out unattached dolls, but if one came in on the arm of a sport, that was okay. It didn't matter what sort of babe she might be—drunks, floozies, kept ladies, all needed an escort at the Metropole. I assented.

"We won't be talking about Masterson much," I warned. "And you'll get tired of uppercuts and low blows and five-ounce gloves and ten-grand purses."

"I'll be at the Metropole door at five-fifteen."

Straight from work. She knew how to spend a Friday night.

She was waiting for me at the door, staying just out of the mist. I escorted her in, smack into layers of cigar smoke. Unlike Shanley's the Metropole was dark, with a row of triple-globe fixtures casting liverish light over the noisy confines. The Considines eyed her from behind their massive mahogany bar. So did fifty sports, half of them figuring I had got me a dish on the side. I planned to cool off that notion.

I steered her into a booth, and she settled beside Runyon. Irvin Cobb—formerly one of our *Telegraph* guys and now a rewrite man on the *World*—and Tex Rickard occupied the other side of the booth. Good company.

George "Tex" Rickard was a legend. He'd won and lost a dozen fortunes in Alaska, finally winning big in Nome. He'd operated the famous Northern Saloon in Goldfield, Nevada, and made another fortune peddling

booze and raking profits off the gambling tables. Goldfield was where he had staged his first fight, between
Battling Nelson and Joe Gans, and cleaned up. I always felt good just sitting in the same booth with him.

"You know Louella," I said. "She's been meeting
with me in dark corners and odd hours to share our
mutual passion."

"Boxing?" asked Rickard.

"Me," I replied.

Louella smiled primly. She was actually something
of a puritan, which was one reason she dug up dirt
and kept company with racy people.

"Well, what have you found out so far?" Cobb
asked, squinting through the smoke. I often wondered
what Cobb would look like in real sunlight. Like the
soft white belly of a mackerel, maybe.

"Nothing. I can't get him to open up. Maybe you
guys will give me the can opener. He's worse than
Lionel Barrymore."

"Bat's a modest man," said Runyon. "He'll praise
others but he won't talk about himself."

"Louella, you ever read Bat's pieces in *Human Life*
about the old gunfighters?" Tex asked.

Louella looked at me, her face a blank.

"A dozen years ago. Earp and Holliday and Buffalo
Bill and Tilghman. I wrote about the qualities that
made them good frontier lawmen."

"Is there anything about you?" she asked.

I shrugged.

"Hey, babe," Rickard began, "do you really know
who Bat is? Really know?"

I was expecting Tex, the foremost fight promoter in
the country, to detail my life as a walking encyclo-
pedia of boxing. But he surprised me.

"Bat Masterson was the most fearless and expert

lawman in the old West," he said. "I know. I spent years out there and all I ever heard was Masterson."

I didn't mind stuff like that and kept quiet.

"This man right here, sitting next to you, made all the rest look like amateurs," Rickard continued. "That's right. This man right here had more ice in his veins than Earp, and was more accurate and deadly with a revolver than anyone else, including Holliday, John Wesley Hardin, Ben Thompson, Luke Short, Hickok, Cody, you name 'em.

"They faced old Bat down over and over, all those wild kids up from Texas, and Bat never walked away. He knew that once he walked, he was done for. The odds might be ten to one, ten wild cowboys with six-guns against one sheriff with his revolver holstered, but old Bat here never blinked an eye. He'd tell them to put their hardware on the ground and walk away because there was a town ordinance against wearing artillery in town. And they'd do it. They were so scared, when it came to a nose-to-nose showdown, they obeyed."

"Crap," I said.

Louella was gobbling all this up, and had started to scribble stuff on a stenographic pad. I signaled the barkeeps for a drink. In fact I raised two fingers; I wanted a double. This kind of talk made me thirsty.

Rickard was all wound up; I could see that. "I'll tell you something else, babe, though old Bat here won't like it. This gent right here wasn't afraid to kill. If it came to defending himself by throwing some lead, he'd do it, and never look back. How many did you plant in boot hills around the West, Bat? Twenty? Thirty? Fifty?"

"Hell, I don't know," I said. "I've filled a few cemeteries."

"Thirty. I've heard twenty-six known, and two or three others out in the sand dunes. Thirty crooks sent to their reward. I tell you, that's some shooting, because old Bat here, he always gave them a chance. They could surrender or draw. All of them drew. Now, there's no one else in the West, on any law enforcement roster, or any badman—not even Hardin, as tough a killer as they come—who's as fine with a six-gun."

Louella stared at me, looking more appalled than admiring.

"Is that true, Bat?" she asked.

"Oh, I never counted."

Truth to tell, I liked moments like this, when old Bat Masterson evoked a hushed reverence, a hidden horror, the top gunmen of the frontier. Oh, some little worm of honesty burrowed through my thoughts, but I corked that line of thinking. I've always been a glutton for flattery.

"You exaggerate, Tex," I said, sipping.

"Naw, I should buy you drinks for the rest of your life, Bat. You're the celebrity."

"I heard that you used to walk into a place and all the troublemakers headed for the back door," said Runyon.

I shrugged.

"It takes skill," Rickard continued. "There's always the hidden gun, the back-shooter, the hood that swears he's going to get you some dark night. You were always ready. If someone was slinking around behind you, you just waited and buffaloed him when he walked by."

"Where'd you get all this?" I asked.

"You walk into any saloon in the West and listen to the old-timers, Bat. I heard plenty of Earp stories, and Holliday stories, and Hickok stories, but they didn't even come close to the Masterson stories."

Louella scribbled furiously. I didn't feel like setting the record straight; not just then. Maybe I'd ask her to set the record straight after I died. Yeah, that was it. I'd give her the real stuff, and she could publish it after they'd planted me.

She reproached me. "You told me you didn't kill anyone."

"Check the papers," I said. "If you want to know, just go into the morgues and look. Try these: *The Dodge City Times, The Ford County Globe,* the Trinidad papers, like the *News,* or *Democrat,* or *Times.* That's all you have to do. They all ran lists of Masterson corpses on the front page, like the daily weather report. Some weeks, five, six bodies. Or they'd put the list on the sports pages like baseball statistics."

They all laughed. I laughed and signaled for another double. If I was going to be a legend this night in the Metropole Bar, I ought to drink like one.

"Really?" she asked.

"Don't take him so serious, kid," Rickard said. "He likes to pull the leg of young reporters like you. If he tells you he only wiped out a dozen, that means he's just tidying up the record in his old age."

Louella eyed Tex and laughed. I detected some uncertainty in her face.

"I'll tell you some more, kid," said Rickard. "Them other gunfighters, how'd they end up? Dead meat, saloon keeps, two-bit tinhorns, janitors, cathouse bouncers, pensioners. Like my friend Earp. He used to be a pit man for me in Goldfield. We met in Nome. What did he ever do after he quit the law? He just fed on his reputation.

"But not old Bat, here. This man beside you is one

of the best-educated men I know. Old Wyatt's like me; we can barely write our names. Me, I got through the third grade. Can old Earp write a straight sentence? Nah. I hear he's got a biographer or two hovering around and swapping lies.

"But old Bat, here. Look at him. He's got abilities Wyatt Earp never thought of. He's like me. He's run big variety halls and gambling parlors like the Palace in Denver. He once had his own weekly paper. He once had his own sports arena in Denver. Now he's a top dog for a big metro paper here. And does he know the difference between a—what do ya call them?— verb and a noun? Can he toss the words and sling the type? Can he pen a good story? Just ask Cobb or Runyon here. They'll tell you. Can some semiliterate Earp—it don't matter which—operate anything bigger than a one-bit saloon or write a straight sentence? Nah."

Cobb and Runyon nodded solemnly. Louella uncapped her fountain pen and began scribbling again.

"Here's the deal, babe," Rickard continued. "You're sitting next to the most important man in the entire history of the West."

I could see Tex was in his cups.

I didn't correct him.

Louella waited for me to demur. The hell with that. This sort of stuff was better than a dose of opium.

Then, mysteriously, the talk switched to Dempsey. Rickard had promoted that fight in Toledo that gave Jack the heavyweight crown, and had plenty of future plans for the Mauler. Most nights the talk switched to Dempsey sooner or later, usually after discussing cathouse bouncers, a valuable and socially desirable trade in which the Mauler learned his art.

Louella got bored, downed the last of her martini,

closed her pad and stuffed it in her purse, and beat a retreat.

"Strange broad," said Tex. "I guess she'll write you up good and proper. I sure told her a thing or three."

"Yeah, you did, Tex, and none of it would survive in sunlight."

"You mean it ain't so?"

I laughed. I knew I wouldn't wrestle very much with my conscience. That was my problem: I liked the legend, even if it was a lie.

CHAPTER 6

Maybe it was the whiskey. I departed the revels at the Metropole early that evening feeling irritable and took a hack back to the flat. I didn't find Emma nor did I expect to. I lit the place up, turning on lamps in every room.

I glanced at my pocket watch. They still had ten minutes of the fifth act, and curtain calls, and she would snack with the gals after that. I wanted her just then. Something was going on in my head, something akin to discomfort, pain, restlessness. In those moments I needed just to talk and let her be my sounding board. She was good at that. But she was sewing buttons and mopping tears for the Ziegfeld show on Forty-third Street.

I should have dealt with all this twenty years ago. There were two Mastersons, the real one and the bullshit celebrity who was the biggest fraud of the twentieth century, give or take one Buffalo Bill Cody.

Tonight, I had listened to a whole honeywagon-load of celebrity talk, knowing it was mostly nonsense. I say mostly. In the middle of the lies and exaggerations and legends was some truth. I had faced down plenty of men—mostly drunks—and won. I will not deny the youthful courage that enabled me to do that.

Hell, maybe I should write my own story. Give Parsons a few yarns to play with, as long as she was poking around, but write the real Masterson story myself. I liked the idea.

I rubbed my legs, which were cold again, and wondered when the diabetes would take me off. I was likely to go blind, they told me. And I couldn't eat this or that, sugars especially, and that was making life hell, too. I wasn't supposed to drink but I did and the hell with the doctors.

Parsons and that story were on my mind, and not even strong drink could help me evade them. This had all started innocuously, just a few yarns about my days as a lawman, and now the thing had grown into something that bothered me. I knew I should just tell the woman to forget it and return to my only pleasures, boxing, horse racing, and looking at cute broads.

I wandered the bright-lit apartment trying to nail down whatever illusory thing was plaguing me, and couldn't. There was something looming there, just beyond my thoughts; something like a worn-out and much-traduced conscience rising from its grave to devil me one last time. Ghosts, hell.

Filtering through my mind came the shadows of the past.

Young Earp: not the old disease-wracked man still alive out in Los Angeles, but the young one with nerves of steel and a will to kill if he had to.

Holliday: thin, actually gentle, desolate that life was

fleeing, bitter about his fate, unshakably loyal to his friends the Earps.

My brother Ed: good, kind, strong Dodge City marshal, shot dead on the south side of town outside the Lady Gay in eighteen and seventy-eight because he had trusted some drunks who had come up from Texas to do what was right.

Jim: a good lawman and lousy brother, who resented my skills and reputation. The thought opened old wounds. I grieved the chasm between us.

The damned ghosts, these and a dozen more who'd floated through my young life. Hell, Louella Parsons had not intended to cause me grief, but grief was welling through me. I had fostered my own legend and now I wanted to disown my own creation. It had all been perfectly rational. If men fear you they don't fool with you. That meant safety for me and peace in my various establishments.

That damned Louella. Why did I keep leading her on when I didn't want her to touch the story?

Thus passed two restless hours, in which I felt like a constipated old fool sitting and waiting and despairing. Then Emma came in, blinked at all the light, and scrutinized me carefully.

"They say diabetics go blind," she said. It was a question.

"Not yet," I replied.

She stood next to me, reading my face. "Drink?"

"Yeah."

She vanished into the Pullman kitchen and I heard her chipping some ice with the pick and loading some whiskey into a tumbler. Then she handed it to me. "I don't think this is going to help," she said.

"You're right, babe." I sipped and it tasted good.

"You'll tell me what's eating you when you're good

and ready." She removed two wicked-looking hairpins and then lifted her wide-brimmed hat and set it aside.

"I wish I knew. All I know is that ever since Louella Parsons started worming old yarns out of me, I've been as itchy as a case of shingles."

I listened to her puttering around in the kitchen, and then she returned with a glass of ruby port and settled beside me as I knew she would. She could lower her head into my shoulder until her glossy hair spilled over my cheek and heal me more than fifty docs and their powders.

"How did the show go?"

"Three winos and a tramp out front. Half-empty house. No one laughed. No encores, no curtain calls. The cops nabbed a purse snatcher in the balcony."

She was pleased that I asked her and captured my free hand. "Okay, guy, you're in the limelight."

That was her cue.

"I thought maybe I should cut down the old Masterson legend a bit by injecting a bit of truth here and there. You know. Just a few facts. For posterity. But Emma, I think I like the legend more. I'm worse than Cody."

"You didn't make the legend, Bat."

"I'm an accessory to the crime."

"That bothers you."

"I don't know. Now it's ghosts. Maybe that's why all these lights are on."

I must have rambled on for half an hour, talking chaotically, not quite identifying what lay just beyond my thoughts, like some open coffin of the mind I didn't want to look into. I don't know where legends come from, or even how I felt about becoming one. I don't know why people compared me to Wyatt or a dozen others, opining that yes, this one was better than that one, quicker with the gun, cooler in danger, killed more men, things like that.

Where did all this nonsense come from, this crazy adulation, the yellowback novels, this hero worship of sullied idols? I sure didn't know, and sometimes the looks I read in people's faces when they met Bat Masterson just curdled something in me. But other times I reveled in it. I saw worship, and few men can resist something like that. How the hell did I get to be a hero?

And what the hell did all this have to do with anything?

I sure did ramble, not making sense of anything, and then I felt Emma squeeze my hand in hers.

"I'm going to bed," she said.

"What do you think?"

"Come to bed, Legend."

"That sounds like an invite," I replied.

CHAPTER 7

I dropped by Louella's cubicle the next day to tell her I would write my story myself. She had surrounded her desk with Chinese silk screens to ward off the icy air funneling over her glossy dark hair.

"I'll be right with you, Bat," she said, cupping a hand over the mouthpiece of the phone that was usually glued to her ear. "I'm talking to Boris Karloff."

"Louella, I'm going to write my own story," I said.

She nodded. "Yes, Boris, send the glossy right away."

I didn't wait. She had gotten the message.

I'd write the damned stuff myself and make sure it was true. And just to prove it, that morning I pulled out a pad and sharpened a pencil and started to write:

A True Account of My Life
By William B. Masterson

Twenty minutes later I still hadn't written one damned word. So I decided to begin at the beginning:

"I was born on November 6, 1853, in the parish of St.-Georges, county of Iberville, in Quebec, and was christened Bartholomew, a name I don't use."

That's as far as I got.

Ten minutes later I tried a new tack:

An Account of My Life as a Frontier Peace Officer
By William B. Masterson

I figured that would focus on the important stuff, so I concentrated hard, pencil poised. And didn't write one sonofabitching sentence. I knew then and there that I couldn't write my story that morning. Not a word came to mind. Not an image. Not an idea for a lead. Maybe I would never write it. Or maybe I just needed to give it more thought.

The next day I tried again, and the motor was just as dead as it was the first time. I had never before been stuck like that, but now I was as mired as a scribbler ever gets. I began to grow testy.

Sure, everything was all right. At least that's what I told myself. But I lost interest in my column. Who the hell cared whether Firpo won the next one? I'd seen so many fights they all blurred together.

One night at the Metropole, Tex Rickard braced me. "What's the matter, Bat? You all right?"

"Yeah, I'm all right."

"You ain't with us all the time. You're off somewhere."

The rest of them told me to see a doc, as if docs could cure anything. I guess I'm too tough on docs. Old McCarty, out in Dodge, sure patched up plenty of men—gunshot wounds, busted arms, contusions, all the usual results of mayhem. But when it came to diseases like consumption or diabetes or cancer, he was as helpless as the rest of us.

So I just told Rickard I'd been having a tough time with the diabetes, and boozing too much, and all that. He reminded me a cure for my boozing was just around the corner. The cure was going to fix up every damned drunk in the country, too. I figured that cure was worse than the disease. The hour was coming when the solid old Metropole Bar would be dark and locked.

But that wasn't why I was always off somewhere, not hearing the guys, not writing my column until the deadline loomed over me like a catamount on a limb. It was this legend thing.

Emma noticed it too, but she was smarter than my pals. "Come on, Legend, get back to your writing," she'd say, but I could see worry in her face.

Then one Sunday she corralled me just as I was about to head for the Garden to watch a workout between a couple of thugs from Hell's Kitchen.

"When are you going to write your memoir?"

"I'm not," I said, and shut the door behind me with just enough of a bang to convey my irritation. That's one thing we both were good at. I knew exactly how peeved she was at me by the way she banged the door of the flat. It had been some time since either of us had slammed it, but this time I came close. She would read the bang-gauge and know.

She'd started calling me Legend, which irritated me. She knew how I felt about that so she made a joke of it. Legend! Come to bed, Legend! What're you gonna write today, Legend? Do I get to kiss Legend this morning?

I bore all this with dignity and silence.

I'd invited her to share an apartment in 1888, when she did a tour at my Blake Street joint, the Palace Variety Theater and Gambling Hall, in Denver. We'd known each other for years and had shared a bed several times before. She was a song-and-dance gal. I liked her looks. She liked mine, or maybe she liked my money. I was flush in those days.

The Palace was no two-bit outfit. It was the most important resort in Denver. My theater seated 750 and had heavily draped boxes on either side of the proscenium arch for those who preferred privacy. Everything in it was wine velvet and gilt, but that was nothing compared to my gambling salon.

I had twenty-five dealers and ran every green-baize game of chance that had been invented. The place was lit by a gas chandelier with five-hundred prisms, and behind the long bar a sixty-foot mirror shot the dazzle back into the room. I served one hell of a free lunch at midnight, which kept the crowd at the tables.

I booked the biggest names in variety, including my old friend Eddie Foy. But I also booked Donnelly and Drew, the Holland Sisters, Ettie Le Clair, and gals like that. Emma wasn't a big draw; she was the type who did a number to open the show while people were still finding their seats. But I liked her looks, and I liked her quietness. Most of those broads were cast from brass, but not Emma. She had a wry smile, a question in her eyes, and a quality that's hard to describe but I'll call breeding. She was like a kid who didn't belong in a joint like mine. She moved in with me and made me happy.

I must have seemed a big shot to her, owning a place like that, raking in a load of cash every night from all the Denver dudes. The city fathers hadn't shut down Blake Street in those days—though they soon would—and I ran things pretty much as I wanted them. Emma stuck with me, and pretty soon we were calling ourselves man and wife, though we never did get married in any formal way. We just took up with each other.

Most of my male friends barely knew her. She was oddly shy around them; open and happy with me, but quiet and fugitive with them, as if she feared my displeasure if she batted an eyelash in their direction. Which wasn't a bad surmise on her part.

I'm the one man she's completely herself with. I've watched it over and over. When I took her to the Metropole a few times, she turned so reserved the boys wondered what got her tongue. So, finally, we just worked things out: she loved to be with her showgirl friends, I liked my sporting fraternity, her girlfriends scarcely knew I existed, and my pals were barely aware of Emma. Which maybe is why we stayed together.

It wasn't all smooth sailing. She fit like an old slipper with a pebble in it. We're a pair of grouches. Back when we first shacked up, I fooled around some. If you own a place like the Palace, you almost have to fight off the opportunities. Those things hurt her but we weathered all that. Now I've got feet so cold from

my poor circulation and diabetes that she dreads
crawling into bed with me unless I put some stockings
on. She says it's like a block of ice landing beside her.

We don't like Sundays. There's nothing to do and
they arrive like a hangover. We read the *Herald* and
sit around. I used to walk but I'm getting too old for
that. Emma crochets and crabs at me and I snarl back.
Sometimes we go to the moving picture show, but I
need about three good slugs of Jack Daniel's before I
can enjoy Lon Chaney and five slugs to tolerate Mary
Pickford, and a drink is hard to come by on Sundays.
So I keep a good cabinet of spirits and we end up
facing Monday with headaches.

She chose a Sunday that November to spring it.

"Let's take a trip," she said, squinting at me.

"Where? Brooklyn?"

"Dodge City."

"Dodge City!"

"I've never seen it. That was before I met you."

I squinted back, my mind whirling like a Maytag
wringer. Hell, Emma wouldn't set foot outside of a
big city. The rest of the country was like darkest Af-
rica to her. She complained that Denver and Chicago
were too small and cheesy. She thinks San Francisco
is a hick town. She says that she can't get a good meal
west of the Hudson River, and there's nothing but out-
houses and kerosene lamps on the other side of the
Mississippi.

"I'm on to you. It'll help me write my memoirs."

"I want to see Dodge City. I want to see where you
became a national disgrace."

I laughed. National disgrace indeed. "Dodge is a
measly little burg in the middle of nowhere, Emma. It
doesn't have a hotel worth the name. It used to have
Dodge House, a big frame joint that let the air in. But

that burned. The food in Dodge would give you gas."

"Take some holiday time. You need to go there."

"I'm too old."

"What's too old about you? The hardest thing we'd have to do is catch a hack in Chicago to take us from one train station to another. It's easy. I checked. We'll take the Limited to Chicago, red carpet. We'll have a Pullman and you can sleep the whole way, or drink all you want in the observation car, or run a monte game back there if the railroad dicks let you. We'll take any Santa Fe train heading for L.A. They all stop in Dodge, don't they? We'll hole up in some joint there. It can't be any worse than Denver."

"Emma, thanks, but I don't want to go there. Last time I looked around, in 'eighty-seven, I could hardly wait to catch the next train out. Emma, there's nothing there but *wheat farmers*. And you're wrong about pouring drinks in observation cars. Most of the states have prohibition. Hell, most of the time you can't buy booze on a train. Two-thirds of the states are dry."

"Good, it's all settled then. I'll get the tickets. I already talked to the ticket man."

"What's settled? I can't just drop my job."

"You've got so many weeks of vacation backed up at the paper you're likely to lose them. The world can get along without your opinions for two weeks. The fight game can get along without you, even if you don't think so. I'll just tell the girls in the show I'm taking a two-week holiday and they can find someone else to sew up costumes between scenes."

"This is Sunday. Let's talk this over on Monday when the saloons are open and everything returns to normal. Hell, put a cold compress on your forehead, Emma. You'll be all right tomorrow. Why don't you take in a Sunday matinee?"

"We'll leave day after tomorrow, Legend. You need the trip."

"I'll go alone. You'd suffer in Dodge. You are the quintessential non-Kansas female."

"I lived in Wichita, once," she said primly. "I want to end your suffering. You're going to suffer until you go back to the scene of the crime."

I knew I'd go. She had baited her rat trap and sprung it. My Emma is a formidable woman, quiet as a glacier, which means usually silent except when it's rumbling. "All right, all right," I said. "But we're going to have to take our booze with us because we're not going to find very many oases when we get the hell out of New Yawk."

"I knew you would come around, Legend."

The truth of it was, she had struck bone. I wanted to go back there and stand in the plaza and look at Front Street and visit the Long Branch or the Alamo and wander around the old Lady Gay and peer into the old jail, and find out what the hell made me a household name.

CHAPTER 8

November is a good time to travel because the coach windows are closed and cinders don't fly in. The cars are neither too hot nor too cold. I wasn't minding the trip at all in spite of my advanced years. I left all the arrangements to Emma, who showed uncharacteristic zeal in planning the trip. She booked us in a Pullman sleeping car over the New

York Central rails to Chicago, and again on the Atchison, Topeka, and Santa Fe Railroad out to Dodge.

When I warned her that Kansas was as dry as an undertaker's wit, her response was to purchase a wicker picnic valise at Abercrombie and Fitch well equipped with medicinal flasks and assorted paraphernalia. And she bought three quarts of Jack Daniel's and a couple of sneaky pints just to be safe.

Any state that could harbor a Carry Nation deserved its pain. The state had been under the influence of Prohibition even when I had lived there, but no one paid much attention until the turn of the century, when the woman went on a rampage and every milksop male reformer boarded her wagon.

I cannot fathom the urge to prohibit entire populations from imbibing, and consider such efforts a violation of our liberties. Let the teetotalers practice their abstinence, and more power to them. Some there are who shouldn't touch a drop. But that does not mean that such pillars of rectitude have the right to impose their fashion upon the rest of us.

For that reason alone I consider Kansas the most benighted state in the Union, worse even than its neighbor Arkansas, where anything resembling fun is proscribed and driven to the back-ends of cemeteries on moonless nights. But the disease that had its epicenter in Kansas, in the bosom of Carry Nation, had spread through Middle America. Now it was weeks from engulfing the coasts, and I'd been thinking about moving to Khyber Pass or some other civilized place.

Now the sonofabitching Prohibition movement threatens to reduce the Republic to a boneyard. I hope I don't live to see it. There is such a thing as an excess of virtue, which only drives vice underground. From my own readings of the Testaments, I have concluded that Prohibition has no authority in religion whatsoever, and anyone who tries to improve on religion is insulting the gods—or God. What God has put together, let no prohibitionist put asunder.

The Bible's against drunkenness and immoderation, not taking a nip. What are they going to do next? Throw Jesus into Alcatraz for the miracle of the wine, or banish St. Paul for recommending a drink now and then? Or put the book of Proverbs in the prohibited reading list?

At any rate we fairly steamed across the East, a mile a minute, via the Lake Erie route, and debarked the next day in a crisp and wind-torn Chicago. With the assistance of a porter we were soon enough settled in a hack, the booze noisily sloshing around in our bags, and caught the Santa Fe's westbound in ample time at the La Salle Street Station. We knew, upon steaming out of Chicago, that we were leaving civilization behind.

Of the train companies, I rather like the New York Central's service better. They dined us in fine style on white linen, with good pewter service; looked to my comforts and did not prohibit cigars. Short of operating one's own private car, one could do no better.

At my request, Emma booked us as Mr. and Mrs. Bartholomew Masterson, though I had abandoned my true name as a youth and assumed the more public one, William Barclay Masterson. But now I wished to veil myself to some degree. I would not be recognized. My face and body had filled out. My hair had grayed. Only my eyes remained what they had been; at least that is what old friends told me. No one in Dodge knew me as Bartholomew, nor had anyone ever met Emma.

Hell, I knew that there might be a few still alive

who would recognize me. I had heard that Ham Bell, the liveryman, still lived. And I suspected Chalk Beeson, one of the owners of the Long Branch, might still endure on his farm outside of town. But even on my last visit, in 1887, I wandered about quite freely, unrecognized, marveling at the change I saw at every hand. I had stayed on that occasion at the Delmonico Hotel, but the place no longer exists, and Emma arranged for other quarters.

Briefly, in 1912, I had gotten off the Santa Fe train at Dodge, along with some fight-game pals, but I hadn't wandered from the station platform, and ten minutes later we were on board again. That had been the last time I'd seen Dodge. I have a photo of that somewhere.

I would brace myself for change. The city now had six or seven thousand citizens and was a thriving commercial center of the Southwestern Sahara.

The Santa Fe offered accommodations much more primitive, especially in the dining car and observation car, but we endured all that as far as Kansas City, Missouri, when suddenly night fell, if I may speak figuratively, for in fact it was merely afternoon and I was looking forward to a bourbon and branch. But minutes before starting for the fateful state line, the steward issued a last call for drinks; he would shutter his oasis to comply with the edicts of the sovereign state of Kansas, and we would see no more pleasantry.

"Well, Emma, from now on, we're in for it," I said. She had amiably whiled away the hours drinking ruby port and reading *Harper's Monthly* and *Smart Set* and *Vanity Fair,* exclaiming at the frank brassiere ads and deploring the Edna St. Vincent Millay poetry and rejoicing at every word Henry Mencken and George Jean Nathan penned.

She merely smiled smugly. Safe in our Pullman bedroom was our own oasis, sufficiently stocked for a fortnight.

I must say that, even two or three days into this venture, I scarcely knew why I was aboard this express train and what the hell I intended to do in Dodge. Visit the haunts of my youth? Why? Refresh my memory? Why? But this had all spun out of my control, and we were rocketing westward at a mile a minute or better on the straight stretches, and I was little influencing my own destiny.

I had finally concluded that I was visiting Dodge to refresh my memory, for if I intended to pen my memoir I needed to visit the scene of the crime, as Emma put it, once again. Hell, I was aware of maggots slithering through that theory, but it was the best I could manage.

The best reason I could come up with was curiosity. What had the citizens of Dodge wrought after various peace officers had reduced it to somnolent safety? And yet another thread of curiosity tugged at me: What did all those wheat farmers and dry-goods clerks think of the wild times?

Well, maybe we were going to Dodge for no reason at all. Life doesn't require reasons. Emma had scarcely seen the place, and even though I warned her there was nothing to be seen, she still wanted to lay eyes on the spot where Legend had been born. This pleasant detachment worked to my advantage. If Dodge offended, we would catch the next express East and stamp Kansas dust from our feet.

Emma winked at me.

"I warned you," I retorted.

"I'm fascinated," she replied. "Are we in the same nation we started from?"

"No," I said.

We steamed into Dodge at the unholy hour of one in the morning, and I would have missed it altogether but for the ubiquitous conductor, who tapped our curtain with polite authority.

"Dodge City in fifteen minutes," he proclaimed, and I knew that history was being born that hour. A wave of nostalgia flooded me and I stared out the window into absolute stygian gloom, in which not so much as a farmhouse lamp gave evidence of civilization. We dressed swiftly and surrendered our sloshing portmanteaus to the porter, but I insisted on carrying my Abercrombie and Fitch picnic valise with the bulk of our contraband in it. If we were going into the smuggling business I didn't want Emma to get caught. She looked cheerful, but one in the morning was always her best hour. She was a regular one-woman party about two in the morning.

"Where are we staying?" I asked her.

"The Harvey House."

"One of those?"

She smiled delicately. At least the Harvey House would be comfortable, though I feared I would be smothered in finger food.

The Santa Fe passenger train squealed to a stop in a whirl of steam, and we descended into a sharp night, the platform lit only by dim electric lights at great interludes. Immediately north loomed a vast red-brick structure, the AT&SF station built after I had left. Beyond, to the north, I could see almost nothing, but within a few yards lay Front Street, the scene of various episodes that had turned me into a dime-novel hero.

A porter gathered our luggage and escorted us into an amazing lobby, lit by electricity, decorated in southwestern motifs, all tile and gloss and white-glove clean. My grudging appreciation of Fred Harvey's railroad hotel and restaurant chain inched upward. The adjacent dining room, called "The Vaquero," was dark and cordoned off with a velvet rope.

"Pretty nice, Bat," said Emma, satisfied with her savvy travel arrangements.

"We'll see," I retorted.

A clerk who could barely pass for eighteen welcomed us politely. He had slicked his hair back with some sort of pomade that stank. "Just sign right here, sir," he said, handing me a nib pen and inkpot.

Bartholomew Masterson and wife, I wrote. *New York, NY.*

He turned the register around. "Mr. Masterson. Familiar name here to old-timers. You wouldn't be related to, who was it? Yeah, William B. Sheriff once, sort of a badman himself."

"Could be," I said.

"That one musta died long ago. That was the old days. You staying how many nights?"

"Four, I believe."

Emma nodded.

The clerk scribbled on a form, showed me the price, looked me over, and inquired whether I wished to pay upon departing—in which case I could charge the restaurant meals. I nodded.

"You say this Masterson was a badman?" I asked.

The youth looked uncomfortable. "We're not supposed to talk about that, sir. Those days are gone. Everything is just as wholesome as the town fathers can make it."

"What days?"

The youth looked like he was desperate to escape the grilling. "The very early days, sir, before this became a modern city. The gambling and saloons and cowboys. This is a good progressive town, law-abiding."

"What about this Sheriff Masterson?"

"I couldn't say, sir. Our pastor says this town has a vicious and corrupt reputation to live down and the best thing we who are the town's future can do is never say a word, let it die away until there is no memory of it, rub it out forever so that we may be at peace with God. We once had a lecture at the WMCA about the progress we've made. We're a city of churches and good clean living." He eyed us happily. "Welcome to Dodge, sir. The wheat farming capital of the world."

I took his proffered key, and the sleepy porter led us up a flight of stairs to our room. Four days was going to be much too long. Four hours was going to be too long.

CHAPTER 9

The Harvey House room could not have been more comfortable, save for the fact that the Santa Fe rails ran between the bed and the washbasin, and assorted express and freight trains highballed through five or six times, fretting our sleep. We dallied late the next morning, being late risers in any case but trying to placate our aggrieved bodies as well. We would endure.

We presented ourselves at the Vaquero at slightly after ten, only to have a well-coifed Harvey Girl in-form us that the dining room would be closed until noon. Breakfast was served from six to nine daily.

"Where might we breakfast?" I inquired.

"It's too late, sir, but you should be able to find an early lunch almost anywhere."

"Where might one discover a cup of coffee?"

"That, sir, we would be happy to provide to our guests. You may drink it in the lobby."

We retired to the ornate lobby while a freight train rattled by, and she brought us two honest doses of java and an ingratiating smile. We had heard about Fred Harvey's famous girls but this was the first live specimen we had encountered.

She wore the standard uniform: black Mother Hubbard dress with white apron and collar and cuffs, black stockings and shoes, and a white ribbon in severely combed hair. These femmes, drawn mostly off of farms and lured by the excitement of the bustling railroads, earned $17.50 a month plus room and board and tips, lived in dormitories under chaperoned supervision, and delighted travelers across the United States with their poise and cheerful attentions to comfort.

"She wouldn't get far auditioning for Florenz Ziegfeld," Emma whispered, and then chuckled. The thought of a chorus of Harvey Girls on the New York boards was too much. Emma had an instinct for the ridiculous.

Thus did we arm our aging bodies against the sharp cold of Dodge, that early November day of 1919.

When we were sufficiently revived by the Maxwell House, I tendered my gun hand to Emma and we pierced into the sunlight. It occurred to me that it was the first time I had set foot in Dodge without being heeled. The sight bewildered me. The tracks, for instance. Where there had been just one in the eighteen-seventies, which my brother and I had graded under contract, now there were two through tracks and sidings on either side. Where the old wooden Santa Fe station stood, I now confronted this massive ramparted and turreted redbrick building that housed the Harvey House, a passenger station, and division offices. But that was only the beginning of my bewilderment.

There before my aging eyes was Front Street, but hell, it could have been Keokuk or Peoria for all I could tell. The fires of 1885 had swept away the blocks east of Bridge Street, including the old Dodge House, the cattlemen's hostelry in the old days, the Long Branch, and a host of other familiar haunts. Brick buildings had replaced the old flammable shacks of the frontier town, but the last time I visited in the late 1880s, things were little different from before. The rebuilt Long Branch Saloon was in its accustomed spot and all was well with the world.

This time I looked in vain for the Long Branch without discovering where it had lit.

"What's the matter, Bat?" Emma asked.

"I'm looking for the Long Branch Saloon."

"But this is a Prohibition state."

"The Long Branch survived that modest impediment for decades. It's not there."

"Where was it?"

"Ah, about where that Pioneer Barber Shop is. Let's go look."

I escorted my lady a few yards north and paused before the Pioneer. Sure enough, tonsorial enterprise revealed itself in a row of barber chairs. And the current proprietors were using the famous old back bar and mirror as the repository of their tools. I sighed. Desecration. It does not pay to outlive one's times. Heaps of hair lay on the floor around each chair. The denizens eyed us passively, and I hastened Emma away from the sacrilege. If Chalkey Beeson was still alive, and still owned the building, I intended to thrash him.

I gazed across the tracks, southward to where the calaboose and city hall once stood. But they no longer existed. I had presided over the most porous jail in the West, with a dirt floor and plank ceiling that could easily be breached by anyone with knife or spoon or shovel. The commissioners would spare me nothing to lessen the porosity of the jail, with the result that I lost a significant number of the sonsabitches I had remanded to the tender mercies of the justice courts.

"It's gone," I said.

"What's gone?"

"Everything."

"Well, what did you expect?"

"Something."

I was getting irate for no good reason. Towns change. Fires scorch away the bones of pioneer burgs. Populations grow. But Dodge had lodged in my mind just as I remembered it, and what I was seeing aggravated me.

"Let's get the next express East," I said. "I don't like this."

"Bat, we're here. Show me the city."

"You'll have the wrong impression."

"Grant me some imagination."

Grimly I hiked west along the tracks looking for a certain spot that had vanished. What I wanted to find was a shallow embankment, just high enough to shelter me from a barrage of bullets emanating from the corner of the old jail; bullets that whipped over my head and proceeded to shatter glass all along Front Street, including the windows of the Long Branch, where customers dove out the back door and Beeson opened his safe and hid behind the steel rampart of its door.

But I couldn't find the spot. There were now several tracks, and the roadbed was half a block wide.

"What are you looking for, Bat?"

"Somewhere around here I shot it out with some sharpers named Peacock and Updegraff who were thinking of killing my brother," I said. "All I got out of it was an eight-dollar fine and a night in the pokey that no longer exists, over there where that big brick city hall stands now."

"I never heard that one."

I smiled. "The things I haven't confessed, Emma, would swamp the Government Printing Office."

She smiled that smile of hers that hooked me so long ago at the Palace in Denver.

Memory helped me. I could see it as if it were yesterday, but I doubted that I could convey all that to Emma. "Jim was in trouble," I began. "Some friends of his sent me a wire to come help him out. I was in Tombstone with the Earps, dealing at the Oriental, just back from doing some posse duty for Wyatt. But I came at once. That's a long trip, and by the time I got up here—that was in April of eighteen-eighty-one—I thought he'd probably be dead. Dodge didn't wait around for slow rescues."

"What kind of trouble?"

"Oh, he'd been canned from his job as city marshal by the new mayor, Webster, and had bought into the Lady Gay Dance Hall . . ."

The smirk on her face told me her thoughts.

"No, it really was a dance hall, though the tarts were pretty thick around there. At any rate, his partner was a man named Peacock, whose brother-in-law, Al Updegraff, worked the bar and milked the partnership for all it was worth by drinking up the profits and serving too many free shots to his pals.

"It came to hot words and then threats against Jim's life. That's when I got the wire. So I hustled back here, pounding the rails and riding stagecoaches hour after hour—no direct route from Tombstone—and arrived here on a Saturday morning.

"I thought they might be expecting me so I jumped off the train while it was still rolling, and was walking beside it when I saw two pairs of feet walking on the other side of the cars. That's when I stepped around the end of the train, and there they were—Updegraff and Jim's partner, Peacock.

"I yelled at them that I wanted to talk, but they beat it to the jailhouse, and once they got behind it they began banging away. That old jailhouse was built of big timbers spiked together.

"I was out in the open. So I dived behind the railroad embankment—which I can't find now—and we traded shots. Their lead blew out the windows in George Hoover's Alamo saloon and the Long Branch and McCarty's drugstore, while mine just splintered wood around the jail.

"Then the southside sports joined in, and enough lead was peppering Front Street to awaken every catnapper in town, and pretty soon the northside sports were blasting back at the southside sports. Updegraff went down, a bullet in his chest.

"Well, after my hammer was clicking on empties, the mayor, Webster, ran up with a shotgun and hauled me off to the jail. Updegraff lived, unfortunately. I pleaded guilty of feloniously discharging a weapon on the streets of Dodge. Even Updegraff agreed that I hadn't shot him; fire from the Front Street saloons had nailed him." I stared at her. "So much for one man-killer episode, eh?"

She sighed. "Well, Legend, I was sort of hoping to see the notch on your revolver."

I laughed. I never notched my revolver—except for the New York suckers who wanted to lay out fat money for my Colt. My revolver business had tickled Emma so much that she began hunting down Colts, and I usually had two or three of the jim-dandies in a drawer. It looked to be a good way for W. B. Masterson to make a living.

I hiked along the tracks, looking for the place where I had dived behind the embankment, but the earth had been moved, and I couldn't place it. It was all changed. Just plain disappeared. And since the jailhouse had vanished, I couldn't even conjure up the event for Emma, at least not by showing her some old bullet scars. I minded that. It was like I hadn't remembered anything right; like I was sliding into senility.

I peered wearily about, trying to find one thing—just one damned thing—that remained of old Dodge. I thought maybe some of the one-story buildings on the west side of Front Street dated back to my time, but I saw nothing familiar at all south of the tracks, and wondered what the hell had happened to the old sporting district where the cowboy sonsabitches up the trail from Texas drank and gambled and whored.

Every last building over there was new to me, and I had a pretty good notion of why. Well, we'd get over there soon enough, but first I wanted to show Emma Boot Hill.

CHAPTER 10

I steered Emma through a bustling burg I did not know. Had it not been for a few familiar names on the fronts of redbrick buildings, I would have sworn I had never been there before. What had happened to the old places along Front Street? The mercantile, Wright, Beverly & Co., the Alamo Saloon, Hoover's Wholesale Liquors, Zimmerman's Hardware, Lone Star Saloon, Saratoga Saloon, Jack Collar's dry goods and coffin store, the Alhambra, Beatty and Kelley's restaurant, Old House saloon, Mueller's boot and shoe?

Now Front Street boasted banks, jewelry, and furniture stores. And on the south side of the tracks a huge grain elevator dominated the city. The streets were paved with brick or wooden block, or asphalted. Motorcars roared up the grade from the river bottoms as effortlessly as a locomotive. I scarcely saw a horse or wagon.

Ahead, I spotted the spire of a formidable school building perched squarely on Boot Hill and remembered that the old boneyard had been shut down and moved late in my sojourn in Dodge.

"We aren't gonna see it," I said. "Boot Hill's a schoolyard now. They moved the stiffs out to Prairie Grove Cemetery."

"Well, cemeteries aren't my favorite haunts."

I was irritated. "I was going to show you those markers. Not a one of those people planted there had been killed by a peace officer. Not a damned one. They'd been shot in saloon brawls, cathouse fights, gambling troubles, love triangles, things like that. There were only twenty or thirty up there but the legend grew larger than real life. The dime novels said I filled those plots myself."

We struck the top of the hill, the highest point in Dodge, with a commanding view of the river and the bottomland. Now it was a grubby yard, and some youngsters were whirling around it while their teachers watched. The kids were playing Red Rover. Emma looked fondly on the fair-haired youngsters and I knew exactly what she was thinking.

From a badman's boneyard to schoolyard. I was feeling disoriented. From up there, I beheld a new county courthouse built of stone, with pretentious pillars on its façade, a new hospital, an array of brick buildings whose purpose eluded me, a city of six thousand or so, stretching across both sides of the rails. On the south side stood an old hotel I knew, the Great Western, if that's what it was still called. The familiar sight comforted me. An army recruiting office occupied the corner of Chestnut and First, with a National Bank of Commerce occupying another corner.

The wind drove us off the hill and down the unfamiliar streets to the tracks. My heart was hammering too fast. The air blew thinner in Dodge than in New York. I steered her down to Front Street again, and then across the double tracks and sidings, wanting to discover just some small memento of the wild south side, some subdued aroma of sin, some shack that had once sheltered a nymph du prairie. But I already knew I'd have no luck. The town fathers had gotten there before me with torches and wrecking balls and moral furor.

"This is where they came, Emma. Those youngsters from Texas. Twelve or thirteen hundred every summer, driving more longhorns than anyone could count. Those cows, they were pretty. Every color you could think of, from blue to brindle, and majestic horns, mean bastards that'd hook some unwary kid. Those cowboys lived a rough life and liked to play rough. But they brought in the beeves, and the beeves were tallied and loaded into stock cars and shipped East, month after month, hundreds of thousands, until the whole town stank of cowshit and money."

"Looks pretty tame."

"I don't know why I came," I said. "This isn't refreshing any memories."

"I think it will," she said. "Things come back."

We walked Locust Street, the old Santa Fe Trail, but I found not even ghosts on hand to celebrate the wild times. Ham Bell's livery barn stood but was now a motorcar garage. I found not a trace of Bell's Varieties dance hall, or the Lady Gay, once half-owned by my brother, or the Comique, where Eddie Foy and a host of other entertainers strutted, or any of the cowboy saloons: Peacock's, Beatty & Kelley's Dodge City Restaurant, Sturm's, the Hub, Sample Room, Nueces, Occident, Alhambra, Crystal Palace, Lone Star, Old House, Oasis, which was once owned by Bill Tilghman, Congress Hall, or any of the rest of the joints I had patrolled as a deputy city marshal or sheriff.

These were south of the famous dead line, the Santa Fe tracks, which separated the reputable part of Dodge from its wilder precincts. Saloons existed north of the line, including the Long Branch, but we made sure decorum reigned, weapons were checked, and rowdiness curtailed. Cattlemen residing at Dodge House usually frequented the northside spas; the hired hands kept the other side of town in an uproar from June to November. We kept a lid on, more or less.

All gone. Not a trace. Where fancy parlor houses and bordellos stood, where rotten little cribs congregated, warehouses and automobile parts dealers now resided. I walked sadly through this mortuary of a way of life, with Emma eyeing me acutely, sensing things from my silence. But there was nothing to see, and this was a civilized, nondescript, prosaic century.

I wanted to find the spot where Ed was shot outside the Lady Gay, but it wasn't the same anymore. There was no Lady Gay. I sighed.

"Let's go," she said. "I'm hungry."

I stood there on Locust, a place as alien as the Congo, trying to remember where I'd buffaloed drunks, pinched gun-toters, talked half-soused drovers into quitting for the night, pulled apart screeching prairie nymphs, howdied with Squirrel Tooth Alice or Big Emma or Doc's gal Kate Elder, hoisted a few with old friends like Wyatt and Morgan Earp, run a faro game, passed time with Luke Short or Doc Holliday, visited with Dog Kelley, the mayor in those days.

I couldn't make sense of anything. Now it was a sprawl of feed stores, International Harvester equipment dealers, Firestone dealers, and bleak vacant lots pretending to be respectable. But they weren't half as respectable as the great old saloons.

"Let's eat, Bat."

I nodded and let myself be led back to the Harvey House. I was full of years, and suddenly weary, though we hadn't walked but a mile or two.

"It's been forty years," she said. "You can't expect things to be the same."

"I expected change, but I also expected to find plenty of the old town around. It's all gone."

She smiled a knowing smile, and escorted me across the dead line, which didn't seem so significant anymore, to the massive redbrick station and hotel. I was hungry. We hadn't had breakfast.

The Vaquero served us a dandy Waldorf and juicy beef blue-plate special, and I repaired my body and soul there. The trim Harvey Girls were endlessly eager to please and hovered about us like fluttering geishas. The food surprised me. I had always considered Oklahoma and Kansas to be the Bad Food Capitals of the World. But the relentless Fred Harvey had heroically overcome local tradition. Will Rogers once told me that Fred Harvey had introduced good food and girls to the West, which lacked both. I had met Rogers in 1915 when he was in a Ziegfeld show.

Emma decided on a siesta, which I found tempting, but resisted. I had an afternoon's investigation in mind, so I left her in our room and ventured out again into the crisp day.

I had to hunt for the office of the *Daily Globe,* which was what the paper was now called. In my day it was *The Ford County Globe,* and it had mostly been friendly to those of us who enforced such law as there was in Dodge. But the paper wasn't at its usual haunt on First and Chestnut, and I had a hell of a time hunting it down.

It turned out to be in the old digs of *The Dodge City Times,* now defunct, a paper I was happy to see in its grave, along with its sonofabitch editor Nick Klaine, who was the bane of my existence after a brief period of friendship. The only Dodge he could imagine was one that sold bonnets to farmers' wives.

I was at home in newspapers. I sized up the *Globe* with one glance. It had two Linotypes and a flatbed press, some Ludlow headline type, and the usual pungent odor of hot type metal and ink. The place was black; generations of ink had permeated the walls and floor and desks and skin of the compositors and printers and editors and ad salesmen. I knew all about ink. The *Telegraph* was printed in the Black Hole of Calcutta.

"Want an ad? Got some news? Subscribe?"

The graying man addressing me appeared to be in charge.

"Neither," I said. "I'd like to dig into your old editions. The very oldest, when it was *The Ford County Globe*."

"I think we can arrange that. You some historian?"

"Reporter," I said. "I'm digging up history."

He hesitated, looked me over, and then nodded me back through the plant, past a kid breaking down pages, and acolytes hovering about the altar of a venerable Cleveland press. "Stuff's back here. I guess you just want to read," he said, observing that I was not equipped to take notes.

"Yeah," I said.

The morgue resided in an alcove off the editorial area, with yellowed papers bound in gray volumes and shelved in orderly stacks.

"I'm Jess Dennis," he said. "Own the place. Came here in 1910, from Wichita. Nice progressive town."

"Bartholomew Masterson," I replied.

He startled. "You related to William Barclay?"

"I'm sure that I am."

"That's what you want to read about? Those days?"

"Yup."

"You're not going to publish stuff about that around here, are you?"

"I live in New York."

"But you're related to the brothers—Ed, Jim, and Bat. I don't know about this."

"Some trouble?"

He paused, assessing me. "Might be. You could get me in a jam." He paused again and made up his mind about something. "I'll tell you a story. I don't know you, but your name's enough. When I moved here in 1910 I began going through the old papers, especially the early ones.

"They were great. There the devils were, right there on the pages, the cowboys, the saloons, the peace officers like the Mastersons and Earps, Bassett, Deger, Tilghman; the murders, the gamblers, the ladies of the night. Wild times, Texas cowboys. Ben Thompson, Clay Allison, Luke Short, Charlie Goodnight; hard men, thirteen hundred cowboys every summer, hundreds of thousands of longhorns; the dentist, Holliday, and his concubine Big Nose Kate.

"Well, I got it into my naive noggin that this was great stuff, and maybe I should reprint it and put it out as a booklet and make a few bucks. So between times, and Sunday afternoons, I dug it up and set it and got it into a booklet.

"The whole shebang. Hop Fiend Nell, Charlie Bassett, your Masterson relatives, gamblers like Short and Thompson and Holliday, Mayor Dog Kelley, Scar-Faced Lillie, Cockeyed Frank, Horse Thief Ben. I had the Earp brothers, Wyatt and Morgan, murder, knifings, robberies, saloon brawls, bordello mayhem, Boot Hill, buffaloed cowboys in that wooden jail, all of it.

"I thought it'd sell like hotcakes. Wonderful stuff. I printed up a thousand and hawked the book in my paper and sat back waiting for folks to lay out their four bits and take a piece of Dodge City history home. . . ."

Dennis shrugged. "It didn't happen. I didn't sell but a few. Old Chalk Beeson bought one, and so did Ham Bell. I wondered what the trouble was, Mr. Masterson, and then the answer visited me one sunny afternoon.

"A group of town fathers arrived. I knew the whole lot. Businessmen, mayor, an alderman, chief of police, two ministers, head of the local chapter of the WCTU, Knights Templar, Elks and Odd Fellows and Masons and Moose, high school principal, head of the YMCA, a couple of wheat farmers outside of town, the librarian. I could see what was coming and so can you.

"They advised me that Dodge was a clean and wholesome town, the finest in dry Kansas, filled with good people, a church for every taste, Sunday schools, good baseball teams, a fine economy based on grains and meat, progressive and pure, blessed by Kansas sun and Prohibition. True blue American.

"And they wanted me to quit muckraking, digging up the filthy past. This was the twentieth century. The shameful frontier shantytown was long gone. This was the land of liberty and virtue, where wives and daughters were safe, children innocent, morals elevated, and business making us all rich."

I laughed. Dennis took that for encouragement.

"They wanted me to stuff the entire printing into the stove. Dodge's past was a thing never to be mentioned. The young people scarcely knew it existed and it would be best not to lead them astray. Next thing, if they got to reading that booklet, they'd be fooling with vices like smoking Cubebs, playing billiards, falling into perdition.

"Well, the upshot, Mr. Masterson, was that they wanted me to bury the past. *Deep*. Their spokesman— bigwig here who'll go nameless—he put it delicately. 'Mr. Dennis,' he says, 'it'd be a pity if a fine, progressive, morally upright paper like the *Globe* were to lose advertising and subscriptions because of this momentary folly.'

"I sure got the message, and from that day onward, the *Globe* has never even whispered about the times forty years ago. Neither does my competitor, the *Democrat*. So, sir, read if you want. There's no harm in it. But spare me my livelihood."

"Would it be all right if I published something in New York?"

"Oh, sure, no one here's ever seen a New York paper."

"Well, good, Mr. Dennis." I offered a hand. "My friends call me Bat."

CHAPTER 11

W hen I told Emma that we could expect a guest before heading down to the Harvey House restaurant for dinner, she began straightening the bedclothes and fussing about in a perfectly clean room.

"You should've seen the guy when I told him I was Bat," I said. "He started pumping my paw like a well-handle and after that he was digging out old bound volumes and fussing around, and saying he thought I'd died thirty years ago. But I told him no story. I don't want a story, at least not just now."

"You thrive on it."

I didn't disagree.

Jess Dennis arrived at five, looking as parched as a

Kansas wheat field in a drought. I had invited him and his wife to dinner, but he said his lady couldn't leave the children. So I invited him for a toddy first, and then dinner without his mate, and he squinted around the pressroom, and then nodded.

"I have to be careful," he whispered. "Being the editor of the paper and all."

I nodded.

I had spent a pleasurable afternoon paging through old *Ford County Globe*s, focusing on the police beat and court reports. There was plenty of stuff I had forgotten about, old names that rose up out of the mists, long-lost friends and enemies, some whores of friendly acquaintance, a little gal named Annie Ladue I was living with in 1880. I had almost forgotten Annie. I had forgotten too many women.

Dennis could spare little time to join me but in odd moments he asked whether I was freshening my memory. Mostly I was getting mad all over at the paper's owners, Lloyd Shinn and Dan Frost, who had made a career out of criticizing me and my brothers when I wore the badge. So many names. Dave Mather, Shotgun Collins, Rowdy Joe Lowe, Kinch Riley, Charley Ronan, Dick Clark, every one of them gamblers and plenty tough.

What an afternoon, flooded with images, tatters of news, memories, stuff long forgotten, old rages and joys, emotions long dead and buried erupting up like spirits on All Souls' Eve, leaving me drained and once or twice on the brink of tears. Another world, another century, another time. God, how the world had changed.

I descended to the Vaquero and begged some ice from one of the Harvey Girls, and just to avoid suspicion, some tea as well. By the time the editor knocked on our door Emma's private saloon was open for business.

I made the introductions, and Dennis nervously checked the drapes and locked the door before accepting some bourbon on ice. He had tidied up his attire and wore a Sunday deacon outfit.

"This is an oasis," he muttered.

"That bad?"

Jess nodded. "We have sort of an underground railroad up from Texas and once in a while I get lucky, but Bat, this is a long-term drought and I don't see the end of it."

"Getting worse," I said. "When this goes national, I'll just check out. It's gonna last a century. You know where all this started? Evanston, Illinois. That's where the WCTU operates."

Dennis downed one and Emma refilled. He looked grateful.

"I like this burg, but not that holy-cow of it and I've thought a dozen times of pulling out. Trouble is, it's prosperous. I get ads, sell subscriptions, keep growing. I'm making good money and it keeps getting better."

"If you want to announce my presence in town, that's fine with me," I said. "Maybe some old-timers would come out of the woodwork and I'll get to reminisce."

"Suppose I ran an item. Frontier sheriff W. B. Masterson's in town for a visit. I'd have to word it carefully but I could do it. Just so long as I don't rake up the past. People are pretty sensitive about it."

"Why? I don't get it."

"It's because they're ashamed of everything that went on around here before, oh, eighteen-ninety, and it's been burned, wrecked, and rubbed from memory.

"There are schoolchildren here who have never

heard of the wild times, the south side or the longhorns or the cowboys or gamblers or the nymphs."

"It's history, isn't it?"

"Not for these people, it isn't. They don't condemn the old days; they pretend the old days never existed. They talk about macadamized motorcar roads, and getting wheat to market, improving phone service, getting electrical lines out to the farms, putting bathtubs in farmhouses, racial purity, a world without war, and getting more good folks into the county."

"So the old sheriff is irrelevant. Fine with me."

Dennis downed his second and Emma fortified his tumbler with more ice and Tennessee. Emma and I exchanged glances. This would be the last. A slightly boozy editor of the county sheet wouldn't improve our stay in Dodge.

"Who's alive I might know?" I asked.

"Doc McCarty and Ham Bell."

"I'd like to see 'em."

Dennis nodded. "I'll arrange it."

"How does the town treat them? Bell ran the Variety Theater on the south side, and some of that stuff was pretty flashy, lot of showgirl leg showing. McCarty patched up more bullet and knife wounds than any army surgeon."

"Fine old pioneers, good rootstock, founders of Kansas."

"One more thing, Jess. Are there any of those old yellowback novels about me floating around here? They're a pack of lies."

"If there are, they're hidden in bottom drawers somewhere, Bat. You know, I can't get over this. When you first introduced yourself I figured you were a nephew of the old boy. That was forty years ago when you were around here."

"I was sheriff at age twenty-three."

"Well, that explains some of it. You know, everyone in the country's heard of Bat Masterson, the man who kept the lid on the wildest town in the West. I just couldn't believe it. You had to be a fake. It wasn't until we talked some that I believed you."

So the legend lived after all, flowing like an underground river through a city doing its upmost to forget the past and embrace the future and climb upward on an ivory staircase called Progress.

"What does this town really believe, Jess? What do these wheat farmers and merchants want?"

Dennis puzzled that for a moment. "That this nation, the United States, is a sacred place with a sacred destiny to throw its light over the whole world. That it's going to abolish sin and evil, and usher in prosperity, virtue, and a sort of heaven on earth. That's what this century is for; making a utopia not just here but from sea to shining sea."

"What are they gonna ban next in Kansas?"

"Anything carnal. Boxing, for example. Divorce. There shouldn't be divorces. Smokes. Pool halls, billiards, the road to perdition for boys. Cards. Whist. Gin Rummy. Dancing, especially the new kind. Jazz. Blues. None of that jungle music for white people. Art galleries. Immigrants. None of those Mediterraneans or eastern Europeans or others who'd mess up the country."

I knocked back a slug of booze, hoping it would calm my brain and subdue my aching body. Was this the future? I had walked into the wrong century.

We imbibed awhile more and then I proposed a meal downstairs. Jess Dennis agreed at once, and Emma began rinsing the tumblers and storing the contraband in the Abercrombie and Fitch outfit just in case one of those sainted Harvey Girls came in to tidy us up.

Dennis dug in his suit coat and extracted a packet of something, dug his fingers in, plucked a pair of tiny squares, and popped them onto his tongue.

"Sen-Sen?" he asked.

Sen-Sen was the tangy breath-cleaner and booze eradicator that had hid the vices of a million schoolboys from their ma and pa.

The Sen-Sen bit my tongue. Emma popped hers and sputtered a bit. "Nice flavor," I said.

"Yeah," Dennis said. "It's handy to have."

I treated him to what the menu announced as Kansas City steak, probably from beef butchered there in Dodge. One thing about those Harvey Girls; they put on a feed. Emma had turned silent again, which was characteristic whenever she was with men in public.

At least they hadn't banned coffee in the Harvey chain.

"What are you going to do here?" he asked.

"Look at those wheat lands. That's where I shot and skinned buffalo for Tom Nixon. That's where I hunted horse thieves and rustlers and men with reward money on their heads. I doubt that I'll recognize a thing after forty years. I was going to show all this to Emma. She's never seen the place where they turned me into a dime-novel sheriff."

"I don't know whether I want to," she said.

"She's an adopted daughter of Gotham," I explained. "Sews buttons for Flo Ziegfeld."

"Who's that?"

I stared across Grand Canyons. "A New York showman," I said slowly.

"I should get home," Jess said. "It was good to meet

you. Thanks for the evening. I'll run an item in the morning paper that you're in town—if you want."

"Sure, if you feel like it. Maybe it'll bring some old friends to the Harvey House. I don't see any harm in it."

But I had the sense that I had spoken too soon.

CHAPTER 12

The knock caught me half-shaved. I set down the straight-edge and wiped away the lather. Emma was still abed. I answered the door in my white longhandles and trousers, and discovered a blue-uniformed policeman without.

"You Mr. Masterson?" he asked.

I nodded.

"Chief sent me over to make sure you're not heeled. Illegal to carry in this town."

"Why would he do that?"

"You're a notorious character, he says. You have a piece?"

"No."

"He said you would."

"I haven't carried since Teddy Roosevelt made me the U.S. marshal for the lower district of New York."

"You a marshal? How come the chief says you're a notorious man?"

I sighed. "What else did he tell you?"

"That's not your business. You mind if I check this place out for a piece?"

I eyed Emma, who was staring big-eyed with the

bedclothes up to her chin. "Yes I mind. You have no cause."

"Chief said you'd resist. I'm gonna look anyway."

I smiled. "Harvey House's north of the dead line."

"Dead line? What's that?" he asked, pushing in and eyeballing the room.

"The tracks. Dodge had an ordinance against carrying, but we only got serious about it north of the tracks."

"What do ya mean, *we*?"

"I was, at various times, a deputy city marshal, a Ford County sheriff, an undersheriff, a U.S. marshal . . ."

He wandered the room, eyeing the suitcases suspiciously. "Never heard of that. There's no such thing as a city marshal. Just a police chief and men."

"Forty years ago the police force consisted of a city marshal and some deputies. My brothers Ed and Jim were on the force or marshals. I was, briefly."

"That don't square with what the chief says. He says you're a notorious man, owner of saloons and brothels and a tinhorn and bad news for Dodge City. He'd like you out of here."

"Mrs. Masterson and I are visiting, as we have every right to do."

"Well, we'll see about that. What's this?" He was pointing at the oasis.

"That's an Abercrombie and Fitch picnic valise."

"Pretty cold for picnics."

"You done?"

"I guess so. Sorry to bother you. Just remember, don't carry in Dodge City."

I ushered him out, grateful that he didn't find the booze and pour it down the sink, or worse. I didn't like the intrusion one bit and wasn't used to being visited by a copper a few hours after I arrived in a burg.

I completed my toilet and headed down to the lobby, intent on buying a *Globe* so I could see what occasioned the unwanted visit.

The paper carried an innocuous front-page story under the heading, "FORMER LAWMAN VISITING DODGE." It went on to explain that I'd been Ford County sheriff and undersheriff in the 1870s, and was planning to write a memoir, visiting historic sites, and so on. I found nothing in the item that might excite the local constabulary and knew at once that the Legend had been at work. Bat the Legend lived underground like a rat in the sewers of Dodge, even though Bat the Man had been long since forgotten. Well, when I wrote my memoir, the Legend would be laid in its coffin.

After Emma and I had breakfasted—keeping the Harvey Girls at their posts long after closing—I discovered some telephone messages awaiting me at the front desk, including one from old Tom McCarty, Dodge's first civilian doctor, and a man I knew well, having summoned him on numerous occasions to patch up the wounded or write out death certificates. I would call him, introduce him to Emma, and we would reminisce.

But I was waylaid by a frail young man in the lobby. He seemed earnest, wore rimless glasses that filtered the images reaching his soulful brown eyes.

"Mr. Masterson? I'm Ed Steinke, the school superintendent. They said you were eating."

"Well, pleased to meet you," I said insincerely, offering a paw which he pumped as if he were drawing water from a well. I introduced him to Emma, whose hand he neglected to pump.

"Mr. Masterson, I read about you in the paper, and

I thought to myself you should be the grand marshal of our parade."

"Ah . . ."

"I'd never heard about you until I read the paper. I come from Topeka, have a degree in school administration. I took a position here in nineteen and seventeen. So I had to look you up. I learned that you fought the Indians and tamed the buffalo herds so the land could be settled and civilized. The students would enjoy meeting you."

"Parade?"

"Yes, we have a Thanksgiving parade. The students do, each Wednesday before the holiday. That's tomorrow. We march from the park through the downtown to the Dodge City Mill and Elevator south of the tracks and east of here, where we have a blessing of the grain and a public thanksgiving for the harvest and a moment of silence for our first settlers and pioneers."

"Just how do I fit into this?"

"Well, we honor the pioneers, and you're one of our pioneers. The students make marvelous floats, tableaux vivants, featuring our Ford County history. We would like you to ride on one. And Mrs. Masterson, too, of course. It's a wonderful event. The high school band plays hymns and Sousa marches. Each student society, such as the Thespian Club, dresses in its own costume."

"And you have consulted with city officials about all this?"

"Well, it's not their province. The schools do this. Our farm children—or their parents—bring in the flatbed wagons. Some are drawn by teams, but most are pulled by tractors, Hart-Parr, mostly. The wheat farmers put much store by them. This evening they'll work like beavers putting all the tableaux together."

"Well, I'll just oblige. Emma?"

She nodded, her eyes clouded.

"What have you in mind?" I asked.

"Oh, this is grand. A real pioneer sheriff. I thought you were all long gone. I'll announce it to the *Globe*."

I smiled. My leg ached from the ancient wound. "Where and when do we report?" I asked.

"Wright Park. At the Hoover Pavilion."

Those names were familiar. "George Hoover?" I asked, thinking of the old saloonman who arrived in early Dodge, selling whiskey by the tin cup from a barrel.

"The same. A fine, substantial man. Upon his death a few years ago he bequeathed a goodly sum to the city for the pavilion, which is one of the architectural gems of the city. I don't know much more about him."

I did.

"Ten o'clock. We're leading with the 'Spirit of Dodge City' float by the ninth grade. We'll put you on that. It's a tableau of the churches of the city. Truly inspiring."

I sighed.

With that, Steinke pumped the well-handles, pleaded that he needed to return to his office, and retreated.

Emma's eyes were incandescent.

"Mind your manners," I said. "It isn't every day I get to be a marshal of Dodge City again."

From the Harvey House lobby I rang up the operator and got McCarty's maid or wife or daughter or nurse.

"Want to talk to Tom," I yelled into a bad connection.

Moments later I heard that familiar voice. "It's Bat," I bellowed.

"Bat Masterson, eh? What's the death toll now?"

"The papers say twenty-six."

"Oh, pshaw, you should take more credit."

"Well, what do you think? You signed the death certificates."

"Of juvenile cowboys massacred by your six-gun, at least thirty. Of seasoned veterans of the Western Cattle Trail, five or six. Of cooks and bartenders, four or five. Of politicians, at least a dozen, all Democrats, most tortured before the coup de grace. Of gamblers, at least fifteen. Of cattlemen, at least ten. Of miscellaneous horse thieves, burglars, and vagrants . . . why don't we just agree you filled Prairie Grove Cemetery? I'll swear to it before the movie men."

"Do you think that would bring me up to Wyatt Earp, Tom? Legend-wise?"

"I'd have to study on it."

"How's business? I see they have a hospital named for you."

"Business slumped after you left, Bat. I had six concussions your last month in office. The next month I treated one dog for a broken leg, and one woman for summer complaint."

"I'm going to be the grand marshal tomorrow so business should be pretty good again. Can you meet us for dinner here?"

"Why don't you come here? I have a few medicinal tonics that I am allowed to dispense to patients. I'll invite Ham Bell and the missus. What the devil brought you to Dodge?"

"Old age, Doc."

He laughed. "I write old-age prescriptions at five," he said.

"We'll be there. Give me some directions."

He named some streets I had never heard of, but I got the gist of it.

That was a good day. Emma and I strolled a city that was as new to me as to her. We wandered through Wright Park, saw George Hoover's monument, discovered a welcome arch that celebrated the returning veterans, learned that Ham Bell operated an enterprise called the Land and Auto Company, which had the first motor-driven hearse in Dodge, examined a fancy new courthouse, discovered a Santa Fe Trail marker placed on Second Avenue by local historians, inspected the handsome McCarty Hospital, strolled the lobby of the Great Western Hotel south of the rails, examined the City Furniture Store and then a frame cottage next door where I once lived, and not alone. I didn't mention that to Emma.

We stopped at the *Globe* and read a few more back issues. Bloodthirsty Emma hunted down all the shootings, stabbings, brawls, and mayhem she could find, while I studied the court reportage. Then it was time for medicinal tonic at the spacious home of Doctor McCarty. It would be a good evening.

CHAPTER 13

Well, damn. It was good to lay eyes on skinny Doc McCarty and beefy Hamilton Bell, the three of us along with Sally McCarty relics of the early days of Dodge. I had not been close to any of them back when I was a lawman but we certainly had plenty of contact. Many was the time I'd help a drunken Texas idiot up the ladder to Bell's hayloft to sleep it off. And many was the time I summoned the doc to sew up the nightly puncture wounds in Dodge. He extracted a pound or so of lead a month during the high times, and kept the souvenirs in a fruit jar. But I had never been invited to his table until this night, four decades later.

One might suppose that we had a grand time reminiscing about the old days, but the truth of it was that we gingerly dodged early Dodge, a place too earthy for polite twentieth-century company. There were ancient grievances and divisions that welled up to bite our tongues. It was the politest damned meal I'd ever eaten.

Emma retreated into herself as she was wont to do when among Bat Masterson's male friends, and Sally retreated to the kitchen soon after we had polished off a cobbler dessert. Ham had come alone and I did not ask him about his marital status, supposing it would come up in the course of the talk, but it never did.

There were things I itched to know. What had happened to the old southside district where the cowboys had roared away their nights? Had its destruction been the result of design, or fire, or something else? And why weren't those buildings put to other uses instead of being leveled?

Were the various town fathers so determined to rub out Dodge's infamous past that they knocked down all the old landmarks, such as the Lady Gay Dance Hall and Saloon, the Comique, the Variety Theater, which Ham Bell had briefly owned, the old parlor houses, and all the rest? I expected change, but what had startled me was the total absence of every last bit of wood and brick that spoke of another era.

But we maneuvered our dinner talk away from all that. Perhaps they supposed that Emma would be offended. Not one anecdote, not one memory of old

Dodge enlivened our dinner table banter that evening, which focused myopically on the present.

We talked of Hamilton's automobile agency and the slick new Chalmers roadster parked outside. We talked of Doc McCarty's hospital, about his son, Dr. Claude McCarty, carrying on the family tradition. We talked about my diabetes, and the ailments of the aged. We talked about the wheat fields south of town, still fertilized by the manure of the great bedding grounds of the trail herds up from Texas. And so the reunion passed like a convention of the Grand Army of the Republic, mostly ghosts, with the transformation of Dodge as much a mystery in my mind as it had been before.

Ham Bell drove us back to the Harvey House in his roadster around nine, a late hour in modern Dodge. We did the pump-handle handshake routine and wished each other well. He drove away and I supposed I wouldn't see him again. That's how it is with old people. Everything we do is a good-bye of one sort or another. I had an impulse to weep, and was instantly embarrassed by it.

"Well, Legend, I don't think this wild place ever existed," Emma said, nestling into me.

There was a certain reality in that.

I lay awake that night trying to understand what lay between the nineteenth century and this one, what was the difference between Ham Bell and Louella. But I made sense of nothing.

The next afternoon we reported dutifully to Wright Park, which was humming with preparation under a bold blue heaven, the Kansas air as sweet and sharp as I had always remembered it. I didn't quite know what would be required of me and started to hunt down Ed Steinke. But he came rushing up, and began stammering something.

"Slow down, Mr. Steinke," I said.

"I'm sorry. I overstepped," he blustered.

"Overstepped?"

"The invitation to be grand marshal. The students already had invited others, you see. The grand marshals of the parade this year will be our returning soldiers. They'll lead the parade. They've made great sacrifices, and the young people—".

"Quite all right," I said, relieved. There was, of course, a question in my mind about this. Surely the school superintendent would have known about the veterans. Whatever the truth, evicting old Masterson from the festivities had been smoothly done. I would have given ten-to-one that someone whispered something about old Masterson to someone and they had concocted an excuse.

"We'll be proud to have you next to the reviewing stand and close to the city officials," Steinke said.

I smiled. "We'll just watch from the streets," I said.

The superintendent looked relieved. We retreated.

"Struck out," she said.

"What do you make of it?"

"You ain't exactly the king of England here," she replied.

"I just think I remind them of something. I think maybe some families around Dodge have a few old skeletons in their closets. Did all the prairie nymphs leave town when they shut down the south side? No. Some of them are the mothers and grandmothers of the citizens of Dodge. I probably remind them of that."

"And maybe you added to the population of Dodge?"

Her lips were pursed primly.

"At least a hundred," I replied.

We headed down the streets until we reached Bridge and Front, where the parade would cross the Santa Fe tracks. I hoped my legs would support me long enough to witness this revelation of modern Dodge City.

About the time my pins threatened to quit me, we heard the thrum of marching bands descending Bridge, and soon enough a color guard walked by, followed by a platoon of men back from the Great War, all in uniform but none carrying weapons as they might have on the Fourth of July. Behind them, in two open roadsters, came more soldiers, the wounded. One had no arm, another no eyes, another bore terrible scars across half his face.

That stirred me. Honoring and thanking these men was the appropriate thing for this city to do. I took off my hat and held it to my chest. Hell, those men had done more for the country than old Masterson would ever do, and I paid them respect.

A band consisting of elderly veterans from the state soldiers' home that had been Fort Dodge in my day banged away with drums and bugles. Then came the first float on a great flatbed haywagon drawn by a tractor. "The Spirit of Dodge City," it said, and the theme was church spires. About forty people had crammed onto it, all of them in choir robes, some black, some white, some white with purple collars, some purple with white collars. They were all singing gospel music.

That's where the old sonofabitch Sheriff Bat Masterson with his showgirl wife Emma would have ridden. I smiled.

The next float, entitled "The Path of Civilization," intrigued me because it was getting personal. This wagon was drawn by a team of draft horses and dealt with the buffalo and redskins. It featured a stuffed buffalo and assorted dead Indians lying about in feather and fur. Over them stood several gents dressed in fringed buckskins and looking suspiciously like my old pal Bill Cody in full regalia. These gents cradled rifles in their arms, revolvers at their hip, and stood about with their eyes feasting on horizons, looking invincible.

I reckoned that was supposed to be me. Only I had never worn a fringed leather outfit in my hide-hunting days and didn't stand around in a field full of dead Indians. Every time I got to Dodge I burned my stinking cotton clothes and bought a new outfit.

"That's me," I said to Emma. "Slayer of man and beast."

"Sure," she said.

A high school band followed, drilling the "Washington Post March" at us, and the members of various fraternal organizations followed, bearing guidons and banners. An upcoming young man could choose, in a town like Dodge, to join the Masons, Elks, Moose, Rotary, Lions, Kiwanis, Odd Fellows, Knights Templar, or Optimists.

The next wagon was a monster and drawn by a Hart-Parr tractor. On it was a prairie schooner, a Conestoga wagon, and this one was labeled "Santa Fe Trail." Mother stood over a black kettle, stirring supper and looking determined. Father stood sternly, cradling a shotgun, which struck me as a peculiar weapon. Daughter was helping Mother. Son was chopping wood, which struck me as even more peculiar. Long stretches of the trail lacked so much as a twig. It dawned on me that these people didn't want a pile of buffalo chips on their float.

Well, that was pretty good. Most of those wagons

had passed through before my time and before Dodge existed, but the city lay smack on the trail and I saw more than a few roll by.

Pioneers were featured on the next wagon. Women in bonnets running spinning wheels and standing before woodstoves; people in various occupations: a dentist extracting teeth, a doctor surrounded by flasks, a merchant in an apron before a scale, a schoolmarm at a blackboard, a teamster waving a whip. I watched, fascinated. A dozen frontier occupations didn't show up on that tableau vivant. The legend on that one said, "The heroic and courageous men and women who settled an empty land and built a new civilization that will survive forever. They will always have our thanksgiving."

There was something to that. I guessed that was as close to celebrating Bat Masterson, buffalo skinner, railroad grader, lawman, gambler, as any that this parade would produce. I don't remember thinking much about building civilization, though.

The next one was labeled "Ford County Animal Husbandry," and featured a pair of shorthorn cows, a dairy cow, a couple of sheep, a haystack, a gent in bib overalls with a pitchfork in hand, and his wife with an egg basket upon her arm, the whole encased in a barbed wire fence.

Not a trace of a trail herd or a longhorn or a cowboy. I smiled.

The high school band stepped smartly by, playing Sousa.

The next one bore the legend "Granary to the World," and depicted all those wheat farmers who had plowed up every square foot of arable land. They had piled a disk plow and a tractor on that one, along with farm husbands and wives, each dressed for church and carrying a Bible.

We watched a railroad float, a Dodge City commerce float, a Soldiers' Home float, a Kansas farmhouse float, and a few more before my knees began to buckle. The sharp wind was chilling me as well.

"I have to sit," I said.

Emma helped me back to the Vaquero, where we sat alone, nursing coffee while the muted blare of the parade served to entertain us.

"Well, what do you think?" I asked.

"Bat, those floats weren't very honest.".

"Honest?"

"Making the past heroic."

"That's how they feel about the pioneers."

"Certain pioneers."

Emma had a way of making a wry statement and I spotted the merriment in her eyes.

I asked the Harvey Girl who was refilling our cups what would happen when the parade reached the grain elevator.

"Oh, they'll make some speeches about being thankful for all that came before, and all the future will bring, and the compact we have with those who have gone before us; sing some hymns like 'Rock of Ages,' and end up with a blessing from all the ministers in town."

"You want to see it?" I asked Emma.

"I've had enough," she said.

CHAPTER 14

T en minutes of lying in my room on that fateful November day was all I could stand. I was feeling out of sorts. The old wound in my leg was hurting along with a dozen wounds in my heart.

"I'm going over there," I said.

"Okay, I'm going to shop for a cream separator and some chicken wormer," she replied.

With that we went our separate ways. I found a quiet crowd enduring Kansas and elocutionary wind. They had rigged up a stand of sorts in front of those wheat-jammed shafts, and there, to my surprise, was old Hamilton Bell declaiming into an electrical amplifier that boomed his familiar voice out upon the throng.

Hell, he was got up in a black broadcloth suit, wore a homburg, a broad cravat, and had the sober demeanor of a Rockefeller. I remembered when he was shoveling manure.

"This great city is at the dawn of its life," Bell was saying, which astonished me, because he had spent about forty-five years in this place, nurturing a city from prairie sod.

"The past is nothing. America is about the future and nothing else. I have lived to see marvels. I witnessed the first lightbulb, the first motorcar, the first airplane, the first telephone, the first radio. We have plunged into a century that will expand our lives beyond imagining. Think not of the past but of what's to come, for we are fortune's darlings, with a brand-new land to nurture us, a new way of life.

"The business of America is the future. Each year I watch new motorcars arrive, each better and stronger than before. Each year I watch new Santa Fe engines steam through, each bigger and more powerful, more able to fulfill the needs of mankind. Dodge lies at the junction of two mighty railroads, the Santa Fe and Rock Island, and we should include that among our blessings.

"We are making a new nation. We are a new people, building new institutions based upon private liberty and responsibility and less government. The past is dead. Let us steadfastly keep our eyes and vision upon the things that make this country the Hope of the World."

He went on like that. Hamilton Bell, livery barn operator, owner of a variety theater catering to wild cowboys, owner of the first horse-drawn hearse and then the first motor hearse in Dodge, a man living in the future, seeing wheat, morality, a market economy, and God in the road ahead.

That Dodge City crowd listened raptly. I supposed that everyone who wasn't tied down in a business office or shop was present. I saw Jess Dennis taking notes.

I listened awhile more but with little patience, and finally turned away when they got to the singing. All I really wanted was a whiskey sour with my friends at the Metropole.

Since I had come to Dodge I had discovered three paradoxical things: Americans buried and rejected their history. Americans had created an official above-the-counter legend of stalwart, heroic, larger-than-life pioneers who settled the land and made it bloom out of their own towering virtue and courage. And Americans had fostered another under-the-counter legend of a lawless frontier full of badmen and wildmen. Men barbarous and dangerous and brutal—Billy the Kid, Wyatt Earp, Doc Holliday, and a gambler and sheriff named Bat who, according to legend, had killed at least twenty-six mortals.

Damned if I could fathom it. There wasn't much truth in either the official or the unofficial frontier, so why did these legends persist? I had come to Dodge to make sense of my past, only to discover a profound mystery. I had the feeling they would invent those legends, no matter what the truth had been, because they somehow needed the legends to explain themselves.

I abandoned the hushed crowd and walked a few blocks west, wishing I had brought my cane. The bullet that had passed through my leg when I was very young had left its eternal mark. I wanted to stand in the very heart of the old southside district and come to terms with the warehouses and vacant lots there; to understand the Carthaginian Peace the town fathers had imposed on an area that had once enriched the town.

People don't credit me with much education because what I got over the years was mostly home-grown, but I had studied a few things, including Roman history. The Romans had so hated Carthage that when they finally defeated the sea-girt city in 146 B.C., they razed and burned it to the ground and forbade anyone to live there. And that is what the town fathers had done to the old district in Dodge, apparently with the same sort of fear and loathing that had inspired the Romans during the Third Punic War.

I reached the corner where the Lady Gay and the

Comique Theater once stood, and closed my eyes to the dreary warehouses there. That was the heart of the southside district. The memories eluded me for a moment, and only the prosaic reality of the Kansas wind caught my attention.

I had to conjure up everything. This, right here, was where Ed was murdered by two drunken Texans he had mistakenly trusted. This was where a barrage of bullets meant for Wyatt blew through the thin plank walls of the Comique Theater, narrowly missing Eddie Foy, who was reciting his favorite number, "Kalamazoo in Michigan." I was inside the Lady Gay, dealing Spanish monte with Doc Holliday, and we both flattened on the floor when things started popping.

Wyatt dropped to his knee in the dark street, skylighting the rider, and shot his man. On the far corner of this block Dora Hand died of a bullet meant for Dog Kelley, our mayor, and I had swiftly formed a posse to go after the killer, whom Wyatt and my brother Jim deduced to be a young cowboy named Jim Kenedy. He was a wild punk connected to the powerful King Ranch and had boasted he would kill Kelley.

What Kenedy didn't know was that Dog Kelley had gone to Fort Dodge for medical help, and had turned over his little cottage to two showgirls he admired, one of them sweet and virtuous Dora, who had gone to sleep in Kelley's bed, never to wake up. We caught up with Kenedy and grabbed him, but only after some gunplay that hurt him bad. His daddy more or less got him off, but Jim Kenedy's life went downhill from there.

The gaudy Lady Gay, gone without a trace. I could walk into the Lady Gay any summer day and see most of the gamblers on the circuit there. I could look over the green tables and see deadly Ben and Billy Thompson, Cockeyed Frank Loving, Johnny Allen, the square-playing and honorable Dick Clark, assorted Earps, slim and handsomely dressed Luke Short, Sam and Lou Blonger, Rowdy Joe Lowe, and many more. And over in the attached Comique theater I could see Fannie Garretson, Dick Brown, Fannie Keenan, and all the rest. And across the street in Ham Bell's Variety Theater I could see the Queen of the Fairy Belles, Dora Hand, poor dead Dora, murdered by mistake.

I was not above some rough horseplay in those joyous days. A certain Dr. Meredith approached the sheriff of Ford County, one Masterson, wondering whether the city would welcome his lecture on phrenology and venereal disease. I am ashamed to report that young Sheriff Masterson responded positively, lured the innocent to the Lady Gay Dance Hall, and arranged a lecture there, which was dutifully attended by all the solemn sports in Dodge upon pain of a night in the calaboose if they declined.

Sheriff Masterson and City Marshal Earp escorted the gent to the lectern, an upended crate, and other notables were seated on the stage, all of us well heeled. No sooner had the good doc started talking than some lout in the audience called him a liar. I asked the gents to listen, but things got out of hand.

As the *Globe* put it, "Chairman Masterson drew from beneath his coat-tails a Colt's improved, nickel-plated size 44 shooting instrument and formed himself into a hollow square in front of the horrified doctor, determined to defend or die."

The defense was successful, though much powder was expended and all the lamps were shot out and the ceiling was thoroughly ventilated. Chairs and tables sailed, screams and explosions rent the gloom, and everyone stampeded for the exits. In the ticking silence that followed, I got a lamp relit, and found the phrenologist and healer of social diseases curled in a fetal position on the floor. We could not persuade him to complete his lecture.

Ah, Dodge, dammit, what did they do to you?

Those people giving thanks over at the grain elevator would have been appalled. But few, if any, ever heard of that bit of Dodge City history and maybe that is just as well. Civilization has the duty, the obligation, to rub from memory whatever barbarisms lurk in the collective memory. Let them give thanks to God for a bountiful harvest, a new nation wrought in virtue and liberty, and the chance to bloom, and let them forget the rousing we gave to an earnest lecturer on venereal disease.

I imagine one day some humorless, axe-grinding historians of the frontier with fancy degrees from fancy universities will examine all this and conclude that we who lived on the border were desperate, miserable, broke, delusional, impoverished, rapacious of nature, immoral, and brutal.

The joke's on them. They will miss the fun we had and the sheer joy of living that permeated our brief halcyon, and so they will miss the heart of it. They will miss the gambling spirit, the way we shrugged off defeat, the pleasure in taking our chances, and so they will miss the very spirit of the times.

I tried to conjure it all up, the fun, the smoke, the lamps, the smelly cowboys, the rattle of dice and wheels, the clatter of glass, the ripples of applause and laughter from the variety shows, the thump of boots on plank floors. I tried to conjure up the moments when I pulled out my six-gun and laid the barrel over the cranium of a dangerous drunk or the times I'd disarmed a Texas bonehead threatening mayhem upon our city.

I remembered going after train robbers, including Dave Rudabaugh, and nabbing two of them out in the lonely wilds and the other two right in town. I was a good lawman. I usually got my man and often traveled hundreds of miles to do so. I ignored minor infractions or offered no more than a quiet warning. I preserved public safety.

It wasn't hard to remember these things. They had been duly written up in the *Times* and the *Globe* and I had studied them just a day or so earlier. But then the yarn-spinners had twisted and bloated them out of recognition and they became something else, with young Masterson a cold and willful killer of men whose infractions scarcely merited death. I could not stem the tide of all that nonsense and had finally tried to turn it to my advantage. Let them think of me as an engine of blood.

Standing there on the corner of Locust and Bridge, I regretted that I had not ever put the record straight—and wondered if it mattered whether I did or didn't. I was no closer to understanding.

CHAPTER 15

Thanksgiving loomed, and Emma and I would be celebrating the feast by ourselves. I rented a Chalmers roadster from Hamilton Bell's automobile agency, intending to see the countryside on the Thursday holiday. We would celebrate the feast in the Vaquero later in the day. I did not tell the clerk that I had driven a motor vehicle only two or three times, and he probably guessed as much when I stalled the engine several times as I engaged the clutch. I admired the machines, but had no need for one in the middle of Manhattan, where hacks are plentiful.

Emma was waiting for me in the room that Wednesday afternoon, looking distinctly ready for some medicinals.

"I bought some porcelain eggs, a cream separator, Doctor LeGear's Poultry Worm Powder, Oshkosh bib overalls, White Russian soap, a McCormick combine, two tractors, a Home Comfort range, and a hay rake. They will all be delivered," she said.

Emma was getting bored with Dodge.

"I rented a roadster so we'll have something to do tomorrow."

"Any chance of switching tickets around and heading home?"

"Yes, but I want to do some things on Friday."

She registered that with disappointment. "We need ice," she said.

I headed down to the restaurant, asked for a pitcher of ice water, and returned to the room for the evening libation. Emma took to the Jack Daniel's like a camel at an oasis.

Her spirits improved by the minute, as did mine.

"I think I know how to get through tomorrow," she said.

We set off in a frosty cloudless dawn, armed with spare gasoline and several tire patches. We took the wicker picnic valise but not the flasks. Instead, we loaded it with sandwiches and a Thermos of coffee. I steered the roadster over the steel bridge spanning the Arkansas River, heading south upon well-graded dirt

roads flanked by wheat fields and occasional farm-
steads. Upon this very land the great longhorn herds
up from Texas had bedded while their owners dickered
with buyers or waited for the railroad to supply the
stock cars to carry the cattle East.

The last time I had seen this country not a building
or a fence existed, but only the stretching plains, never
quite flat and always full of surprises such as hidden
glades, springs, wandering creeks, rock outcrops with
caves that harbored the dens of catamounts or wolves.
I had wrestled the hides off of buffalo here while I
was with Billy Dixon's outfit. But the landscape had
so changed as a result of the endless farming, broken
only by a few livestock operations neatly fenced with
barbed wire, that I could scarcely conjure up those
brutal days when I toiled from dark to dark and then
blew my meager pay in the shantytown of Dodge after
a badly needed bath and haircut and shave and the
purchase of a set of new duds.

Emma stared at the emptiness placidly but I knew
this country tried her patience. I was awash in memories, but she had no connection to the land and saw
only the bleak skylines, the stubble of spring wheat,
the amazing green of winter wheat, the sad stumps of
harvested corn, and the herds of Herefords and Angus
and shorthorns that had long since driven out the rangy
longhorns. It was going to be a long Thanksgiving for
her.

The roadster hummed without trouble once I got the
spark adjusted right, and I began to relax. It wasn't
going to rain and we weren't going to mire. The garage had supplied a robe, which Emma had tucked
about her skirts. I lost my fedora to a gust of cold air,
stopped the machine, and retrieved it. Thereafter I let
it rest on the floorboard.

Ahead, on the misty horizon, lay Oklahoma, the Nations back in my day, and beyond, the Texas Panhandle, where one of those fateful moments of my life played out. Emma didn't know about that one, so I decided to tell her, though it was not the sort of story a man would usually tell his wife.

"If we were to drive another hundred miles or so," I said, "we'd reach the panhandle of Texas. We won't get that far. I'll turn around in a while. But something happened to me down there that I'll tell you about. That's where I was shot in the leg; where I got the scar and the limp—and where I almost lost my life."

"Woman trouble," said Emma.

"How did you know?"

Her eyes glowed. "I can read, you know. It was in *The King of the Gun-Players*." So she knew. My friend Al Lewis had written the article in 1907, sensationalizing me and building the legend of the killer. In this one case, Lewis was more or less right. I did probably kill one man in my life, in self-defense, in 1876. I was not then a peace officer.

"Then you know. I shot an army sergeant named Melvin King, who had just shot me near the groin, put a bullet through a girl named Mollie Brennan, and was about to finish me off. Yes, all that lies ahead, over the horizon there. Long ago."

I circumvented a quagmire, knowing that if I attempted to drive through it we would spend the rest of Thanksgiving there, awaiting a passing farmer with some draft animals or a tractor to pull us out of the gumbo.

I lapsed into silence. Even then, remembering the red haze of pain, the fear, the doctors' pronouncements that I would not live, and Mollie's death from a bullet through her abdomen, fostered silence.

"Tell me," Emma said.

"I was twenty-one. I had been a scout for General Miles, who was chasing renegade Comanches. Many of the hide hunters were helping out. He set up a winter camp on Sweetwater Creek in the panhandle, built Fort Elliott, and soon enough the wild little town of Sweetwater sprang up to cater to the troops and the scouts and hide hunters.

"There was a joint called the Lady Gay, same name as the later one in Dodge, that dished up rotgut, gambling, and girls. I fell for a girl named Mollie. So did Sergeant King, who regarded her as his own, and who also regarded hide hunters and civilian scouts as fair game for his revolver."

"Was Mollie pretty?"

"To a twenty-one-year-old boy in from the wild country and months in male company, Mollie was beautiful beyond words."

"Did Mollie have a profession?"

"I imagine," I said. "Mollie liked me. I fancied she loved me. Well, you can imagine the rest."

"No, tell me."

She had me cornered. I didn't much mind. "Sure, babe. I wanted time alone with Mollie so I paid the guy who ran the joint to let me and Mollie have some privacy after the joint closed. He lent me the key. Mollie, she was willing.

"But King got wind of it somehow. Next thing I knew, someone was hammering on the door, so I opened it, and there he was, drunk, violent, and with a six-gun in his hand. Mollie shrieked and tried to shield me. He shot me and I went down. He shot Mollie in the gut. I pulled out my own six-gun and shot him in the heart as I lay on the floor. He was dead when he hit the floor, but I don't remember it. There were other shots as people rushed to help me. Mollie died a few hours later. Somehow the army surgeons stanched my blood and I survived."

"Oh, Bat, that's a good story, not a bad one. Were you in trouble?"

"No, there were plenty of witnesses and the army ruled that it was justifiable homicide. King was a mankiller and I came close to being another of his civilian victims. He knew who he could kill and not get into trouble with the brass. It took two months before I was on my feet, and I had a limp that comes back when I'm tired."

"I am sorry that she died."

"I have lived with it all these years."

We drove silently awhile, the coy November sun keeping us barely comfortable. We did not see a single mortal and often went several miles without seeing a farmhouse. This was all part of the country under my jurisdiction as Ford County sheriff. In those days, much of the unorganized territory in the state came under our supervision. I had crossed this country many times with posses, in search of horse thieves, bandits, train robbers, and killers.

The engine coughed, and I stopped at once. I unscrewed the cap, ran the measuring stick in and pulled it out to gauge how much fuel we had, discovered only a gallon remained, and filled up from the two canisters I had brought along. I had a little trouble cranking the machine to life because I hadn't set the spark and choke and throttle in the right spots, but eventually the roadster coughed to life.

"We'll go back now," I said.

"I was worried."

"We're only five or six miles from a farm."

She sank into melancholia. I stared one last time

toward the horizon, aching to see Sweetwater, which
became Mobeetie; and also Adobe Walls, where another episode in my young life had spun out. That was
where a couple dozen hide hunters and a few shop-
keepers catering to the hide business fought it out with
Quanah Parker, the Comanche chief, along with a formidable army of his own and allied warriors. In the
end, our Sharps buffalo guns and our skills honed from
dropping buffalo at long distances drove off the much
larger force of wild Indians. That was where the Masterson legend began. I had fought well and my Sharps
rifle had found its mark time after time.

I have come to regret all that: the killing of the
herds, the invasion of the homeland of those people,
the destruction of their food and shelter. When I was
young I didn't give it a thought and if anyone had
asked me I would simply have said it was the march
of progress, and a better race was driving off a primitive race. But I am old and I see with more vision
now. Maybe I will write a column or two about that
when I get back to the *Morning Telegraph.*

I yearned to drive the rest of the way, see Adobe
Walls and whatever was left of Mobeetie, and let my
memories rush through me. Only reluctantly I turned
the roadster back to Dodge. Once we started back, into
a fine fall afternoon, Emma began to smile.

CHAPTER 16

The heavy overcast the next day reminded me that November is the least favorite month of practically everyone. Emma's and my mood matched the sky.

"Do you want to get out of here?" I asked, over poached eggs and toast and marmalade at the Harvey House restaurant.

She started laughing.

"All right. I want to talk to someone this morning. We can catch a train any time after noon. But Emma, I want to go to Trinidad."

"Trinidad?"

"I did some lawing there and so did Jim."

"Not New York?"

"I could put you on the train East if you want. I've started something I want to finish. Maybe I'll figure out who the hell Bat Masterson is."

There had been defining moments in our long union, and this was one.

"Let's get on the road. Trinidad, here come the Mastersons, jugglers and ballroom dancing."

"My travels won't stop there, Emma."

She smiled. "I think Flo Ziegfeld can live without me."

That was my Emma.

"Okay, kid, get us some tickets. And we'll have to deal with the hotel."

My destination was the fancy big city hall across

the tracks. I hiked over there, feeling my old leg-wound once again. I found the city police bailiwick at once, and entered a brown barn of a room with a pair of iron-barred cells at the back. I made myself known to the blue-uniformed bald clerk with a rap on the counter. No one else was in sight.

"Like to talk to the chief," I said.

"He's upstairs talking to the county bookkeeper. Is this some emergency?"

"No. I'll wait if he's coming back soon."

"I'll tell him. Who should I say—"

"Masterson."

He eyed me as if I belonged in one of those empty cells in the back, and vanished up a stairway. Law enforcement was pretty casual in Dodge, and the closest thing to crime these days was probably some bindlestiff off a boxcar stealing longjohns from a washline.

The room had three desks, the chief's larger and with a desk lamp. A rack with half a dozen shotguns and rifles was screwed to one brown-painted plaster wall. A brass spittoon flanked each desk. Some big round ashtrays held the stubs of slimy cigars. A fly-specked feed store calendar proclaimed that this was still November 1919. Some file cabinets and two telephones, one on the clerk's desk, the other on the chief's, completed the spare headquarters.

It seemed a long time. The phone did not ring. I wondered how many cops were out and whether they patrolled in Fords or on shoe leather. I guessed that one copper was patrolling Dodge.

At long last the clerk and a lean and trim chief rattled down the stairs. The chief was not young, had mottled pink and brown flesh that ran to ridges and valleys around his face and neck, and the eyes of a mongoose.

"Masterson, I've been expecting you," he said.

"Then you knew more about me than I know about myself," I replied.

"I was expecting to haul you in."

He waved me back to his desk. I followed, faintly irritated. I knew this type. He was a classic. We seated ourselves, armchair gladiators.

"I don't believe we've met," I said cheerfully.

"Delwig Bjorn. Have you come to tell me you're leaving town?"

"Well, you cut right to the chase," I replied.

"You didn't answer my question."

"When I'm ready."

"Why are you here?"

"To find out why you think I'm notorious. That's what your copper said I was."

"You've a criminal record, you're a gambler and associated with illegal boxing."

"United States marshal, most recently appointed by Teddy Roosevelt for the Southern District of New York; Ford County sheriff, undersheriff, deputy city marshal of Dodge, deputy city marshal in Trinidad, brother of a slain Dodge policeman, brother of a Dodge City marshal and U.S. marshal and Ford County deputy sheriff, deputized federal posseman in Arizona."

"And a little soiled on the cuffs."

That puzzled me, and he saw it.

"I've been through your records, city and county," he said. "When I learned you were in town I pulled some old files. Pretty good stuff. You were fined for illegally discharging a firearm at a certain resident in the city of Dodge and you were lucky a murder rap wasn't hung on you. You were part of the Dog Kelley administration that was soft on vice. You ran for sheriff, won by three votes, and next time around you got whipped badly.

"You ran faro and monte and other games while wearing the badge and so did your brothers. One brother bought a half-interest in the notorious Lady Gay as soon as reformers discharged him from our force. You've been trouble everywhere you've gone. You got into big trouble in Denver. You were very nearly arrested for insurrection during the railroad war in Colorado. You owned a joint called the Palace in Denver that reformers called the worst cesspool in the city. Is that enough?"

"Nope."

"You got into trouble running a bunco game in New York City."

"And it was dropped when they took a closer look."

"Yeah, maybe."

"No maybe. If you want to make me mad in one hell of a hurry, just accuse me of being a crooked gambler. I sued that sonofabitch who accused me, and I'd sue you. The rube skipped town out of reach of my suit."

He eyed me cheerfully. "My patrolman reported you had a wicker picnic valise in your room and when I asked him what was in it he couldn't say. I'll tell you what's in it. Illegal booze which you illegally imported into this state."

I smiled.

He smiled back, the pink and tan blotches curling into triumphant ridges. "I'll make you a little wager, Masterson. I'll bet ten dollars that you have illegal booze in that wicker case. We'll go look. If you don't, I'll pay you. If you lose, we'll haul you over to the court and you and the missus will get yourselves fined, usually twenty-five and costs. Apiece."

I said nothing. He would need a search warrant and probable cause.

"I knew it," he said, grinning. His teeth were spotless.

"I'm thinking of writing a memoir. There seems to be some legends about me that don't quite add up. This is a good place to separate truth from falsehood."

"Memoir? Who would read it?" he asked.

That was a low blow.

"Probably not you," I replied, "but not for the lack of trying."

I could punch below the belt too, but he didn't get it. He just sat there, his mongoose head weaving in rhythm with mine, studying me, showing me nothing.

"What else did you discover about me in the old records?"

"There was some misappropriation of funds when you were sheriff."

"Yes, and what was the conclusion of the county investigators?"

"You managed to lay it off on a clerk."

I laughed. Before me was a Bjorn-again bloodhound. "What else makes Masterson a notorious man?"

"You've killed what? Twenty, thirty?"

"What does your record show?"

He was grinning wickedly. "That you managed to cover it all up."

"Twenty or thirty? What's in the record?"

"Nothing."

"And what do you make of it?"

"That you dented a lot of skulls, Masterson."

"That's what Doc McCarty kept telling me."

I was sort of getting to like this guy. "Chief, tell me something. How many men have you killed?"

That surprised him. He wasn't used to being on the receiving end.

"None."

"How many would you like people to think you've killed?"

"None."

"Then we're about even. Before I became a peace officer I killed a sergeant in self-defense at a dance hall in Sweetwater, Texas. There were witnesses. I was cleared immediately."

"I know."

"Name any others. You've just gone through my records and probably studied a stack of old dodgers too."

"That doesn't mean there aren't any," he said.

"Yes, it does mean there aren't any, dammit. Where does this mankiller rap come from? Newspapers, articles, dime novels. Would you like a legend like that hung on you?"

He sighed. "Cigar, Mr. Masterson?"

He liked me. I took it, a puke-yellow five-center, bit the end off, and lit it. I don't much like cigars. But the smoke is obnoxious and that is useful.

"In those days," I said, "peace officers weren't paid enough to buy beans with. You had to have a side income or starve. Most of us ran games. When your reform mayor, Webster I think, posted the rule that peace officers could have only one job, my brother bought into the Lady Gay, a partnership. I made a living dealing. That's how it was in those days. I was no different from all of the peace officers, Deger, Bassett, the Earps. Don't single me out."

"I never have, Masterson. Now, are we gonna look at that wicker case in your room?"

"Nope. Unless you think that harassing a newspaperman will make you a big cheese in a city that doesn't welcome me; a pissant city in which some of my old friends turned into bitter critics—people like Nick Klaine, the first editor of the *Times,* and Mike Sutton, county attorney who switched sides. Hell, it seems like even now, forty years later, things haven't changed much."

"Cool down, Masterson. You're welcome here. People are a little sensitive, that's all. The town fathers buried the past in an outhouse vault years ago, and I don't plan to pump it up. If I pinched you, half the reporters in the country would land in Dodge City, and city hall wouldn't like that. Just hurry up and do whatever you're up to before you get me into trouble."

"I'll get out when I've answered the questions in my mind. Unless, of course, you run me out."

It was a question.

"You have a right to stay here."

"That is correct," I said, propelling some cigar smoke at him. "I am an old man looking for some understanding of my life. You can help me. Last Wednesday I watched the Thanksgiving festivities, which included a celebration of some mythical people labeled Pioneers. I saw those tableaus go by. Farming, Santa Fe Trail, Buffalo Hunters, the Army, all of them. Your high school youngsters honored the settlers, and that's what I'd expect in a Thanksgiving parade even if a few things were missing, like the cowboys and trail drives and longhorns. I didn't really expect them to do a float honoring the dance hall girls."

Bjorn smiled thinly.

"That's one side of it. The other is that fanciful

writers think up tales about me and persuade themselves that I've killed twenty, thirty men and lived a
life of depravity. Like that cuckoo in the Kansas City
paper. Like the friend of mine, Al Lewis, who did one
of the hokum gunman articles about me and a screwy
novel, too.

"That's the legend you've bought and believe even
though you know it's not true. Your own records show
the falsity of it. There's over-the-counter history, and
under-the-counter history. Both as crooked as a bunco
steerer. Why?"

"Darned if I know. This is the twentieth century,
Bat, and no one cares anyway."

So we had moved to a first-name relationship.

"Somebody must care about the Old West. Every
novel that Zane Grey writes about the frontier is a
national bestseller. Bill Hart makes five-reel cowboy
movies, guns firing and bodies falling, and the public
lays out millions of dimes. If no one cares, why is
that?"

"I got work to do, Masterson."

"Sure, big stack of papers here on your desk. You
give me a good answer to the mystery and maybe
we'll hop on a train this afternoon."

"I want an autograph. You're the most famous man
in the history of Ford County."

"Sure," I said.

He handed me a blank sheet, which I tore in half
so he wouldn't write some Declaration of Indepen-
dence above my John Hancock. "Best wishes to Del
Bjorn," I wrote, and signed it. He studied it for criminal intent and decided it wasn't something to lay before a grand jury.

I extended a paw. He shook the notorious gunman's
hand.

I actually had learned nothing, but had made a friend.

Dodge was still as mysterious to me, and as brooding, as the Sphinx.

CHAPTER 17

I headed for the offices of the *Daily Globe*, hoping Jess Dennis would spare me some time. He was busy, but decided he could use a sarsaparilla and we headed for a soda fountain. They had a lot of those in Dodge, marble affairs serving up ice cream and fizzy stuff.

I ordered a phosphate.

"Maybe you can solve some mysteries for me, Jess," I began. "Let's talk about that Thanksgiving parade. The young people were honoring the settlers. Nice floats, handsome pioneers on them. I saw tableaus for everything in the history of Ford County except one thing."

"The south side?"

"No, I wouldn't expect them to depict any of that, especially in a parade giving thanks for our blessings. What I didn't see was any depiction of the trail herds up from Texas, the drovers and cattlemen, the old Dodge House where millions of dollars of business was transacted. Nothing about the brave boys who drove cattle for months on end across total wilderness infested with dangers, through storms and stampedes, through wild Indians and outlaws, and got them here safely.

"They were heroes too, Jess, maybe even more so than the local settlers. The cowboys were the bravest and finest men I've known. They deserved a float. And those herds jacked Dodge into a city. I would have liked to see just one float with a hell of a big old longhorn on it."

"That's the taboo chapter here, Bat."

"But I'm not talking about the saloons and cribs and dance halls and gamblers. I'm talking about brave and skilled men who pretty near made this city and this county."

Dennis stared a long moment. "I'm afraid the young people scarcely know of them," he said.

"Yes, and why?" I persisted.

"That's the buried chapter, Bat. It's because the cowboys and trail herds are associated with evil, sin, lust, murder, greed, and all the rest of it. It's not only been erased physically; it's been rubbed out of memory, as if there were some fear, or horror, of it, or as if the knowledge of it would corrupt everyone here."

"And I suppose that's why they've never heard of old Bat, either."

"I'd·wager you could poll the senior class at the high school and not a one would have heard of you, or the Earps, or Holliday, or Tilghman, for that matter."

"Okay, my other question is, why do people believe all this stuff? I can't travel around the country or check into a hotel without running into it."

"Let me ask you a question in return, Bat. Did you ever do anything to discourage it? Like responding to untruths that were said about you? Or writing some pieces to correct the legend?"

"No."

"Then you acquiesced in it, and to that degree you created it yourself."

"I imagine I did. It was handy."

"It's not too late to correct it, Bat."

"But what the hell good would that do?"

"That's for you alone to say. If you want to, you will."

"I don't think anyone cares, twenty years into a new century."

"That's right, Bat. No one does."

"I care. I was a good peace officer."

"Then say so. I'd even publish your piece myself in the *Daily Globe*."

"You? Even if the town fathers landed on you for it?"

"Sure, I'd do it."

"That's admirable. I'll think about it."

"I gotta put out the paper, Bat. But before I do, I got a question for you. Why'd you leave Dodge?"

"I lost the sheriff race to George Hinkle in eighteen-seventy-nine. Lost badly. They'd accused me of crookedness and I figured the charge was so phony I didn't reply. I guess I should've."

"Ever since you got here, I've been paging through old papers. I found an issue of the weekly *Globe* that ran a letter you wrote from Trinidad in 1883 taking the *Times* and Nick Klaine to task. I won't go into all that, but you were plainly pretty bitter. Remember it? You called our city and county officials vampires and murdering bands of stranglers who'd controlled Dodge's political and moral machinery. Stuff like that. You were pretty hot."

"I was plenty hot, Jess. My friends switched sides and joined the new reform mayor, Webster, who wanted to shut down the whole south side and get rid

of the Texas cattle trade and put their own people onto
the police force. Klaine, Mike Sutton—he was county
attorney—men I thought were my friends. I was sick
of this town, sick of this county, and I'd just taken a
licking at the polls, so I got out."

"But not for the last time."

I smiled. "Not for the last time. When Luke Short
asked for help, I helped him. So did a few others."

Jess Dennis smiled, as if that were a bond between
us. "Some day I'll get up the nerve to run that story
as a history column. You got any more questions,
Bat?"

"No, I guess not."

"Could I have an autograph?"

"Hell yes."

I signed my name in his stenographic pad.

"You're a legend, Bat, and I just want you to know
how much this means to me. Just talking with you;
just hearing some of the old stories. I'll never forget
this."

"You're a good man, Jess, and I'm glad we met."

Emma had booked us on a two-twenty local to Trinidad, so we ate a leisurely lunch at the Harvey House,
said good-bye to the Harvey Girls, checked out, and
waited in the November gloom for the westbound.

"Well, what did you find out?" she asked.

"Oh, that the chief really likes me, and that the town
has banished a chapter of its history from memory,
and that I probably made the phony legend myself just
by letting it stand. I also found out that no one gives
a damn, and this is another century, and what counts
is trains and telephones and indoor plumbing and ra-
dios and automobiles and bigger wheat crops."

We boarded five minutes later.

The train mourned its way across doleful prairie

country, sometimes flat, sometimes convoluted, mostly tan and wan under the burden of the fall's frosts. We passed into Colorado, still following the Arkansas River to La Junta, and then cut southwest to Trinidad, which nestled in a corner of the mountains just north of Raton Pass. We sat with a dozen silent strangers in a rattling coach, and hammered our way over the empty plains, which seemed little different in 1919 from when I had first taken this great railroad West. The drummers all looked ready for a drink.

"I was in Trinidad for only a year or so; just want to see it," I said when Emma was looking dolefully into the twilight. "It holds some memories."

"And after that?"

"We'll see. This Legend still doesn't know how his life spun out, and he wants to know."

We steamed into Trinidad in a moonless darkness so we couldn't see how the town nestled hard into the red-rock mountains. There was scarcely a level acre in the whole place. It was now a coal mining town with a bitter history of labor strife, but it was also a ranching town, a supply center for vast cattle enterprises in every direction.

Six or seven thousand people were jammed into a town no larger than Dodge, but that only gave Trinidad an urban air that seemed to shut out the howling wilderness. We stepped out of the car onto a steel conductor's stool, and into red gravel. The station bulked in the dim light and I looked at once for a hack, and found there were plenty.

"Is the Ritenburg House still a good place?" I asked.

The driver shrugged.

"That was informative. You have gabby shoulders. We'll try it."

The place would bring back some more memories.

An undersheriff named McGraw, actually the man who ran the whole department for Sheriff Juan Vijil, had died in the Ritenburg after being shot on the street by one of my policemen, a man named George Goodell, who harbored a king-sized grudge. McGraw had picked the fight and drawn first, so Goodell escaped the consequences.

I didn't tell Emma any of that. She was soldiering along with me, looking after my health, making sure I ate right and was warm enough, which I never was with the bad circulation. I didn't want to add any nightmares to her burdens.

Everything had been jammed together in Trinidad and it looked the same as ever, but most of the old saloons and gambling parlors were apparently shuttered. When I was the city marshal, the burg ran wide open. In fact, I operated a faro game there to fatten my lousy salary. I remembered the old joints, but especially the Bonanza, a house that specialized in high-stakes games for high rollers.

Trinidad was loaded with familiar faces when I was there, some of them old friends from Dodge; others were familiar to me as bunco steerers and crooks I'd run out of Dodge. The joints even reminded me of those in Dodge: the Bank Exchange, the Tivoli Saloon, the Boss Saloon and Brunswick, the Grand Central Bar, and many more. I was at home in them all. Tomorrow I'd see whether any had survived as ice cream parlors or near-beer joints in dry Colorado.

My stay in Trinidad was largely devoted to rounding up confidence men and vagrants and swindlers and running them out of town. I shut down or cooled down a few whorehouses, kept a lid on various species of banditry, and tried to pacify half a dozen ferocious newspapers, every one of which was looking for ways to fault the constabulary for one thing or another. My brother Jim was in town the whole period but we didn't see much of each other because things were a bit frosty between us.

But I wasn't coming back to Trinidad to relive any of that. Most of it was ordinary police work. The things I remembered about my sojourn there really were rooted somewhere else, in a wild Arizona mining town called Tombstone.

After leaving Dodge, I had drifted some, going up to Leadville and Gunnison, and dealing faro in the Oriental Saloon in Tombstone for Wyatt Earp. And that's where the trouble began that washed its way through Trinidad and sent me up to Denver to rescue Doc Holliday.

I wanted to relive that and discover if there was anything worth remembering about it. I didn't create any legends in Trinidad. Or maybe I had. Maybe I kept Doc Holliday from an informal execution.

The hack dropped us off and I escorted Emma through a chill night into the old place and booked us in. I didn't much like the look of it but we wouldn't be staying long.

CHAPTER 18

We weren't in our room but twenty minutes, and fixing to head for the nearest ice cream parlor, when we were greeted with a sharp rap on the door.

I opened to a young dude, maybe twenty, dressed

to the nines and looking proud as a peacock.

"Mr. Masterson?"

"Yes?"

"Are you the old lawman, Bat Masterson?"

I owned to it.

"I'm Harry Gustafson from the *Trinidad Daily News*. Are you up to an interview?"

"How'd you know we're here?"

"I get a lot of tips from desk clerks. I make it worth their trouble."

"That's the time-honored method," I said. "Emma, you suppose we could repair to a soda parlor and let this gent have at us?"

"You bet, if he buys."

"I'll buy," said Gustafson.

"All right, take us to a good joint," I said. "This is my wife Emma and she does the negotiating in our family."

It took him all of one minute to steer us into a neighborhood street-corner saloon, with boiled eggs, peanuts, and popcorn available for the asking. The only thing missing was booze. He selected a hardwood booth for us that I knew would persecute my tailbone, and took our order for some malt near beer, below one-half percent alcohol and legal.

When he returned we did some serious sucking for a moment. Travel inspires that. Leaving Kansas absolutely necessitated it. I sipped, hoping the pain in my arthritic joints would numb a little.

"I can't believe I'm this lucky," said our host. "Everyone in the country knows who you are."

"And they all think my ticket expired years ago."

"Well, I did. But that's all the better. This'll be the story of my life. I've been a reporter four years and

I've covered murders and stuff, but never a big story like this."

"This is a big story?"

"Yeah, Mr. Masterson, you're a legend."

"How so?"

"You've killed twenty-six people."

"Where'd you get that?"

"Clippings. Our morgue's full of them. We got a Masterson file an inch thick."

"Why, may I ask?"

"You know what people around here think about? Old West peace officers like you. And the Earps, and maybe Hickok."

"Not Buffalo Bill?"

"Aw, he was a showman. You're the real McCoy."

"Why am I the real McCoy?"

He looked puzzled. "I don't know," he said, and signaled the keep for another round. The habitués of this Prohibition-spawned fraud of a corner pub were probably miners. Some were playing billiards but most sat in the booths or on bar stools and sipped their near beer. There wasn't much conversation and they were probably listening to us.

Gustafson continued: "All I know is that I've heard of you all my life. Trinidad boasts that you were the city marshal here. There's not a boy grows up here that doesn't know all about you."

"What do they say?"

"That you could shoot faster'n anyone else."

"I never tried to shoot fast, Mr. Gustafson. I did try to hit what I aimed at and that was usually a weapon or a shoulder. Most often, a horse. Shoot a horse and you've stopped an escape. I shot innocent horses and the Humane Society considers me Exhibit A. I don't recollect shooting at anyone in Trinidad. You've checked the old clippings. What the hell did you discover?"

Gustafson sighed. "No, you didn't kill anyone here. Mostly you rounded up vagrants and bunco men and ran 'em out, and kept the lid on, ah, certain resorts."

"Well, what is it you want to talk about? I'm game. But I'd better warn you, this Masterson"—I pointed at myself—"isn't the Masterson you've heard about. Never was."

I sensed the beginning of disappointment in the young man. I think he was hoping for a sensation, a front-page story. But this scribe turned out to be no Louella Parsons.

"That's good," he said quietly. "Maybe you'll let me write the first true account of your life. Maybe I'm the luckiest guy in Trinidad. Mr. Masterson, you probably just don't know how much you're admired here. It really has nothing to do with shootings and gunplay and all that. It has to do with the way you faced stark danger over and over and made the world safer. Everyone I've ever talked to about you thinks you are a fine American."

I liked that. Between sips of fake beer and some dried-up bar sandwiches and fat dill pickles, I talked while Gustafson loaded his legal pad with his own hieroglyphics. Like many reporters, he had evolved a personal shorthand. I felt at ease. Emma was listening quietly, also at peace, munching pretzels. This neighborhood saloon was a haven for peaceable men who asked little more than the companionship of their fellow coal miners.

"Okay," said Gustafson, "tell me how you rescued Doc Holliday."

"That's quite a story, and it involved some maneuvering and maybe some manipulation of the law. You want to hear all of it?"

"I sure do if you have time."

Emma nodded. She liked this man.

"All right. I spent a while in Tombstone dealing faro for Wyatt Earp at the Oriental. That was where the high-stakes games were usually played. I made plenty of money, twenty-five a day and five an hour overtime, because dealing faro is tough work. You can't make a mistake, not one, and you have to be on the watch every second. The Oriental was a great place, with old friends like Dick Clark and Lou Rickabough and Bill Harris and Luke Short coming in and out of there all the time.

"I had known the Earps and Holliday in Dodge but I drew close to them in Tombstone. I never liked Doc much but I like him more now than I did then. He'd been dealt a bad hand and was playing it out as best he could. He was actually a quiet man with a dry wit and good southern manners and a surprising gentleness.

"Well, trouble was brewing down there. Real, serious, murderous trouble, between an outlaw bunch out in the county, expert at cattle rustling and stagecoach robbery, and the businessmen and financial and banking interests in town.

"Hell, people keep calling it a feud or vendetta, but none of these definitions really fills the bill. It wasn't just the Earps feuding against the Clantons, as if it were some sort of family fight, and not just a vendetta, and there was more to it than gangs fighting for turf or spoils.

"It was more, much more. The outlawry in that desert waste was so pervasive it threatened business and finance and the mines, which is why Wells Fargo got into the act and most of the businessmen in town had formed themselves into a vigilance organization with the intent of stamping out the crime wave that was threatening Tombstone's very economy.

"Look at it this way, Gustafson. The city's merchants and mayor and such big outfits as Wells Fargo put their chips on the Earps, who were city police and also had a deputy U.S. marshal badge. Morgan was riding shotgun for Wells Fargo. But the cowboys, or outlaws, had some law on their side in the person of Sheriff Johnny Behan, so both sides could conduct manhunts under the cover of law, as posses.

"Law on two sides. Hunting licenses, murder licenses, all legal. Think of that. The hunters could hunt the hunters with a license to kill. So this whole thing was much more than a vendetta. You know how the dictionary defines a vendetta? A feud between clans or families. That's much too narrow a description of what was going on.

"I was in on the opening deal. After a stagecoach robbery attempt in which a couple of people were killed, Wyatt, who was then a deputy U.S. marshal, organized a posse that included me. All we could go on with a federal badge was United States mail robbery, but that's all we needed.

"We knew who we were looking for—Harry Head, Bill Leonard, Jim Crane, and Luther King. Well, we rode four hundred hellish miles. My horse dropped dead under me. We got King, but the rest got away. And King managed to escape from Johnny Behan's lockup, a put-up job, so it was all for nothing. You might say that was the beginning.

"Well, I got out before the whole thing broke open. Jim was in trouble in Dodge and I hurried back to help him and just never went down to Tombstone again. If

I'd gone back, I would have been right in the middle of it all. It had boiled down to the three fighting Earps and Holliday against an entire cutthroat mob, all of them skilled with six-guns, courageous, reckless, and deadly.

"The odds against the Earps must have been ten to one, maybe worse. Curly Bill Brocius, Ringo, the Clantons and McLaurys, Stilwell, and the rest amounted to an organized outlaw army larger than even Wells Fargo, with all its resources, could hope to handle privately.

"That desperado army was set to run the county, pirate the mines' bullion, operate with impunity from ranchos and mountain hideaways, and bleed citizens and companies of their hard-won wealth. If I'd stayed on I might not be here talking to you right this minute. It was that desperate."

"But you were here, right?"

"I was here, watching it unfold, sometimes wondering whether I should get down there and help out. Well, you know how it broke. The fight at the OK Corral, the butchery of Morgan, the wounding of Virgil, Wyatt's ruthless stalking of the killers with little color of law to protect him, Behan's warrants for the Earps and their allies, and then suddenly Arizona Territory was much too hot for the Earps and Holliday and some of their men.

"They came through here in May of 'eighty-two, stepping off a Santa Fe train up at El Moro and walking here about as quietly as men can slip into a town. That's when I got the story and discovered the trouble they were in. Behan had warrants out for all of them, but there was another set of warrants too, out of Tucson.

"Wyatt had shut down his posse in Silver City, sold

the horses and beat a retreat, coming up here by stagecoach and train. A Tucson grand jury had warrants out
for Wyatt and Doc, for the slaying of Frank Stilwell.
From here they spread out, Doc hitting the gambling
circuit in Pueblo, Denver, and other Colorado towns,
while Wyatt and Warren Earp headed for Gunnison to
lay low. They were in big trouble. And it wasn't long
before Wyatt asked me to help."

"And you did," said Gustafson.

"I sure did."

"Doc was in trouble."

"He was good as dead."

"Want another malt?"

"I'd have to drink this crap for a week to get one
good whiskey sour out of it."

Gustafson smiled.

CHAPTER 19

O kay, I'm a sucker for flattery. Harry Gustafson
believed in me, didn't care about how many
people I planted six feet under, and considered old Masterson a good American . . . unlike the
typical citizen of Dodge, who probably would have
banished me to Argentina if possible. Well, that cut
two ways. I would like to ship Dodge City to Costa
Rica as an international goodwill gesture.

Emma liked him, too. She even talked now and then
between pretzels and hard-boiled eggs instead of clam-
ming up the way she usually did. She loves me, and
she can scent a malicious bastard about two miles off.

"Harry," I said, "you won't understand this, but you're graduating magna cum laude from the College of Mastersonology."

He laughed. "Tell me about the rescue of Doc."

"Well, all right. Now there's two ways of looking at this. You can say I bent the law and manipulated the justice system to spring a wanted man. That's one way of looking at it. Or you can say I simply balanced the scales of justice to make sure that everything came out square and fair.

"If you believe that, you have to believe that law and justice are two different things, and some officials use the law for their own ends. That's what happened in Doc's case.

"Doc thought he was pretty safe in Colorado from those Arizona warrants. He set up shop in Pueblo with some gambling pals. But he was spotted by a certain dubious gent named Perry Mallen, who approached him with some song and dance about Doc being in danger from Frank Stilwell's brother.

"A few days later Doc and I and a couple of others went up to Denver for the races, and checked in at the Windsor—some joint that was. I've never seen such a hotel west of New York.

"Well, poor Doc was walking near the hotel when he was ordered to throw up his hands. This gent, Mallen, cuffed him and hauled him off to the cops where Doc learned he was being held on Arizona charges for the killing of Stilwell.

"Doc, in the lockup, immediately sent for me, and I set to work. Doc wasn't my favorite man but he was a friend of the Earps and on the right side of the law, and I figured it was up to me to do something or Doc Holliday was a doomed man. He wouldn't have lasted ten minutes in the hands of Johnny Behan."

"You helped a man you didn't like?"

"You know, Harry, it's a funny thing. The older I get, the more I like Doc's memory. I wish he was sitting right here, right now, so you could see for yourself what sort he was. When you get past his rough side and see the young man slowly dying from consumption, and see how the booze cut the pain, and how he had no future, and couldn't practice dentistry because people didn't like a consumptive coughing in their face, and how Doc attached himself to the Earps and remained a loyal and valuable friend every single day of his life, risking his life for them, then maybe you'll see the Doc I'm remembering more and more, and not the meaner man."

Gustafson was writing all this down at a great pace so I let him scribble a little and downed another hard-boiled egg. The gents in the next booth were listening and eyeing me furtively, as if I were some sort of purple and orange parrot out of the Nicaraguan jungle that had alighted in their street-corner clubhouse. I had seen that look before. An American legend sees stuff like that.

"Well, I went to work. I went to Frank Naylor, an attorney there, and he got a writ of habeas corpus, and we sprang Doc the next afternoon. But the miserable rags that get called newspapers in that rotten town— and believe me, I know what I'm talking about—got on the case and next thing I knew, I was reading that poor old Doc was a vicious killer. Now, in fairness I have to say a few of those scandal sheets rallied in Doc's defense and had plenty to say about what was going on down in Tombstone."

"Yeah, I got some old clips here," Harry said. "They describe him as a gentle, well-dressed, and well-educated man."

"He was all of that. Meanwhile, this lobster, Perry Mallen, is giving the press a cock-and-bull story about being a Los Angeles sheriff and tracking Doc for seven years because Doc had supposedly murdered Mallen's pal, someone named White, during a stage-coach robbery. I smelled the odor of skunk in all this."

"Mallen turned out to be a bounty hunter, right?"

"And a fraud. Not a true word in him. Well, Doc was in bad trouble. If they extradited him to Arizona he was a cooked goose."

"So I figured it was time for me to set up a diversion. I got ahold of my friend Jamieson, can't remember his first name, dammit, city marshal in Pueblo, to cook up a charge against Doc for a bunco game or something like that. Which he did. Now when there's a local warrant outstanding, it's not so easy for another state or territory to extradite. So I hoped that would do it.

"Well, a friend of mine, Sheriff Bob Paul, of Tucson, a damn good man, showed up in Denver with extradition papers for Doc, but our governor, Frederick Pitkin, wasn't around and Paul had to wait.

"That extradition hearing had been set for the thirtieth of May, and when I got wind that the governor was back in town the evening before, I figured I'd better act, and fast.

"So I got an interview with him and let him know what was what; that Doc Holliday would not get a fair trial, that he had been a deputy U.S. marshal in a bona fide posse during the Earps' manhunt, and that Holliday would be a dead duck if he were sent back to Arizona Territory.

"I guess that did it. The governor denied the extradition and Doc was sent down to Pueblo to answer the bunco charge. He put up three hundred dollars of bail bond and the trial was postponed. Not once, but time after time. He headed out to Gunnison to be with the Earps and it was all over. He died in Glenwood Springs before the trial ever came up. It worked pretty good."

"And you saved Doc's life."

"I believe I did. What was left of it. He didn't have long to live, Harry. Five years, and most of them pretty desperate, sick and alone and unable to practice dentistry, and in the end coughing so much no one would let him deal or run a faro game either.

"He got awfully sick up in Leadville. I did what I had to do. The man had stood beside me and stood beside the Earps. You can believe I threw a wrench into the system or you can believe that I balanced the scales of justice a bit. I don't care which."

The kid closed his notebook and sucked suds off that fraud called near beer. "That was quick thinking. You helped a friend."

"I'd do it again. No regrets, pal, even if I twisted the tail of the whole system. That Mallen fellow turned out to be a cockamamy character. He ended up bilking a few Denver residents and hightailed out of there. He just wanted some of Johnny Behan's reward money, and when it didn't happen he looked for other victims."

I felt Emma's hand touch mine under the table. The love of a man and a woman is the best thing that life has to offer. It hasn't been the best of unions but we've endured.

Gustafson turned to her. "How does it feel to be married to an American legend?" he asked.

"I didn't know I was until the last few weeks. He was just my Bat. I had no idea when we met that he was anything other than a gambler. So all this is strange to me and I've learned much about my own husband this trip that I never knew.

"I'm proud of him. I'll tell you something. He's a courageous writer and if you want the true legend of Bat Masterson, you just read his columns in the *New York Morning Telegraph*. He fires words just as well as he fired lead. That's the real legend."

I gazed, amazed, at my usually silent Emma.

"What's this trip really about?" Harry asked.

"I don't know. Truth for sure. Summing up a life. Figuring if I counted for anything. Wondering whether this legend that follows me around will be the ruin of punk kids with six-guns, meat for more crazy novelists.

"I started out to set the record straight but now I don't know why I'm on this odyssey. But here I am. I know this is important. I'm not just looking at my past. I'm hoping to tie up some loose ends, answer some of life's big questions, such as why I'm such a hero to a bunch of people. Why people here like me, but in Dodge they would gladly have hustled me out of town. When I get back to New York I'll let you know."

We talked awhile more. Gustafson would have a pretty good story. He wrapped a scarf around his neck and headed for the paper to write it up in time for the morning edition. It was pretty late for a half-sick old man, so I escorted Emma back to the hotel, keeping an eye out for footpads, but we made it.

"What's tomorrow going to be like?" Emma asked, after we had shut our door and cranked open the valve in the hot water radiator.

"Not much. Walk around Trinidad. This isn't Dodge, and the neighborhoods haven't changed much. You know something? Meeting Gustafson was a stroke of luck. He got me to talking and by the end of the evening I had what I wanted. A sense of my life here, my one year in a city I never cared much about. This was just a way station on my road to the future. I wasn't put on earth to be a city cop."

"Want me to get some railroad tickets? Ready to head back to New York?"

I didn't answer. Instead, I opened up our portable bar in the wicker picnic case and poured one hell of a nightcap. I figured that it would take about two drinks to soften her up. And after that damned near beer, I was ready for some real ninety-proof booze.

She smiled as I handed her the whiskey. She sipped, smiled, and sipped. I swilled mine back and poured another.

"Here, let me top yours," I said, aggressively splashing a good dose into her silver-plated cup.

"Hey, what are you trying to do?"

"Soften you up."

An eyebrow shot skyward. "You're too old; you'd have a heart attack, and I'm an old broad, and it's too late to make babies. Where did this come from? You had some gorgeous girlfriend here you're remembering now?"

"Oh, several, but I wasn't thinking about them. You're all I ever think about."

"Likely story, Legend. Let's see, you bumped off twenty-six mortals. How many women did you lay . . . in their graves?"

"Too many to count."

"Where am I in this lineup?"

"Nine hundred seventy-two."

She swallowed the whole load and thrust the cup at me, looking downright coquettish. "So soften me," she said.

"I already have. You willing to extend this trip a bit? I'm thinking about a side excursion to Los Angeles."

"Los Angeles!" She started laughing and gave me such a hug as I haven't had in twenty years. Getting old is not always hell.

CHAPTER 20

We caught the Santa Fe Chief at twilight and swiftly broke out the ninety-proof Tennessee and washed Trinidad out of our minds. Then we repaired to the diner for a dinner as the train topped Raton Pass and rolled into New Mexico.

The whiskey sours were tonic for body and soul. I idly contemplated the assassination of the entire directorate of the Woman's Christian Temperance Union as an act of public service.

"You realize, William Barclay, that we'll have to get a wire transfer of cash in Los Angeles. Where will this end? Bora Bora?"

"Not a bad idea. I want to see you wearing a grass skirt just low enough to cover your varicose veins. Are you having a good time?"

She smiled cheerfully. "What are we going to do in L.A.?"

"Chase the legend," I said.

The lonely New Mexico high desert faded into gloom and I had a sense of passage through a land as empty as it had ever been, the train a tiny oasis in a wilderness, rather like a steamboat traversing a sea of solitude. One who has lived in the wilds, beyond the rim of civilization, knows what wilderness is really about: loneliness. Utter solitude. How few of the Runyons and Parsons of the world grasp that.

Over filets mignons loaded with sauteed mushrooms I toyed with the thought of getting off at Las Vegas. I had spent a little time there; a good, rowdy, gambling sort of town populated by every species of sharper on earth until the vigilantes hanged the superior class and drove the rest up to Trinidad, where I had to deal with them and did. I decided against it. I was pursuing a legend, not a scrapbook of memories. Las Vegas was nowhere and always will be.

I thought also of hopping off at Albuquerque, shuttling down to the Southern Pacific, and catching a westbound as far as Benson, Arizona, and then, quite probably, an anachronistic stagecoach down to Tombstone for a look around unless someone has laid some rail since I left. Maybe they had a spur line going down there now. I didn't know. The town had burned down a few times but maybe I'd recognize some street names or something.

"You're thinking about Tombstone," she said after she had demolished a garlic salad. She had a way of reading my mind.

"Do I think with my lips?" I asked.

"No, you started looking gunfighterish."

"What kind of look is that?"

"Slits for eyes, keen burning gaze surveying the hands of everyone in the joint; checking for bulges under the armpits of suit coats, squinty glances at people passing through the car, and a poker face, lips curled slightly downslope. You see, Legend, you can't escape me."

"How do I look when I'm not being gunfighterish?"

"Like a man who's examining every female figure in sight. Like that sultry blonde who came down the aisle a moment ago in a tight dress, followed by her Latin gigolo with the pointy mustache. A fire lit in your orbs and then faded. Well, are we going to Tombstone?"

"It's a temptation, babe. But I think not. I'll tell you what Tombstone is now. It's a sleepy little sand-in-your-soup dump living on evil memories and hating the Earps. And the food is bad."

"You have a hundred bad-food capitals, Bat."

"Yeah, and I'm right every time. Tombstone's dead. The mines shut down when water flooded them. Dust blows down Allen Street. The old gambling palaces are either charred wood or decaying to dust. Such people as remain are mostly kin of the old outlaws and cowboys and still despise Wyatt, Morgan, Virgil, Doc, not to mention Wells Fargo, which had a big hand in cleaning up the place.

"I could go there, peer into dusty abandoned buildings, try to conjure up some memories, recollect how little I was there—a few months—and how much of that time was spent riding in a posse with Wyatt until we were all ready for a hospital. But that's not the real reason, babe. Tombstone is another man's story, not mine."

"Yeah, and that's why we're going to L.A."

"I haven't seen Wyatt and Josie in decades. He lives with a legend of his own, as false and foolish as the one that chases me. I want to find out what he thinks of it; what he says to people who brace him with Boot Hill counts and try to buy his old revolvers and tell him they'll pay him a young fortune for his Buntline Special—which he probably sawed off at the first opportunity if he ever got one at all, damn worthless things. And talk with Josie, too."

"It will be good to see them again."

"Yeah, it will. Talking to Wyatt's one reason. The other is seeing the film companies and find out what they know about the Old West. They're the ones telling the stories now, reel after reel. Not old farts like me. They do pretty good, actually."

Her face lit. "You mean get on the set and watch them shoot?"

I nodded.

"You didn't have to soften me up for that," she said.

"I want to see if Bill Hart or Ben Turpin or the Gish sisters know the barrel from the butt of a revolver."

"You mean I'd get to meet them?"

"If Wyatt and I can arrange it."

She slid into fantasy and I knew she was already wandering through sound stages, meeting show people like herself, having a grand time.

I thought about Wyatt. I'd been thinking about him for many years, and with advancing age had formed some private conclusions, things I would never say publicly. He had assets. Courage greater than any man I've known; coolness in terrible circumstances; an intuitive skill as a peace officer when it wasn't overruled by bad judgment; a deadly skill with any weapon. All those things had made him a bona fide legend and he deserved his far more than I deserved mine.

And yet, I could scarcely say that Wyatt had much of a life. He had tried his hand at several things and the only ones he was any good at were running a gambling game and operating a saloon. He made money with the Dexter Saloon in Alaska, and a little more with saloons in other mining camps. Tex Rickard employed him as a gambling pit boss in Goldfield.

At bottom, he had become a night watchman, a human rottweiler looking after someone else's mining property.

What else was there? His ventures into horse racing were financial strains. His prospecting and mining were mostly ruinous. He staked out the Happy Day mines but I don't think they were worth a plugged nickel and were little more than a place where he and Josie could camp out.

I'd heard he made a little in Kern County oil, but I've often wondered what he and Sadie, as he called Josephine, lived on. In 1911 he was nailed on vagrancy and bunco steering charges, and I suspect that whatever they lived on was supplied by her family. He lived in genteel poverty in a small rented bungalow in the heart of the city.

He was not much more than literate, and developed no new skill or business. He followed the fight game, as I did, but made little of it. He had been near-broke much of his life. Like ninety-nine percent of mankind he was content to drift rather than to progress, or master new skills, or educate himself, or grow into a better life.

I wondered whether he was very bright. Certainly not bright enough to write a coherent memoir of his life. I wondered what I would find in Los Angeles. Probably a penurious Wyatt, feeding on a few Hollywood friends who celebrated his legend. I hoped I was wrong.

But of this I said nothing, not even to Emma. I might be off base and we would have to wait and see. For all I knew, he might be up in Oakland, where he spent time with his wife's friends and family.

I've always felt a stab of joy traveling through New Mexico and Arizona. The two were states now but still had the feel and look of territories. I stepped out upon the platform of the observation car just to breathe in the air. I couldn't see much but it didn't matter. We were in Hopi and Navajo country, and I knew that when the moon rose I'd see vast arid plateaus, oddly shaped buttes and mountains, and a land of mysteries.

Then I headed for the Pullman car, number 1036, which I had memorized so I wouldn't wander into someone else's bunk. Emma had preceded me and taken the upper berth, knowing that my pins were wobbly and I wasn't much good on a ladder anymore. I removed my shoes and slid them under the aisle curtain, pleased that they would have a new shine in the morning. I managed to squirrel around in there and get to bed between the clean and starchy sheets, and thought of her up there.

We had had a pretty good marriage, more because of her steadiness than anything I brought to it. If we were ten years younger she probably would be with me, jammed into a bunk barely big enough for one instead of up there. She had a standard line now:

"But Bat," she would say, "you'd have a heart attack."

Which was probably true, but she hadn't considered the beauty of checking out in flames.

We steamed into L.A. late the next afternoon, after passing through seas of orange groves, the fruit ripe and ready to pluck. It seemed an odd and perfidious place, one I didn't understand, an ersatz copy of Paradise executed by a hop fiend street painter. We finally puffed to a halt at Union Station and I stepped into the Los Angeles air, which was balmy, spicy, and fragrant with oranges, as if the city were engaged in a perpetual wedding.

"Where'd you book us?" I asked Emma, as the red-

cap gathered our bags and lugged them down the platform. I leave all that stuff to her. She understands
cities.

"The Hotel Cordova, Eighth and Figueroa," she
said. "It was that or the Alexandria, but I like the
Spanish name."

"Is that near here?"

The redcap replied. "Just other side of town," he
said.

We fought our way through an army of real estate
agents, subdivision hawkers, and land investment
touts, all offering free motorbus rides to nirvana or
paradise or the Elysian fields, where we would find
properties that would double in value every few
months. Los Angeles was booming and had topped
half a million people. The motorcar, along with ubiquitous red streetcars, had welded the subdivisions into
a vast metropolitan whole.

"Mister, you and the lady are about to get rich,"
said one bulbous-nosed broad in a perky dress. "You
just let me show you Alameda Heights, nice little bungalows, very private, doubling in value—"

"Do they allow saloons?" I asked.

She turned pouty.

The redcap fought off the piranhas and deposited us
on the curb of Alameda Street. There he fetched us a
hack and we were whisked through what appeared to
be the center of Dubuque, jammed with trucks, an occasional dray, and snazzy roadsters, none of which had
a top and all of which had horns.

"Where's the real downtown?" I asked.

"Maybe they don't have any," she said.

"Los Angeles doesn't really exist," I said.

The driver braked before a gaudy white Moorish
structure and I had misgivings. I'd seen high-priced

bordellos that resembled this outfit. He shifted the gears to neutral and unloaded our stuff on the sidewalk. I paid him his four-bit tariff and a dime tip, and lugged a bag into a cavernous lobby before two predatory bellboys descended and snatched our possessions from us. I looked to my wallet for ransom money. At least that part of it was no different from Manhattan.

I checked us in, William Barclay Masterson and wife, and we ascended to the third floor in a whining brass-furnished cage operated by a Vaseline-haired simian, and we were duly deposited in our room after traversing gloomy tile-floored halls. The Cordova seemed to be manufactured of white stucco smeared over chicken wire, but maybe that was the way of the world in Los Angeles.

Emma headed for the window, which opened westward on a vast and hazy panorama with a blue line of arid mountains to the north. I was eyeballing palm trees for the first time and some shaggy-barked giants I understood to be eucalyptus. It was the damnedest place imaginable for Wyatt B. S. Earp to call home. I stood there squinting into the dying sun, wondering why the hell I had come there and what the hell I expected to discover.

It was time to call Wyatt and find out.

CHAPTER 21

Josephine answered and I told her it was Bat, and she told me to lay off, she was sick and tired of that stuff, why did everyone do that? Couldn't they let old people alone?

. "Josephine, this is Bat Masterson. William Barclay. Let me talk to himself."

"You don't sound like Bat. Where are you?"

"In Los Angeles."

"You don't belong here."

"Truer words were never spoken. Now if the old reprobate is available, put me on."

"This is a hoax. You're trying to sell insurance, or maybe you're another blackmailer."

"Put him on, Josie."

"I will not. He's not well."

"You mind if I come out there and you can inspect me at the front door?"

"Yes."

"All right. He calls you Sadie, right?"

Silence.

"And you met my wife Emma in San Diego, right?"

Silence.

"And you and I first met in Tombstone when I was dealing for Wyatt at the Oriental and you were still running with Johnny Behan, right?"

I heard a scuffle and what sounded like the earphone banging on the floor or a desk, and then Wyatt's voice.

"Yes?" he snarled.

"This is Bat."

"Yeah, and this is President Wilson."

I started laughing.

"How did you get here?" he asked truculently.

"By paddy wagon. I want to buy your six-guns, Earp. Especially your Buntline Special for my collection. I'm a serious collector. I've got Bill Cody's Buntline with the three-foot barrel, and I want yours. I know you have it. It's in the bottom of your trunk. And I'd pay anything for the gun that perforated

Johnny Ringo but I'd settle for the one that got Curly Bill.

"And if you don't have any notched artillery on your shelf, just sell me a certificate of authenticity and I'll pick out a Peacemaker in a pawnshop and put it into my private museum. Name your price, Earp. I'm good for it. And I want an affidavit saying you wiped out thirty-seven badmen. I'll pay you in gold so you can keep it off the tax forms."

"Not here," he said. "We'll meet you for lunch at the Alexandria Hotel on Sixth Street at noon."

He didn't want us to see the bungalow. "My treat," I said.

He didn't argue. "What are you here for?" he asked.

"To see you, Wyatt."

There was a choking sound on the line. "I never thought I'd see you again," he muttered. "I'm coming heeled and if this isn't Bat, L.A. will have its man for breakfast."

"That's the nicest compliment I ever got," I said. "Bring Sadie."

"If you aren't Bat she'll attack with hatpins."

"She sure protects you."

He didn't reply to that. "Good blue-plate specials there," he muttered.

"Wyatt, is this Alexandria a fancy place?"

"It's the movie place. Some of the actors live there and they shoot the pictures out Washington Boulevard where nothing's built up. Some of them take me to lunch there, like Bill Hart, so it's a place I know."

"All right. Good to talk to you. We'll be waiting at the Alexandria," I said.

I hung the earphone on its cradle and turned to Emma. "Josephine's got a Chinese Wall built around Wyatt," I said.

"You don't need one," she retorted.

That was my Emma.

We spent the morning walking the streets and dodging streetcars in air so incredibly balmy that I wondered why I had chosen harsher climes all my life. I could not fathom why the City of Angels had risen just there, hard by a dry river, with a topographic lump called Bunker Hill on the other side. But hell, I wasn't going to argue with the city fathers.

The place bustled with life and joy, and to the north and east great blue mountains barricaded a mean world from this corner of paradise. It would be a good place to die, I thought. Room-temperature coffins forever.

I understood this citified part of Los Angeles. I wondered whether I would ever understand life in the little bungalows in vast tracts in the hinterlands. Thanks to Mulholland, they had brought in enough water from the Sierras, but I just wondered whether the whole thing would dry up some day.

There in the tawny tile lobby of the Alexandria were Wyatt, old and lean and bristly and tall, and Josephine, softer and rounder and shorter, an improbable love and union. We shook and went through the rituals. There we were, two notorious peace officers and their showgirls, two or three feet in the grave.

"You're either Bat or a good imitation," Wyatt said. "The eyes. Same as ever."

"You look pretty fine," I replied, "for someone who's had a pound of lead fly by him."

"I never stopped a bullet," he said.

We headed for the dining room, a high-ceilinged affair that echoed and amplified the conversations within it. I surveyed the room, as I always do, and had to do some pretty serious pokerfacing. This might be

Los Angeles but I wasn't going to admit that anything was peculiar.

At one table six cowboys, each with a six-gun tucked into tooled leather, were chowing down. I hadn't seen so many spurs and bandannas since Dodge City. If that wasn't enough, another table held a complement of harem girls in gauzy pantaloons and tight little vests. Their bare arms were loaded with copper jewelry. I eyed them carefully while Emma stared. And if that wasn't enough, another table featured a gaggle of people in ball gowns and tuxedos. I'd seen plenty of those in New York but not on a weekday noon.

"Movie people," Wyatt said. "They live here and change costumes here."

The sight absolutely fascinated Emma, who was squinting at one harem costume that had ripped along a seam, revealing a creamy and flawless limb too young for varicose veins or creped flesh.

"I could sew that," she said. "Should I tell her?"

"Pretty nice leg," I said, which was ample answer. Emma sniffed.

"Don't you look, Wyatt," said Josephine.

Wyatt couldn't look without turning around. "You're safe, Sadie," he said.

I ordered double whiskey sours all around, intending to loosen up this noonday party. God had endowed Californians with a little sense. Josephine's disapproval built brick by brick up her face until it was a rampart. "Wyatt shouldn't," she said.

"Old marshals get exempted," I said.

"He's not in good health," she persisted.

"Sadie, I'm going to have a drink," Wyatt said.

We spent the next ten minutes agreeing with each other. We agreed the world had gone to hell. We agreed we hadn't seen much of each other since Wyatt dealt faro in Denver in the mid-nineties. The rest of our meetings had been on the fly. I had visited them once in San Diego and we had run into each other once in Luke Short's White Elephant Saloon in Fort Worth where we both had sat in on a high-stakes poker game they're still talking about down there. Once we had gone down to Mexico together to pick up a fugitive.

We agreed that all the good men were dead and the wild times had vanished and that the new breed of peace officer didn't hold a candle to the old ones. We agreed that getting old is hell and we shouldn't have to ache so much.

We were old men reminiscing and we should have had a grand time digging up old yarns, but I sensed that Wyatt was not a happy man. And the more he sipped that drink, the less serene he seemed.

"These bloodsuckers," he said, waving at the crowd of actors lunching around us. "They come to me for advice and I give it, and I don't get anything for it. They tell me I'm the most celebrated man alive from the old days and they put the things that happened to me in their movies, but they don't give me a dime for any of it."

"Who's 'they'?"

"The film companies. The producers and those people."

"Why don't you sell them the right to do a story about you?"

"They'd just do it anyway. They come over to my house and tell me what a famous man I am, Colonel Earp they call me. They get me to talk about Tombstone or the killing of Morgan, and all that. They get me going and then steal everything I said and put it in their pictures."

"Do they keep asking how many people you killed?" I asked.

"Yeah, and the truth is I don't know, but it's about a tenth what they say."

"They ask me too. You know what I am? One of the best boxing experts in the country but they never ask about that. All they want to know is bodies."

Wyatt was getting steamed up. "They ask me to show them a fast draw and I tell them I wouldn't know how, and they don't believe me. Those actors all want to whip out a revolver and shoot some fatso through the heart. I wouldn't help them if they paid me."

We ordered club sandwiches all around and I noted that Emma had slid into one of her silences as she often did among my friends. Only young Harry Gustafson had lured her out of her quietness. Josephine wasn't saying much either but she was listening sharply, no doubt for the faintest slur upon Wyatt issuing from my mouth, which she would no doubt recite to him later in high dudgeon. I did not satisfy her lust for indignation.

"What do I get out of all this motion picture attention?" Wyatt asked. "I get free passes. I get to go watch them shoot out in Inceville. They even give me lunch in the cafeteria."

"What's Inceville?"

"Oh, that's just a name. Tom Ince—the producer, you know—bought a big ranch out in Santa Ynez Canyon in the mountains beyond Santa Monica a few years ago, and there's where the picture shows about the Old West are made. They've got a regular ranch set there, and all the livestock and stuff anyone would ever need.

"They bus actors out there by the carload, so much a pound. That's why the whole business is moving out that direction, mostly around that Hollywood subdivision. That's a Temperance place. Cecil DeMille was one of the first. He rented space at Hollywood Boulevard and Vine and set up shop. Air's good there, plenty of fields and sun and it's so far out from here the land's cheap enough. That's all because of the western pictures over at Inceville."

"We'd like to see it. Emma and I have never seen a film being made. She's a showgirl, too."

"Well, don't go. They'll just job you and ask for advice and try to get you to show them how it was done. Or they'll just dog you for ideas and stories so they can steal them. If you want to go out there, don't call on me for it. I'm your friend and I'm not about to put you into the middle of all that. Those people are all worthless."

"Has anyone approached you about the Tombstone story?"

"Oh, they all have, over and over, tried to worm it out of me. They think I'm some sort of celebrity. They think they can buy me a drink and get my story out of me like I was some old drunk."

"Wyatt, why don't you take things in hand, get some writer to put your story down, copyright it, and then sell it to them for a good price?"

"Oh, the writers are worst of all. They'd just steal my story and never pay me."

"I know some who would give you a fair shake."

"No."

He said it in a way that shut doors. He ate angrily and the rest of us nibbled silently. One thing was plain: Wyatt Earp was a miserable, suspicious old man.

CHAPTER 22.

A fter lunch the women excused themselves and headed for the water closet. The Alexandria's dining room had emptied. Wyatt started for the closet but I stayed him.

"Wyatt, I'm on a trip to look at my life. Here I am, some sort of notorious character, and I keep wondering why. Do you ever wonder why people keep coming to you?"

"I am well known in some circles."

"Do they want to buy your guns?"

"I've sold a few Colts. I don't grasp why you're making this trip."

"My doc says I could check out any time, diabetes, hardening of the arteries. Risk of a stroke. People have turned me into a celebrity, only it's all half true. I'm thinking about putting the record straight while I can."

"I might do that. They've got everything all wrong. But I'm not going to let them sell Wyatt Earp to the public without cutting me in."

"You're a brave man, Wyatt. People admire that. You stood up and fought. People admire that. What's wrong with letting people admire you? If they're making films about your life, things you've done, what's wrong with that? Your name will live on, just as it deserves to."

Wyatt's face softened.

"If you don't get paid, so what? Some day this whole country'll know what you did there in Tombstone. You're a hero, Wyatt, and you should let this country have its heroes. Maybe you should just co-operate with them and try to make sure they get things right."

For once his antagonisms dissolved. "It wasn't anything more than duty," he said. "You backed us. That's why you're a friend. We were loyal and our friends were loyal."

"Loyal, yes. If people want to know who Bat Masterson is, I'll tell 'em I'm one of the best players that ever sat down to a poker game and I know the fight racket as good as anyone. Wyatt, is there anything you'd do different if you could do it over?"

He stared down an ancient well. "I could have kept Morgan from getting killed if I'd paid more attention. I knew better. I've told myself over and over I could have kept that from happening. It wasn't over, and I knew it, and it was up to me to go after them and finish the job. That's the only regret I have."

"No regrets over leaving Mattie?"

His face turned stony again. "She left me for a bottle long before I left her."

"I have lots of regrets," I said.

"You think too much."

"I have more questions. This moving picture craze. They're out in these lots shooting blanks at each other and wearing cowboy gear. Why's that? Why does the public lap it up?"

"I never gave it a thought."

"The public devours these two-reelers and these Los Angeles outfits are churning them out. Do you ever watch them?"

"Not if I can help it. They get it all wrong."

"Well, hell, I'm just the opposite. I love to watch."

"If they got it right I wouldn't mind."

"What do they get wrong?"

"All that banging away. I hardly burned powder in all my years as a peace officer."

He spent the next minutes giving me his opinion of the whole movie industry and spilling a lot of information about who was who. He didn't think much of the movie business or anyone in it. When the women returned, Josie proclaimed that it was time for Wyatt's nap. He rose at once. I knew who ran that outfit.

"If you want to look at the filming, Bat, I'll give you a name and a number," Wyatt said.

"I would."

"Bill Hart. You can ring him up at Ince's Culver City Studio. Or talk to Gardner Sullivan. He does script and titles for most of Ince's westerns. Or just call Tom Ince. He's quite a man."

That's how we left it. Emma and I watched the old man depart, ramrod straight, an obelisk beside a sphere.

Wyatt had been too busy being angry to examine his life or wonder what needed to be set straight. Maybe he would come around to it.

"You want me to get tickets to New Yawk?" Emma asked.

"No. We'll go watch 'em shoot a picture."

That was one hell of a smile on her face.

The Alexandria was well fixed with public telephones so I commandeered a booth and had the operator hunt down Thomas Ince. But she had news for me. "Mr. Ince isn't in Culver City anymore, sir, he's with Paramount."

"All right, put me through to there."

Moments later an operator announced that I had been connected to Paramount Studios, home of Mary

Pickford, Douglas Fairbanks, Fatty Arbuckle, and William S. Hart.

"Thomas Ince," I said, expecting to run into blockades.

"Are you an actor?" the lady asked.

"No."

"Well that's okay, then. Mr. Ince doesn't like to talk to actors."

He answered himself, and didn't even sound impatient.

"Mr. Ince, I'm Bat Masterson," I said, and waited.

"Well, what can I do for you?"

"I'd like to visit the Santa Ynez ranch north of town and watch some filming, along with my wife."

"Well, we're pretty busy—"

"I'm a newspaperman."

"A newsman. You should have said so."

"I'm with the *New York Morning Telegraph*. Friend of Louella Parsons."

"Louella! Any friend of Louella is a friend of Thomas Ince Productions, Mr. Masterson. She's the greatest motion picture reporter in the country, bar none."

"I thought you were with Paramount."

"Thomas Ince Productions is Thomas Ince Productions."

"Could you get us out there to Inceville?"

"Sure can. We've jitneys leaving the lot for the ranch all day. You just show up here and hop one, and spend all the time you want out there. I'll have someone tell you what's being shot and who's in each picture. Usually half a dozen pictures going at once. Some ours, some that just rent the property. Catch the streetcar to our lot and I'll leave word with the receptionist."

"What streetcar?"

"Melrose."

"You have time for some questions?"

"Sure, I always have time for a friend of Louella Parsons. You going to do a story on Thomas Ince, right?"

"On westerns, maybe. Okay, are westerns popular?"

"Popular! They're our bread and butter. Millions of people lay out a dime each week to watch a western. Thomas Ince can't make enough of them. The public laps them up. If it weren't for bottlenecks Thomas Ince would be making even more of them. Thomas Ince is doing one two-reeler a week and I'd like to do more five-reelers too, one a week, but there aren't enough labs to process what we shoot, and we can't get experienced people."

"Why are they so popular? Is it because they're a part of our history?"

"Where'd you get that crazy notion? No one cares about history. I'll tell you why they're popular. Westerns and celluloid make a perfect marriage. The moving picture camera was made for fast action. It's no good running footage on a bunch of people sitting around and talking or someone reading a book.

"Action is what this medium's about. The camera's great for shooting guys getting shot off horses, men banging away at each other, pretty girls getting rescued from a burning ranch house. A mess of cattle being herded along. A stagecoach rolling along with outlaws chasing it. Bandits jumping aboard a moving express train to rob the mail. Action. That's what a Thomas Ince film is all about, and no stories on earth are better than westerns when it comes to action. All you have to do to make a great western is just to keep things moving."

I laughed, mostly at myself. This impromptu telephone booth interview was a surprise, and was helping me figure out why Bat Masterson was a legend. "Do your writers pay any attention to the real frontier?"

"Oh, that's how they get ideas. But most real events don't film well. We at Thomas Ince invent our own stories. We're making them more powerful now, using visual images to inject ideas and emotions. A beautiful white-spired church, a graveyard, sunsets, things like that. We're working on it at Thomas Ince."

"You using stories and anecdotes from real people like Wyatt Earp?"

"They're all dead except for Earp. No, our Ince Productions writers just script in as much movement as we can figure out. If I caught a writer stuffing too much history into the westerns, I'd fire him."

"Well, how do you tell the heroes from the villains?"

"Obvious visual symbolism. White hats, black hats. Our heroes shoot faster and win fistfights against ten gorillas, and crawl along the top of freight cars and drop down on the bandits and climb the stairs of a burning courthouse to rescue a pretty girl like Mae Marsh who hugs him as he carries her to safety. Ince films don't explain much in the titles. That's the camera's job. Images are what count in films."

"What about heroes with moral courage; men who do what's right, no matter what pressures they face?"

"No, sir. That stuff doesn't play on thirty-five-millimeter nitrate film. If I see a Hamlet scene in a script I tell my writers to chop it."

"Well, let me ask you this: Isn't the western story unique to this nation? No other country has stories like this, with wilderness, cowboys, Indians, settlers, cavalry, and covered wagons. Isn't the popularity of westerns because they're so American? Isn't that why people fill the theater seats?"

Ince paused, and then replied politely, as if talking to an idiot, which I suspected was not far from the truth.

"Mr. Masterson," he said, "viewers of westerns are too busy watching gunfights to think of anything. Anything at all. They don't sit in their theater seats thinking about America or history. They're thinking about the bullets. I don't like westerns myself, but Hart's a genius and gets better and better so I let him make them for Thomas Ince Productions and they are very profitable."

I heard someone saying something to the mogul and then he told me he had to hang up. "Any last questions, Mr. Masterson? We try to cooperate with the press."

"I have a hundred questions but I'll save them, Mr. Ince. Will I be able to talk to the actors out there?"

"Of course. Any friend of Louella Parsons is a friend of Thomas Ince, Incorporated. Good luck. Be sure to credit all quotes to Thomas Ince, and to spell it right. Thomas Ince Productions, I-N-C-E. Send me a copy."

A click announced a dead line.

I started to laugh, and that was how Emma found me.

"What's so funny, Bat?"

"Any friend of Louella Parsons is a friend of Tom Ince," I said. "I-N-C-E."

"Did he know you?"

"Sure, he'd heard of the *Daily Telegraph,* so the doors opened."

She started laughing.

CHAPTER 23

T he next morning, another monotonously gorgeous day, Emma and I caught the red Pacific Electric streetcar that would take us out to Hollywood, where various studios were rising in the vicinity of Sunset Boulevard.

Others had gone up farther west of town, setting up on acres sold to them by real estate developer Harry Culver. The Triangle Studio was out there, but the company had collapsed and Ince had built another studio nearby only to sell it to Sam Goldwyn. A Metro studio, erected by someone named L. B. Mayer, was going up out there too. I didn't grasp all the ins and outs of it. The motion picture business was a whirligig.

Los Angeles seemed little more than a vast hinterland, with open fields checkerboarding subdivisions of bungalows and commercial streets, all of it glowing contentedly in a sedate sunlight. It obviously was a city where nothing ever happened and never would happen. Not like New York, where all the energies of the country seemed to gather into hectic life. I closed my eyes a moment and tried to think back to the pathetic row of frame buildings in early Dodge City, every stick of wood imported by the railroad, the little town a pinprick in a sea of grass. In the space of one brief lifetime the world had been transformed.

Emma didn't much like streetcars because of the electric ozone smell and grinding noise, but the windows were all open and the trip didn't take long. Ince was right. The car took us right to Melrose and the ramshackle structures put up by Adolph Zukor and his Paramount company.

We pulled the cord and stepped off at the next stop. The area certainly wasn't prepossessing and reminded me of the factory districts of the Bronx. I steered Emma inside and confronted a male receptionist.

"I'm William Masterson. I believe Mr. Ince has arranged our passage out to the Santa Ynez ranch," I said.

"Sure, get in that," the gent said, pointing to a jitney that reminded me of the vehicles used to transport convict labor to work sites.

"This is Mr. Ince's studio, isn't it?"

"Zukor owns it. He bought Triangle and got Mr. Ince, Mr. Griffith, and Mr. Sennett in the bargain, as well as the people they had under contract."

"Ah," I said, getting bewildered. "I'm a friend of Louella Parsons."

"Oh, you're that guy. Get in the roadster there. Nothing's too good for Louella. Chauffeur will take you over, bring you back."

"Louella Parsons is a magical name."

"We call her the Fortune Cookie. Thousands of dollars hang on her favor."

"Is there a chance of talking to William Hart out there?"

"Sure, just buttonhole him between takes."

Moments later Emma and I found ourselves being driven at a reckless pace through urban Hollywood and then over unpaved roads that divided glowing fields and sailed straight over formidable sun-baked hills.

Then, suddenly, we plunged through the jaws of a gloomy canyon with tawny slopes rising on either side of us, the terrain covered with waxy-leaved shrubs that were not familiar to me. We careened past trucks full of strange equipment and into a rolling sea of grass dotted with unfamiliar trees. Ahead lay a whole frontier town. When we finally pulled up we found ourselves in the middle of a bank robbery.

When I heard all that shooting I reached for my piece out of pure instinct, but I hadn't carried for years. There we were, driving into a pretty good imitation of a frontier town, with a two-story red brick bank, a mercantile, a barbershop, a livery outfit and feed store, hitchrails on the dirt street, and little frame houses leaking wood smoke from stovepipes. It threw me back forty years. It was much too clean and orderly, though. A real frontier burg would have junk heaped everywhere. Every alley between buildings was a dump for whiskey bottles, tin cans, and garbage. A livery barnyard would have had a dozen broken-down wagons, spare wheels, discarded harness, and all the other debris people cast aside. And not an outhouse was in sight.

Our driver drove right into the middle of it but stopped just out of camera range. This episode was being shot with two big black cameras up on booms. Some white screens were posted around and I fathomed that they threw light into shadowed areas. Four masked robbers, their bandannas over their noses, were bursting out of the Longmont Valley Bank carrying sacks, and climbing aboard their nags, which had been tied to the hitchrail in front.

Hell, that was all wrong. I'd never been involved with a bank robbery as a peace officer, but anyone would know that the robbers would have a horse holder so they could make a quick getaway, and the holder would have the horses in the alley beside the bank, not in front where any townsman could shoot them down. But I held my peace.

"Oh!" yelled Emma, as the townsmen appeared in windows and up on porches and began firing. "Duck!"

"I'm too old," I said.

The cameramen swung their big black boxes around, following the frantic bandits as they galloped off.

The director, some fellow in jodhpurs, was yelling through a black megaphone. "Get a move on," he bawled. "You're slow."

That's when the familiar actor burst onto the scene from behind Wesley's Mercantile and Dry Goods. He was trotting a magnificent blaze-faced sorrel, and he peered about, squinted, dropped off the nag, extracted a long gun, laid it over his saddle, and began methodically shooting at the disappearing outlaws.

"Cut," the director bawled. He turned to the nearest cameraman. "Print it. There's a slow spot but I'm not going to do it over. We'll cut out a few seconds."

William Shakespeare Hart certainly had a stately presence. I could have used some of that in Dodge. I'm on the short side, and another five or six inches, and maybe a foot-high sombrero, would have been an asset when I walked into the southside dives. But I always told myself that I made a smaller target so it balanced out.

Hart had garbed himself authentically, at least if he was trying to portray a cowboy. I doubted that a city marshal or any peace officer would have duded himself up in chaps, boots and spurs, a vest, a creased Stetson, and gauntlets, much less ride a horse with a silver-mounted and fancy-tooled saddle or carried a lariat. But the gaudy star on his vest suggested that in this opus he was, indeed, a lawman.

It didn't matter. Hart was somehow evoking feelings of respect in me. I had watched him in a dozen westerns playing around Broadway, usually at the Rialto, and hadn't exactly appreciated the king of the westerns. In front of a camera he seemed mannered— no, weird—and I couldn't understand why he didn't just behave like a regular man. On film, he enunciated everything so slowly that a viewer had time to read the titles three times over.

Hart and the megaphone man conversed while the cameramen rolled their boom platforms toward a certain balcony. They were going to do a quick shot of a townsman being shot and falling over the railing to the ground. I watched the stuntman practice the tumble, landing on a haypile just below camera range.

"I thought we were going to get shot," Emma said.

"They're blanks."

Hart wasn't in this scene so I figured this was my opportunity. He lounged on his nag, which stood restlessly, swatting flies with its tail.

"Mr. Hart? Could we talk a bit? I'm a friend of Louella Parsons."

"Well, any pal of Louella's a pal of mine."

"I work with her on the *New York Morning Telegraph.* I'd like to write up something about you. My name's Masterson."

Hart stared. "Not Bat?"

"Yeah."

"Good God! You're Bat Masterson, the old marshal?"

"That's me, and this is my wife, Emma."

"You've come to see me?"

"I guess we've intruded."

William Shakespeare Hart swiftly dismounted, shook

hands solemnly, and approached the fat director with the black megaphone.

"Shoot around me for a half hour."

"Shoot around you! Ince'll complain!"

"Just shoot around me. This is Bat Masterson, one of the last two frontier legends alive."

"Nice to meetcha, old-timer."

"And this is Scott Sidney, our assistant director. I'm directing this. I direct all my films. Now, Scott, I'll be at the canteen with these people, doing an interview."

"Ince won't like it."

"These people are friends of Louella Parsons."

That seemed to settle the matter. Hart tied his sorrel and steered us to a kitchen area several hundred yards distant. "Watch out for rattlers," he said.

We did.

Hart settled us at a crude plank table and brought us java.

"This is one of the great days of my life," he said. "You're a hero of mine. I've tried to learn everything there is to know about you."

"I seem to be a legend here and there."

"You are. You're a man known to everyone who cares about the Old West, as I do. I've made a study of it. I try to make everything authentic. This costume is straight out of old photos," he said.

"It sure looks like what the cowboys used to wear in Dodge City."

He seemed pleased with that. I don't know what I was expecting but Hart surprised me. He was a serious, intense man with a certain presence, a formidable quality I couldn't quite place. He was not a young man. I had not particularly liked him on-screen, but now, in his company, I grew aware of something remarkable in him.

I could see that Emma liked him, too. Emma was like Josephine Earp in that respect; she didn't like to see her man treated badly. Hart was treating me as if I were a visiting conqueror.

"What brings you here, Mr. Masterson?"

"I'm on a little trip to make sense of my life," I said. "It all started when my colleague in New York, Louella Parsons, wanted to interview me. . . ."

I described my voyage of self-discovery to Hart, who listened intently. I told him that some people saw me as a gunman who had killed a score or more of badmen and celebrated it as if killing made me somebody.

I told Hart I didn't much like that reputation and maybe this trip was about setting the record straight. But I was also curious about this whole fascination with the frontier and how the pioneers were being idolized and turned into heroic figures in town after town. I told him what we had found in Dodge where the past had been ruthlessly rubbed out.

"I'm here to look at these western films," I said. "Where does all this come from? Why do hundreds of thousands of people lay out dimes at the ticket windows to see you shoot it out with badmen?"

"That's something worth talking about. I've got to go back to work now, but I'll pick you up at six-thirty for dinner. All right?"

It sounded just fine to me.

"May I have your autograph?" asked Emma.

Hart smiled. "I'll bring a signed photo," he said.

CHAPTER 24

W illiam S. Hart showed up at our hotel in a sporty Pierce Arrow roadster, lemon yellow, with nickel plate trim and plush leather seats. He wore a dark worsted suit and paisley cravat, transforming himself from the screen cowboy to an urbane man of the world.

He whisked us back to Hollywood and drew up to the Blue Lagoon, on Sunset Boulevard, which I judged to be the center of gravity for the motion picture business. I thought perhaps he would have a lady with him but he came alone, which I took to be a sign that he wanted to do some serious talking. Too bad. I would have preferred to see an actress on his arm.

Our entrance was an improvement on Moses parting the Red Sea, and we were swiftly settled in a corner banquette and surrounded by half of the servant class in that town. They produced icy martinis all around and I had no complaints. For a few more weeks Los Angeles would be wet. Next January that would end forever. I suspected that these movie people had stashed a few thousand barrels of booze in private vaults and were prepared for the worst.

Well-wishers gave us three sips of privacy before descending on him, mostly to spread a little flattery or make themselves known to his imperial eye.

He handled all of that graciously. The more I experienced this formidable man, the more impressed I was. He seemed to be royalty but it affected him not at all. The Blue Lagoon was the site of coronations, and, I suspected, of regicides as well. I recognized a dozen faces in surrounding booths. Even Emma, showgirl that she was, stared raptly at Theda Bara, Douglas Fairbanks and his wife, Charlie Chaplin, and one of the Gish girls, I couldn't tell which.

"There's a young man I want you to meet later, Bat," Hart said. "Brilliant. Name's John Ford, and he's made a western film that's going to set the style in the future. If you haven't seen *Straight Shooting,* have a look at it. That man will be king of the westerns some day."

I stared at a young, lumpy, and unprepossessing gent in the far corner, surrounded by female acolytes. I thought I could get used to this town swiftly if I could roll back twenty years. Emma had been reading my thoughts and smiled wryly.

Two chilled dry martinis put us in the frame of mind we were waiting for.

"I'm pleased you came West, Bat," Hart said.

"I'm looking for something that lies just beyond my reach," I said. "Maybe you can help me."

Hart nodded.

"Why do you make films about the West?"

"Money, and personal inclination."

"Why do movie viewers like westerns?"

"They don't have to think. It's pure motion."

"Okay, maybe you can't answer these, but I'm trying to figure them out. Why am I sometimes celebrated, sometimes hated? Why do some people rejoice in the mankiller Masterson? Why have they made a killer out of me? Why do I walk into a place and they introduce me as a man who's put two dozen mortals in their graves? And why does this win me admiration?"

He toyed with his swizzle stick a moment. "Unanswerable questions," he said. "Maybe you shouldn't seek answers when there are none, Mr. Masterson."

"I'm Bat."

"No, sir, you're Mr. Masterson to me and always will be, and I'll tell you why: we shoot blanks; you didn't."

"Then I should call you Mr. Hart. You make a forgotten world come alive once again."

Mutual backscratching, perhaps, but both of us meant it.

"Maybe I can illumine one small corner of the mysteries you are confronting. Let's talk about these westerns we're making here. This industry's in its infancy, you know. Every serious film we make is an experiment. Some day we'll be able to synchronize sound to image and you'll hear actors speaking their lines. But I don't want to talk about technology."

"You mean the pictures will talk?"

"Talk, yes, and record every other sound, too. Every gunshot, every rattle of a wagon, every neigh of a horse. Then someday you'll see everything in color. Then you'll see stories on the screen so real that you'll be transported into the world of the story.

"It'll be the storytelling medium of the masses. More important than novels. It's going to happen. And that's when you'll see the story of the settlement of the West done with such authenticity that you'll pinch yourself and wonder how you were transported back sixty or seventy years."

"I won't be here for that, Mr. Hart. And I'm not sure I'd want to see it. The frontier was a rough, mean place and civilization overwhelmed it fast."

"Rough, yes. Mean, yes. But Mr. Masterson, a legend. Without even being aware of it, brave men like you spun a story of courage and daring, of enterprise, of survival in wilderness, in bad weather, against outlaws and Indians and starvation.

"You see, westerns are elemental. They are raw stories without the veneer of civilization moderating them. The hero of a western is a man on his own who must survive without the comforts and conveniences of civilization, and that includes the comforts of established law enforcement. So you people seem larger than life to those of us who came later.

"We see you as giants striding across a land without cities, a land fraught with danger, a land ruled by anyone with a six-gun and the will to use it."

Hart was talking with evangelical fervor, exploring things he had thought about, things he admired, things he was seeking to inject into his films.

"Everything about character becomes larger in a western," he continued. "That's because all the props of civilization have been pulled away. That's what I try to convey in my pictures. The seriousness, the grandeur of a man all on his own.

"Now Ince doesn't care what I do as long as I make money for him. But I care. And my viewers care. I make a lot of money for him. He's got me on a long-term contract I wish I had never signed. One twenty-five a week."

"That's a lot in my book," I said.

"Not when you're making hundreds of thousands a year in sheer profit for your employer. Tom Mix does better over at William Fox. We don't agree on much. His stories are more casual, comic, relaxed, and devoid of the heroism that I see as the bedrock of my stories. But they're good films. He's excellent at what he does and gives me things to study. He has a large following and maybe he'll surpass me. He's young and I'm not.

"You know, western stories used to be a joke. They were made around New York City on manicured lawns by people who never saw a cowboy in their life.

"Then along came Broncho Billy Anderson, and he started the change toward realism, dressing like a western man might dress, playing a big, rough sheriff. Then the whole thing moved out here and suddenly we could use real western scenery as backdrop, show the spaces and wilderness.

"But we're only just beginning. Great things are coming and then historians and writers of screenplays will dig into history and get it right. And they're going to come across the name of Masterson when they do."

"That's what I'm worried about."

A waiter set our dinner before us and I marveled because we hadn't ordered. Dish after dish appeared, each under a pewter cover, and I found myself trying to choose between steaks and a rib roast and ham and chicken and potatoes, and a dozen other dishes. Emma and I were being entertained Los Angeles–style by one of the kings of the business.

I had rarely had such a feast set before me. Emma was aglow. She wasn't used to being royalty or hob-nobbing with movie stars.

"You were saying," said Hart after a gluttonous interlude, "that you're worried about the name of Masterson."

I dabbed my lips with the linen napkin, trying to frame what this journey was all about. "The legend is greatly exaggerated," I said.

"You are a modest man."

"I spent most of my life as a gambler, usually drifting out of town one step ahead of the reformers."

Hart laughed. He was not uncomfortable with that.

"That's what I was truly good at," I continued. "The

pay of a peace officer is nothing. A skillful gambler can make a good living. I made and lost plenty of bankrolls but in the end I got a comfortable nest egg from my days operating a faro or monte game, or playing poker. I ran a variety theater. I've been a pit boss in gin joints in mining towns. That's what Bat Masterson's about."

Hart cleaned his platter and drained his martini glass, and a refill instantly appeared. We were surrounded by flunkeys.

"A legend can be a kind of truth in its own right, Mr. Masterson. A nation needs its heroes, its sense of what it is and what it wants to be. The finger of fate pointed and you became one. Why not let it go at that?"

"Because truth matters to me."

"But a legend is a form of truth. Let us simply concede that you're a mythic figure, a king of the Old West in the public's eye, regardless of what actually happened. As a mythic figure you inspire a nation. You are an example of bravery, courage under fire, daring, enterprise, a sort of good white knight. And out of that myth of Bat Masterson, little boys grow up tall, men find heart in tough corners. Who knows? Maybe the myth of a tough frontier sheriff heartened the doughboys in the trenches."

"Not likely."

"Ah, Mr. Masterson. Let me plead this. Don't underestimate the virtue of a legend. I like to think that my films are helping this nation find truths about itself, especially the value of a virtuous and brave man and what he can do in desperate circumstances, against all odds.

"I try to portray such a man, but you really were, and are, one. I like to think I'm giving this country

more than five-reel entertainments. I like to think that
I'm being a model, a prototype, of the idealized American, something any youngster—boy or girl—can follow. Have you seen my pictures?"

"Some."

"In every one I play a serious man. Look at *The
Return of Drew Egan* or *The Toll Gate* or *The Narrow
Trail*. I play tough men, never boys. And I like to think
that's important."

"That idea never occurred to me when I was a peace
officer," I said.

"You weren't shooting blanks," he replied.

We parted friends. Emma and I each had a glossy
photo, autographed by Hart, to take with us. On the
way back, driven by Hart's chauffeur, I toyed with a
new idea. A young, brash nation needed its heroes and
would have them no matter what. It wasn't that Wyatt
or I had done anything special but that we were simply
available to a nation hunting for its own version of
manhood. If we hadn't lived, the nation would simply
have turned others into legends.

Our celebrity wasn't anything we sought and wasn't
even closely tied to anything we did. The whole country wanted some ritual story about how it had built
itself, how it had turned a wild continent into a bountiful land, and Wyatt and I were merely actors on the
stage. I learned something from talking with Hart: if
we hadn't lived, the country would have invented us
anyway.

CHAPTER 25

W e were awakened by a rap on the door and I discovered a young man in blue livery standing there. He handed me an envelope.

"Mr. Masterson, I've been instructed to wait for your answer," he said.

"Sure, just a minute."

The envelope contained a handwritten note from Hart asking whether Emma and I would like bit parts in his film. If so, I was to tell the driver, Ace Bandig, and he would drive us to Paramount to be gotten up in costumes, and then out to Santa Ynez Canyon.

"Emma," I said, "you want to be a movie star?"

She peered out from under the bedclothes so coquettishly that I knew the Mastersons were destined for cinematic immortality. She read the note, sighed ecstatically, and nodded.

I returned to the door.

"Sure," I said. "Give us twenty minutes. Do you know what these parts are?"

"Yes, sir," Bandig said. "The bank robbers invade the farmhouse of an elderly couple and treat them badly. But Mr. Hart's changing the script. If you do the part, you'll play a retired sheriff and give the bank robbers a hot time with the help of your wife."

That filled me with joy and fancy. Emma beamed in bed.

"Yeah, we'll be in the lobby as soon as I scrape my face," I said.

And so it was that a half hour later we were being driven out to the Paramount studios, and an hour after that we were in a wardrobe room being handed some pretty familiar-looking garb by a gaggle of costume girls. They got Emma into an old-fashioned dark dress, added an apron, and mussed up her hair.

"Some song-and-dance gal I am," she muttered.

"She needs a rolling pin," I said.

Much to my astonishment they provided one.

They put me into a ranch outfit, jeans, chambray shirt, leather vest, and battered hat. Then they shrewdly added suspenders and ran some white stuff into my mustache.

"Hell, Emma, you look younger than I do by a long shot," I said.

We arrived at the location before noon and we waited around for the lunch break.

Hart joined us at the canteen.

"This is top stuff," he said. "I thought of it last night after dropping you off and before I turned out the lights I figured out what to do with the script. Mr. Masterson, if you'd just hang around Los Angeles, I'd keep you busy as a character actor. And you too, Mrs. Masterson."

Emma's eyes twinkled. Hart had erased thirty years out of her face.

He eyed her rolling pin. "They gave you that? It's perfect. Now here's what'll happen. The crooks are gonna burst into the farmhouse kitchen where you're rolling out some dough for a pie. They want chow, some food to carry in a bag, fresh horses, and any arms and ammunition lying around. Now the first thing you do is get mad and wave that rolling pin at them."

"I've wanted to wave a rolling pin at someone all my life," Emma said.

"Now, Mr. Masterson, you're a retired lawman, see? We'll establish that with a closeup of a star stuck in the frame of your mirror, and hanging on the wall will be your old six-guns, a pair of them in their sheaths, like mine. In fact, we'll just use these that I'm wearing. These are your old guns, see, and they've been retired, like you, but they're hanging right there on a hook on the bedroom door, old friends to you, all right?"

He slipped open the buckle of his gunbelt and handed the thing to me. It was a hand-tooled fancy outfit, with a brace of nickel-plated Colt's Peacemakers snugged in the sheaths. I drew one, saw it was loaded, and extracted the brass. It was a blank, with nothing but a cardboard wad holding in the powder. I examined the rest of the loads. If I was about to be burning powder, I was going to make sure no one got hurt.

Hart watched me, grinning.

"We'll do this after lunch," he said. "In the original script they abuse the old woman, tie up and rob the old man, ransack the place, and take off. Later on I arrive—I'm pursuing them—and untie the old people and get their story.

"But now it's going to be different. They bust in, start bullying the old lady, she gets mad and waves her rolling pin, the old man gets up out of his rocker, sees the commotion, buckles on his six-guns, and appears in the kitchen, weapons drawn.

"The crooks think they can overwhelm him but the old boy knows a thing or two, buffaloes one, shoots the foot of another, and then shoots the hat off a third who is trying to grab the old lady. The upshot is, they steal fresh horses but don't get any chow, and the angry old boy is potshooting them as they ride off. You think you can do that?"

"Hell, I don't know how I can buffalo this man without hurting him."

"Our stuntmen'll show you. It'll look authentic on the screen, believe me. If you still have trouble we've got a balsawood gun that won't hurt a flea."

"I'm not in good shape, Mr. Hart."

"You don't have to be. We'll set up this scuffle so that none of the crooks actually throws you or Mrs. Masterson."

Emma nodded sagely. She knew theater and this was no different. "You better give me a rubber rolling pin," she said, her eyes glowing. "And a bowl of flour to dump on one of these yeggs."

Hart thought that was pretty good.

After a wolfed-down lunch of beans and sowbelly he led us to some interior sets I hadn't seen before. These were nothing but a row of roofless two- or three-sided affairs, like miniature theaters, where our little drama would take place.

They seemed to fuss endlessly with the lighting, setting up reflectors and screens to throw even light into every corner and catch our faces. But the sun shown down serenely, as it did 350 days of the year in this locale, and no one seemed to be in a rush.

"All right," said Hart, this time wearing his director's hat. "We'll get a shot of these outlaws riding up to your place later. They'll get off their worn-out nags and look the ranch house over before knocking.

"Now, Mrs. Masterson—"

"Emma, sweetheart."

"Emma. You get your hands full of flour and start kneading that mudpile there. It looks like dough, I hope. When you hear the rap on the door, you wipe your hands and answer it, and these galoots barge in. You talk to them, saying just what you'd say anyway, 'What do you think you're doing?,' and they'll say they want food fast and don't make a false move.

"Just play the scene out, don't exaggerate any motion or ham it up. Sometimes we write the titles to fit what you say in the scene. The cameras aren't kind to hammy actors so don't get theatrical.

"Keep your faces open to the camera, your bodies too. I don't want to see your backs or the backs of your heads on film. I don't even want profiles. Just keep turning your head and body into the lens no matter what you're saying or doing.

"Now, the old man's in the parlor, through that door, and you want to get his attention, so you look that way now and then, and make noise even if the audience can't hear it. We'll put in titles. Got it?"

This shot didn't involve me so I just parked myself out of camera range and watched. Hart ran Emma and these galoots through a rehearsal but told her not to dump the flour on them yet.

They fussed through the scene and then shot the real one. Emma startled the hell out of me. That old gal put on a show. Those mean devils marched into the kitchen, and pretty soon she was yelling at them and wagging that rolling pin around like a deadly weapon, and pretty quick they got tired of her and began dumping cans off shelves into their gunny sacks. She unloaded the bowl of flour over one galoot and he sputtered and she whacked him with her rolling pin. Ouch, that looked like it hurt, and I sort of had to wonder about my bloodthirsty old Emma.

I watched the camera grinding and the chaos building. The table got overturned, the other outlaws tried

to wrestle her down and finally got the rolling pin
away and my old Emma started calling them names
that never before escaped her chaste lips.

"Okay, cut, stop!"

That was Hart.

The cameraman beamed. Grips looked mighty
happy. The kitchen was one hell of a mess. A smirky
kid was laughing.

"We going to do this again?" Emma asked, a mean
look in her eye.

"Naw, that was perfect, just perfect," Hart said.
"You're a natural. You've just discovered your calling."

Next thing I knew, they were toting the camera and
those screens over to the open-sided bedroom.

"Okay, Mr. Masterson, just a quick shot. You rush
into this bedroom, like this, in a hurry, because you
want to buckle on this belt hanging here on the door
with the six-guns. You do that and start to rush back
to help the missus—but then you notice the old star,
the sheriff's badge, stuck into the corner of the looking
glass there, and something wonderful happens to you.
You sort of feel the power of that badge.

"I want the audience to know what's in your mind
even if you don't say a word. Don't ham it up, just
the slightest lift of the chin, something like that. And
you pluck it and pin it on your vest, taking a precious
moment before rushing to help your wife."

"But that's out of sequence. Don't we start with me
in the parlor hearing this stuff?"

"Films aren't made in order, Mr. Masterson. We put
it all together in the editing room."

"Dammit, I'm Bat."

Hart smiled.

They ran me through this while the crew got the

lighting right, and then they did it for real. The camera was grinding, and I pulled that belt around my waist— I was a hell of a lot thicker in the middle than Hart and I couldn't buckle it for a moment, and finally sucked in enough gut to do it—but I didn't stop acting and that demon kept the camera rolling. I saw that star, pinned it on, drew those big nickel-plated Colt's six-guns, and raced out that door.

"All right, cut. What a good touch! You sucking in your gut to put the old guns on. Great acting!"

"The hell with that," I yelled. That belt was cutting me in half. I released the buckle and felt my south and north halves solder themselves back together.

"We've got a few more shots here, and then you can go back to town if you want."

"When do I get to see this in the theaters?"

"Not long. I'll let you know. Now you can teach me something. Show me how you draw and fire."

I buckled on a holstered cartridge belt a prop man handed me. Then I picked a target, a horse at a hitch-rail. I lifted those nickel-plated sonsabitches and squeezed off some rounds just for fun. All six chambers of both had been loaded, which faintly surprised me.

"Great, great. Show me again. I want to learn how you do it."

"Damned if I know," I said. I hadn't the faintest idea how I drew a gun. I just did it. So I reloaded and whipped them out and fired a few times for the actor.

I wouldn't confess this to my closest friend, but the truth of it was that I was having a hell of a good time.

CHAPTER 26

T he next scene was more to my liking. This time the retired sheriff would burst into the kitchen where two outlaws were wrestling with his wife and two more were loading canned goods into gunnysacks, and tell them to halt and put up their dukes and release the woman.

Hart wanted the outlaws—being played by Yakima Canutt, Jack Hoxie, Paul Hurst, and Charlie Ogle—to resist, to figure they could jump the old man. They threaten to kill Emma if I don't drop my Peacemakers. Two advance on me, and I blast away, dropping one and wounding another before they overwhelm me.

"How come you don't let me wipe them out?" I asked Hart.

"Because I'm the star and we still have two reels of chase scenes after this episode," he replied.

I couldn't argue with that, though it galled me. Masterson *never loses.*

"They'll hogtie you, steal your guns, take off with food and fresh horses, and then in the next scene I'll ride in and rescue you. All right?"

I nodded grumpily. Sure, it was all make-believe. But I wasn't used to losing. If I had to lose, I damned well didn't want my good name to show up in the credits. "Don't bill me as Masterson," I said. "I didn't lose when I was a peace officer and I won't now."

Hart laughed. Hoxie grinned. Hurst, the one covered with flour, smiled like a Ku Klux Klan executioner.

I intended to watch this film, *On the Outlaw Trail*, a few times at the Rialto and make plenty sure that I wasn't revealed in white letters in the credits.

We rehearsed the whole thing several times. This would be a complex scene. Emma, her arms pinned by Canutt and Hurst, was to keep on yelling like a banshee. Hoxie was to be the spokesman for the outlaws, telling me to drop my pieces or see Emma hurt. Ogle was the one elected to die.

They slipped a little wax-paper packet of catsup into his breast pocket, and when I shot him he was to clutch his chest and spew catsup over his shirt. We worked on the buffaloing so I wouldn't brain Canutt. I felt uneasy about that. Canutt just grinned.

They fiddled with the lighting a long time because the sun had rotated west. That's all people on movie sets do, tinker with lighting. Hours go by and they just move screens and kliegs around.

Then, at last, we tried it. I rushed in, waving my artillery, two were wrestling Emma and she was bellowing at them, Hoxie told me to drop my pieces, and I responded by blasting away.

"Cut," yelled Hart. "Slow down, Bat. This doesn't have to play in ten seconds."

We rehearsed again. I wasn't acting like a sheriff. I was acting like an old fool and Hart was growing impatient.

"Bat, dammit, forget the script. You've been a peace officer in situations like this when it took nerve and courage and timing. Now you just forget the lines. These guys are veteran players and they'll improvise, whatever you do. All I ask is that the result be the same. One down, one wounded, you and Emma hogtied on the kitchen floor."

William S. Hart was chastising me, and I was feeling sulky. Why the hell was some play-actor bossing Bat Masterson around like he was a toady? I damn near quit on the spot. Let old Louella write that one up.

I was in an evil temper, even if Emma looked like she had been anointed queen of Hollywood. They dumped some fresh flour over Hurst, and before I knew it the cameras were rolling again, and I was going to burst into that kitchen and get those bastards before they did anything worse to my woman. And by God, let them shoot me if they would; I was old and didn't mind dying, even if I would never get to see this at the Rialto on Times Square.

I was mad. I burst into the kitchen, saw what they were doing with one swift glance, snarled at them to drop their guns and reach—and I wasn't joking. I would show these tinpot actors what a frontier sheriff was made of. They heard me all right, whirled, aimed, and Hoxie—he played the boss robber named Cutthroat—jabbed his piece into Emma's ribs, which elicited a fresh barrage of outrage. I never knew Emma had such volcanic feelings in her.

Then two of the thugs rushed me. I coolly blasted Ogle, two pops to the heart, he clutched his shirt, and a fine spray of catsup stained it. Then as Canutt rushed in, I sidestepped just as I used to and laid the barrel of my Colt's over his temple. I meant to miss, and he meant to dodge, but it didn't quite happen and I connected. He went down in a heap. Fortunately, I hadn't gotten him squarely—my old age saved him from a concussion—but it was a close thing.

They landed on me and I began blowing holes in the ceiling, my hands clenched around those pieces. We had choreographed this so that I fell in a chair instead of the floor because I wasn't fit for rough stuff.

But I kept on shooting until I had emptied the six-guns, which was not in the little scenario. They had one hell of a time wresting my pieces out of my hands, and then they tied me up good, and beat it out of there.

"Cut."

"Untie me," I said.

"You mind staying tied for one quick shot? I come in here, see you both, and untie you."

"I almost got those bastards," I said.

Hart looked at me solemnly. "Bat, Emma, that was one of the best scenes I've ever filmed. You couldn't have done better. This was a memorable scene. Shooting like that even when they were wrestling you down. Shooting every last round."

"I missed my calling," said Emma. She was lying on the kitchen floor, an awful mess. "Bat, you were glorious. I'm so proud of you."

"Of me?"

"You *were* the old sheriff. You were yourself."

"Hey, Bat, did I hurt you?" asked Yakima.

"I should be asking you that."

"My head's solid bone. You didn't even dent it. But you nailed my ear pretty good."

Hart swiftly set up the next sequence in which he discovers us, and then turned the direction over to his assistant. It took only a single take. He expertly slid into the kitchen, gun drawn, saw us, peered about for danger, untied us and lifted Emma into a chair, and got our story. That was it. End of the acting for the Mastersons.

"You really don't want credits, Bat?" Hart asked.

"Hell no, I don't want a bunch of people thinking I took a licking like that."

Emma was laughing. "He's in love with his legend

no matter what he says. Put me in as Emma Walters," she said.

"I'd sure like to bill you as a featured player, Bat."

"I'll think on it."

Ogle was laughing and so was Hoxie and I clammed up.

An assistant led us to dressing rooms where we washed up and changed to our street clothing, and then we watched the shooting for the rest of the afternoon, sitting in canvas-backed chairs they provided for us. It was a pretty good show.

Hart quit about five-thirty and walked over to us.

"Bat, Emma, your cameo is a gem. You could have great careers here as character actors if you want. I know you won't; you'll head back East and write sports columns and keep Flo Ziegfeld's girls costumed and happy. But I just want you to know this was one of the most memorable days of my life, seeing an American legend show us, once again, the qualities that made you a great peace officer."

That man Hart had a way of saying things and I knew he meant every word. That was a compliment I would always remember.

"Could you stick around one more day? We'll process these takes tonight and I'll know first thing in the morning whether we'll need to reshoot any of it."

"Sure," I said. "We'll find something to do."

"Ince will pick up your hotel bill. And you'll each get a check in the mail."

"You mean we get paid for this?"

"Even Tom Ince forks over when I lean on him enough."

We said good-bye right there, and Hart promised to visit us in New York. "Say hello to Louella," he said, and I was reminded that out here, I got through the door as Louella Parsons's friend.

We were taken clear back to the Cordova Hotel by a studio driver, in time for a bath and a late dinner. I found myself in a euphoric mood, as if this day had been some sort of triumph in my long life. It had all been make-believe and yet the acting had evoked something large and eloquent in me that I couldn't quite translate into words.

I knew that the day had been one of the happiest of my life. Those four villains had each come up to me and expressed their pleasure at working with Bat Masterson, a real man with a real reputation. They were good men, skilled at their craft, and their compliments set me aglow. They all asked for my autograph and that turned them all into lifelong friends of old Masterson.

If I had accomplished nothing else with this long, rambling, unplanned adventure, that brief bright moment in Santa Ynez Canyon had made the entire trip well worth it. Maybe the legend wasn't so wrong. What they saw out there in the canyon was an old lawman showing some of his lifelong accumulation of skills.

Emma kept glancing at me, smiling, nuzzling me, and clutching my hand as we sat in that touring car, and I knew she had enjoyed one of the great days of her life, too. Little did I know that as soon as she poured some whiskey sours in our room she would use my moment of euphoria to advance a little plan of her own.

CHAPTER 27

W e had a day to kill while we waited to hear from Hart, and I welcomed it. The filming had exhausted me and I was exploring aches in places I didn't know could ache. So much for being a movie star.

We had things to do: we needed cash and arranged a wire transfer to be delivered to the Cordova. We had to buy railroad tickets, and that's when Emma surprised me.

"Bat, as long as we're on this tour down memory lane, I'd like to do some of my own sightseeing along the way."

That sure caught my attention. It dawned on me that so far, this expedition had been entirely devoted to examining the life and times of Bat Masterson, and Emma had been left out.

"I want to go to Leadville, Central City, and Denver," she said.

"Denver? I can't stand that place."

"Some important chapters of my life played out there. One of them was you."

Well, why not? This journey had begun as a trip to Dodge City to look at the young Bat Masterson but it swiftly expanded to include other way stations along the path of my life. Emma had her own life to look at and I wanted her to. I supposed we could look at Denver again, although when I left decades earlier it was with the encouragement of the constabulary.

There was a lot about Emma I really didn't know, especially her early years. We had known each other a long time and had lived together off and on in several places before we made it permanent. That's how she wanted it then and so did I.

But she was always there, floating around the Rocky Mountains, and so was I, and she never left my mind. The song-and-dance gal had plenty of history behind her before we met, much of it in Central City, Leadville, and other Colorado mining camps. Other beaux, other lives. And I had not pined for her in loneliness, either, when we were drifting apart.

"Emma, that's a great idea."

That earned me a hug and a kiss. "I've done three things with my life," she whispered into my shoulder. "I've been a showgirl, I've been your friend and lover, and I've been backstage with the New York variety shows. I'd like to see how it all began, and how those places look to me now."

"Get the tickets and we're traveling first class."

That won me another buss. I am a lucky man.

"While you're at the railroad station, I'm going to call the Earps. One last lunch or dinner, all right?"

"Sure."

She donned her picture hat with all the fruit and flowers on it. I always considered the thing a floating salad, or portable greenhouse, but she liked it and I have learned over decades of marriage that there are some small jokes that must remain unjoked. She departed blowing whistles like an ocean liner, and I had the operator ring up Wyatt.

Josephine answered.

"This is Bat," I said. "We're spending another day. How about lunch or dinner?"

I was hoping we would be invited to their bungalow. I wanted a sense of how they lived and maybe see some of his memorabilia, if he had kept any. But she promptly quashed that.

"Wyatt's not feeling well but I'll make him come. We are taking you to lunch at the Alexandria Hotel. All right?"

"I invited you, Josephine."

"We will take you this time."

"All right, see you there at noon."

She was all business and her porcupine quills were projecting in all directions. I fathomed that they really didn't want us to see their bungalow and she feared we would discover the depth of their poverty if we set foot there. I sighed. They didn't have to put on the dog for us. They didn't have to pretend. Hell, didn't Josephine understand how it is with old and comfortable friends?

I guess she didn't. I settled down for a catnap and put off the industrious chambermaid who took affront at a rumpled bed.

Emma steamed in late in the morning with a fistful of long, perforated tickets that looked like they would get us across the tundra on the Trans-Siberian Railroad, if not to Guatemala on a United Fruit Company banana boat.

"I didn't want to go back the way we came," she said, "so we're going via Salt Lake and Cheyenne on the Union Pacific, and then down to Colorado."

"Why the long tickets?"

"Leadville, Denver, Kansas City, and New York."

"That's one hell of a dogleg to New York."

"It runs straight through our lives."

I liked that. This accidental trip was fulfilling something in me, something I couldn't quite express in words, but it was becoming something precious and memorable and insightful, as if I were seeing my time on earth from the highest peak. How many mortals have the chance to relive everything? Maybe it would be even more: an epitaph.

We were fixing to head for the Alexandria when a messenger arrived and handed us an envelope labeled *Ince Productions*. The message inside was from Hart and he said the footage was great, and we were free to leave at will. He would tell us when the film was released.

I tipped the studio messenger a buck now that I was a movie star. He stared at the silver certificate as if it were a piece of cheese, and I guessed that a buck didn't catapult me into movie star status. To hell with that.

We found the Earps waiting dourly in the Alexandria restaurant, having been seated. Josie didn't much like to stand. An aura of gloom rested upon them, which I hoped to lift. This was my old friend and colleague. Where had the lighthearted days gone?

"Our treat. You just order whatever suits your fancy," Wyatt said, his voice sepulchral.

I had the sense we were about to eat up their rent money.

Emma and I ordered the blue-plate special. The Earps ordered bowls of chicken soup.

"It's good for what ails me," Wyatt explained.

"Well, you gave us a good steer, Wyatt. We got ahold of Tom Ince, who talked to me because I'm a friend of Louella Parsons, and eventually I reached Hart and spent some time out there in Santa Ynez Canyon watching them film an Old West picture."

"It's all bunk," Wyatt said.

"It didn't seem that way to me. I thought it was pretty good."

"It's all blanks and baloney. I've offered to help them but they just ignore me."

"It's worse than that," Josie said. "They steal everything Wyatt tells them."

"Who's 'them'?"

"Everyone. William Fox. Ince. Sennett. Griffith. L. B. Mayer. Adolph Zukor. Sam Goldwyn."

"And what have you offered?"

"Wyatt's life story, Tombstone, as told by him."

"For a price, I gather."

Wyatt fumed. "I'm not about to give myself away."

I itched to ask him his terms but didn't have the nerve. "Hell," I said, "hire yourself a writer. They don't know who you are."

"Everyone knows who I am."

"Wyatt, that was almost forty years ago."

"I'm known from Sonora, Mexico, to Alaska. I'm known from California to Maine, and people write me for my autograph. I'll tell you what this is. Those sharks in those film companies think they can get me for nothing. They're waiting for me to croak. But I'm too mean to croak on 'em."

"What directors have you talked to?"

Earp crumbled crackers and loaded them into his soup. "Hart, of course, but he can't help me. Young fellow, John Ford, was interested in me for a while. He does westerns, not as bad as some. At least he gets his cameras out into the West."

"What did he say?"

"He said he's always interested in a good story, especially one with clear-cut good and evil in it, and things people admire, like bravery. So I thought he was my man and I told him he could have Wyatt Earp for ten thousand dollars plus one percent of the gross box office."

"For what?"

"For my name and story."

"And he turned you down."

"He said he had to make a profit. Some of the actors come visit. Bums. Some fat man called Hoot Gibson. Young punks wanting to know how to shoot a six-gun. They flatter me to get in with me and think I don't know it. When I tell Josie it's time for my pill, she comes in and chases them out."

"Tell me more about Ford."

"I met him through Harry Carey. Now Carey's a real western man. He's got a big spread up in the San Fernando Valley, Spanish-style adobe house, and all that. He and Olive had us out there a few times along with just about everyone else. Carey gives me nothing but respect, not like all those other swindlers.

"That's where I met Hart, too. He's a good man, and respects me, but he works for that swindler Ince, and there's no cash in it for me. Hart had us out to his Horseshoe Ranch at Newhall, and I respect the man. He's about the only one in Los Angeles who knows anything about the old days, Tombstone . . ."

There was something tremulous in Wyatt's voice. The man ached for recognition—and ached for some cash. He was a walking paradox, a legend living in obscurity.

"Maybe you're asking too much, Wyatt. Emma and I just did some bit parts up there in Inceville for Hart. Just a few dollars, but we sure had fun.

"I played an old sheriff who has to deal with some bank robbers. Hart invented it just for us. Emma was my wife in the picture and she got to dump a bowl of flour on a bank robber."

"Well, I can't do anything like that. They all know who Wyatt Earp is, and so does the public, so I can't do bit parts for peanuts. You can't turn a deputy U.S. marshal into a comedian.

"I wouldn't even do them for Harry Carey, and I count him one of my true friends. He asked me and I wouldn't. 'Hell, no, Harry,' I said. He makes those Cheyenne Harry films, playing himself, with Ford. But Ford says a hero should be loused up. I'm not about to get put on film all loused up. I've never been loused up in my life."

"Ford says that?"

"Sure, look at the way he puts Carey on film. All messed up, wearing rags, a gun stuck in his belt instead of sheathed, stuff like that. A bum. You won't catch me being a bum on celluloid. And it gets worse. Ford always gets Cheyenne Harry in trouble for something, like stealing a horse. So the hero is put in jail.

"What the hell kind of hero is that? A horse thief. So I asked Ford, when he was dickering one time, how come you do that, and he says heroes shouldn't be plaster statues, they shouldn't be holier than thou, and they should have feet of clay sometimes, wet their britches in a bad moment. Some hero. I never wet my britches. So when Ford wanted my story, I put a price tag on it and also control."

The corners of Emma's lips were curving upward just slightly, and I winked. Old Josephine, the Torquemada of the Earp Inquisition, was squinting at us both, ready for the auto-da-fé. Reverence was demanded and offered. I offered it without stint; I might be a minor legend, but Wyatt Earp was an authentic hero.

"No, Wyatt, you never did. You were the coolest man I've ever seen under fire."

"Ford shoots those Harry Carey pictures right there on Carey's ranch and I've watched them," Wyatt continued. "They're so busy they don't have time to listen to a real shootist like me. They started with two-reelers out there and now they're doing five-reel features. Ford wanders around there in khaki jodhpurs and boots and thinks he's God.

"But I'll tell you something. He is absolutely fascinated by Tombstone, and he pours a few drinks into me just so he can hear the whole story over and over. And when I tell him, he always has a dozen more questions and wants to get everyone's name right.

"Some day he's going to steal that story from me and make a film about the OK Corral. He's got it memorized. But it'll be after I'm gone because I won't let that screwy Irishman have it. He'd make Johnny Behan the hero."

Josephine, once Behan's girl, looked particularly stern. Josie's late-in-life specialty was the withering gaze.

"Wyatt, you and Ford could work something out," I persisted. "Bend a little."

"Bend? He's the one who should bend. I've set my price. He can afford it. He earns three hundred a week. He makes so many films I can't keep track of them. He told me he made eight in nineteen-seventeen, and seven in nineteen-eighteen, and this year he's busting all records."

"Wyatt. Hell, man, just write a little screenplay and sell it to Ford."

He turned sullen and I intuited the reason. He couldn't manage a smooth letter, much less a screen-play.

"He doesn't want screenplays. He invents his stories as he goes along. I asked him and he told me so. When the action slows he puts in a gunfight or a jail break.

"He says he writes up a little two-page continuity

for Universal because they want to know what the hell they're paying for, but he just invents as they go along. That's why he'd never buy anything of mine."

I pushed and probed Wyatt from a dozen directions, but he obviously had a grudge and even though a part of him enjoyed running with western actors, he didn't much enjoy not being in the limelight. I hoped he wouldn't go through old age in self-wrought poverty.

The lunch went pretty much downhill after that, and we finally shook hands on the sidewalk in front of the hotel. I didn't expect ever to see Wyatt and Josephine Earp again.

CHAPTER 28

We debarked from the Union Pacific eastbound express into a fierce December wind in Cheyenne. There would be time enough between trains for me to explore my old haunts and see whether Wyoming had outlawed everything except breathing the way most states had.

Emma had booked us into a Pullman compartment and we had wallowed in luxury the whole trip. The price put a nick in our retirement funds but I didn't much mind. This ramble was turning out to be one hell of a trip. We were on our third whiskey sour about the time the train punched into Nevada, and then we hit the diner and feasted on great filets and twice-baked potatoes, served on snowy linen as the express thundered through the arid wastes.

Until dusk overtook us, I gazed out upon a vast

wilderness, little changed by the hand of man, reflecting on what I had witnessed in an ordinary lifetime. Had I really spent my youth skinning buffalo in a trackless grassland? Did I really live now in the premier city of the nation, enjoying electricity and telephones and steam heat?

I found myself in a euphoric mood, rejoicing that we had stumbled into this voyage of discovery while we could, and before age made it impossible. In the days ahead, the things I discovered about myself, the memories, the refinements of my view of myself, would nurture me.

I was so wrapped up in the sweetness of my days, the happy contact with old Wyatt and ferocious Josephine, the adventures with the movie crowd, that I barely noticed that Emma was in a strange mood too, almost girlish with gaiety, a sixty-some coquette, her gaze raking me over and over, something anticipatory in her. I thought she needed another whiskey sour or at least a postprandial cocktail back in our compartment.

When we got back and locked ourselves in, we found that the porter had opened the bunks and we were alone in our tiny world, rocking across a Nevada wasteland without lights or habitat. That's when she kissed me, only it wasn't just an ordinary peck, but the variety much employed by twenty-year-old ladies, and it was then that it began to dawn on old Masterson what his old Emma had in mind.

She had never made love in a passenger train.

For that matter, neither had I.

We tried pretty hard. That's a hell of a thing to say but when you are up in your sixties you will understand. Emma cooed and didn't climb into her bunk. I got a sore shoulder from the weight of Emma's head, but the pain will go away in a month or two. The porter was going to examine that untouched bunk and admire his randy ancient guests.

Cheyenne blew the heat out of us before we could get our bags into the commodious old station. The city sat on a grassy plain, and though mountains were visible in the distant west we had returned to the endless flat land of the blue northers.

The city squatted mostly north of a sweeping bend of the UP rails, and the part of it I wished to see lay entirely within sight of the tracks. But first I checked the bags and located the water closet. When you are my age that is what you do.

We had a three-hour layover before catching a coach to Denver. In Denver we would have another layover, at night, before catching the narrow-gauge Colorado and Southern for Leadville. The C & S had no sleeping accommodations, nothing like what we had just enjoyed. It would be a tough twenty-four hours.

The brown-varnished benches in the Cheyenne UP station weren't designed to lighten the burden of weary sojourners, but we sat there accommodating ourselves to the twenty-degree weather. Los Angeles had been in the seventies. The heavy odors of sweat, steam, burnt coal, and old cigars caught in my nostrils.

"I want to see the old district," I said. "It's all within five or six blocks."

"It's cold . . ."

"If I get cold, I'll duck into places to warm up."

"If you get a hack I'll go with you."

Maybe that was a good idea. Especially if I could find a patient driver who knew something about the early city. I had come through Cheyenne in 1876, at the height of the rush to the Black Hills. I had caught the gold fever while serving as a city policeman in Dodge, and decided to head north. I was going to go up there and stake out a gold claim in spite of the surly Sioux, who were exterminating as many miners as possible.

So I turned in my badge and my job was given to Morgan Earp. I got as far as Cheyenne and found the city jammed with transients, prices stratospheric, no sleeping rooms available, and the sporting district going full blast. The whole city roared, devoured the wealth of gold-seekers coming and going from Deadwood, and spat us out.

Only I made a roll there. I bucked the tiger the first night, won, and kept on winning. Next I knew, my bankroll was growing by leaps and I was reluctant to catch a stagecoach for Deadwood when I was harvesting so much cash at the faro layouts.

I ended up staying in Cheyenne five weeks, sleeping on billiard tables for a buck a flop, and by the time my winning streak petered out, refugees were filtering back from Deadwood with the news that all the good claims had been staked and only a fool would go up there now. And somewhere right about then word came down that Wild Bill Hickok had been shot in the back by a punk named McCall, and the dead man's hand was aces and eights.

I've rolled through Cheyenne many times since then, mostly when I was following the fight game, but I scarcely had time enough to get off the train and buy a cigar before the conductor was hollering at us. This time I had some precious hours to rake up my past and maybe find bits and pieces of it.

"Get a hack. Tell me what you did here," Emma said, and winked bawdily.

She had gotten positively kittenish since last night. One grand thing about this odyssey was that we were turning into youngsters again.

"I don't think we'll need one. Everything I want to see's within three or four blocks."

"I'm game," she said.

We bundled up and braved the wind. Whatever I hoped to find would be on Fifteenth Street in the shadow of the rails. I could see at once that Cheyenne hadn't torn the old district down root and branch, the way Dodge had.

The old buildings stood, comfortable brick structures that still harbored the sort of enterprises one might find along railroad tracks, including some dubious rooming houses, greasy spoons, tattoo parlors, distressed merchandise outlets, and tired little hotels.

I was looking in particular for a big, spacious structure that had housed the McDaniels Variety Theater, a combined theater, hotel, museum, saloon, and gambling parlor called the Gold Room that was roaring while I was there. The Gold Room was where I spent my days in Cheyenne, and for once the tiger was coughing up more than it swallowed. It was owned by some brothers named Greer and I remembered how they hovered about. They didn't care whether I won; they were growing rich by the hour.

I steered Emma down the dreary street, trying to conjure all that, including the whole roaring district, picking the pockets of all the argonauts who stepped off the trains. Every trainload brought new pickings to the merchants and sports of Cheyenne. I found the place—at least I think I did. Memory played tricks. It was a kitchen appliance warehouse now.

"What is this?" she asked.

"This was once the center of my universe," I said.

"I bucked the tiger for five weeks right here and walked away with a bankroll."

"It doesn't look like anything."

"They've outlawed anything resembling fun," I said. "Let's go back. This was a mistake."

We wheeled back toward the big station, glad to escape the wind. I felt low. There was something about poking around in old hellroaring districts that had a dark side, like seeing worms eating a corpse. The modern reality was stark and cold and obscure. The district wasn't mean; it was just empty, as if memory had fled, and the hundred-watt bulbs had been changed to twenty-fivers.

"You don't like it," she stated flatly.

"It's not so bad. I prefer the memories. Rough men in brogans waiting for the next stage or freight outfit north; slippery gamblers in silk hats and white shirts, like rows of shark teeth as the little fish swam by; whores with names like Slanting Annie or Big Chipmunk."

I winked at her. "Showgirls, too. That was some variety house, and the girls wore as little as they could get away with, and got showered with coins after each show. They nearly froze to death with this wind blowing through nonstop."

"What did you want from this?"

"Hell, I don't know."

"Maybe it's best to let things go."

"Maybe. Pretty soon we'll get to Leadville and Central City, and we'll see how you feel."

She caught my arm. "I won't remember the names of all my beaux," she said.

That made me mad, as was intended.

We laughed and plowed into the gloomy station in a whirl of icy air. Cheyenne turned out to be a cipher.

Five weeks in that madhouse hadn't changed my life any or left me with memories. There are many chapters in any life that just don't count, and my brief sojourn in Cheyenne was one of them. If I had learned anything, it was that I enjoyed the sporting life, the hubbub, and gambling. I have always been a first-class man at the gaming tables.

But when we finally got settled upon a varnished waiting room bench I did remember something: while returning to Dodge from Cheyenne, I ran into Wyatt and Morgan Earp, who were headed for Deadwood to try their luck in the new camp. I tried to warn them away from that long and feckless trip, to no avail. There are men, myself included, who ride the tail of comets. I don't think, as I look back on it, that gold or wealth were the reasons for these peregrinations. Just uproar.

Wyatt always claimed later that he had talked me into running for the sheriff's office at that time and claimed that he had persuaded me to try the life of a peace officer then. Hell, I have no recollection of it. And he hardly had to persuade a former copper to become a peace officer, especially since both my brothers were in that line of work. Later, in 1877, I did take a stab at the Ford County sheriff election and won by three votes over Larry Deger, who was a fine lawman. I was a ripe twenty-two when I took office.

We sat in that overheated station, permeated with the stink of old cigars and spit, and then the westbound evening train hissed to a stop. After passengers unloaded, its rear three coaches were decoupled, a solid Pacific-class locomotive and an express car were hooked onto them, and we boarded the coaches for Denver, a city I had no use for and wished I might escape.

But Denver and its hinterlands meant something to Emma. So we chuffed south in twilight until darkness blanked out the stern snow-capped Front Range and the dim-lit, melancholic, maroon-upholstered coach was our only world. Travel had become wearisome to me, even as this journey lit amazing fires in Emma's blue eyes.

CHAPTER 29

W e made it to Denver barely in time to catch the little Colorado and Southern train to Leadville. Back in my day, the line had been called the Denver, South Park and Pacific, and it wound its tortured way over the high Rockies, crossing the divide at Boreas Pass, and almost doubling back upon itself to reach Leadville. It hadn't changed much in four decades.

We ground through the cold high-mountain night, an express car, two boxcars, and two noisy coaches heated with potbellied coal stoves, thundering over trestles, plunging through snow sheds and tunnels where the stars disappeared, groaning up grades that made a man wonder whether the panting and huffing locomotive would stall.

Cold air seeped through the dim-lit coach and I wished Emma and I had blankets. Our fellow passengers were largely single, porcine, gaudy males of the sewing-machine drummer and lightning-rod salesman variety. They were trying to sleep, or sat stolidly through the night, finding sustenance in their flasks. I sympathized with them and wished we hadn't checked our wicker Abercrombie and Fitch oasis. Some spirits would have lubricated the trip just as the brakeman's oilcan lubricated the engine at every coal stop.

At least we didn't run into snow, though in the dim light I could see it had been plowed off the rails and banked to either side. By daylight I would have found it grimy and cinder-laden; by night it was simply a gray ghost or perhaps a gray sea we were plowing through. Emma curled up and rested her head on my shoulder. I liked the contact.

We had both spent time in Leadville. I bucked the tiger, played faro there in 1880, doing well enough to tempt me to stay. But rents were astronomical during that heyday period, the winters were terrible, and I had retreated back to the familiar precincts of Dodge. I knew Emma had been in Leadville for a longer period and I knew she was going to revisit her old haunts and I would catch glimpses of the song-and-dance gal who would have been in her early twenties then.

I couldn't remember where I met Emma. She was on the circuit, going from one opera house to another with her solo act, in and out of the same wild towns where I would alight. Somewhere we had met and that was long before she came to my Palace Theater in Denver, too. We had spent time together, shared rooms, and drifted apart only to discover one another again, through most of the 1880s. Hell, I enjoyed the company of a lot of women, which is why I have been a little vague about all this.

We huffed into Leadville at four in the morning. The little train sighed to a stop after its hard haul over forbidding mountains that radiated contempt for mere mortals. We stepped down into thunderous cold, penetrating, mean, cruel cold that made me wish we hadn't attempted this trip to a city almost two miles above sea level and surrounded by fourteen-thousand-foot mountains.

We raced for the dimly lit station and found it barely heated, with its radiators providing pitiful defense against the painful air. The drummers, wiser to the ways of railroads than we, hauled their baggage with them while we were forced to wait for the sole expressman to deposit our bags at the luggage counter.

"Where the hell are we going to get a room at four in the morning?" I asked Emma.

"We can get a hack and ask."

"What hack?"

The drummers had commandeered the two that had braved the night and the cold.

We claimed our luggage long after the train had departed for the yards. Leadville was the end of the line for the Colorado and Southern, but passengers could connect to the Denver and Rio Grande for points west or east.

"Where can we get a hack?" I asked the Wildroot Hair Oil–slicked kid doling out the luggage.

He shrugged. "Wait for one."

"Can we call? Can we get a hotel to pick us up?"

He pointed at a pay phone. "Ask the operator."

I got a polite lady on the line and told her our plight, and she said she'd call the Delaware Hotel and also get a hack to us. After that things cleared up swiftly and we found ourselves in a well-heated room by four-thirty. The old Delaware, on Seventh and Harrison, had survived. I knew it well, although I noted that it had fallen on bad times. But any port in a storm, I reminded myself, eyeing the hissing radiator gratefully.

I was not well. The thin air, the long trip, the fetid

air in the coaches, and lack of sleep were all deviling me. Maybe it would be a day or two before I would roam Leadville.

Then again, as I considered this skeletal hulk of what was once a joyous, thriving mining town of thirty or forty thousand people, maybe I wouldn't want to see much of it. Part of the trouble with walking through graveyards was looking at skeletons.

We didn't get up until lunch, and even that stretch of sleep didn't cure me of my weariness. My throat ached and I feared I was catching a hellish cold. A glaring white day greeted us and the hotel's thermometer registered thirty degrees on Herr Fahrenheit's scale. Some good java revived me, and by the time we had eaten I discovered the temperature was fifty and Leadville basked under a warm alpine sun nestled low in a transparent blue sky. We decided to tour the old city, and I bundled up.

My first impression was of a lively burg, much diminished in size but generous, good-humored, and amiable. Some of the old saloons along Harrison Avenue were open, their cheery interiors each inviting wayfarers like the Mastersons off the street.

All they could peddle was malt near beer, sandwiches, and fizzy phosphates, but they were there and open. They peddled soda and malts through the front door and I wondered what the hell they peddled through the back door. I wished I could ship every damned prohibitionist in the country to Kansas, and let them choke on their own dust. Kansas and prohibitionists deserved each other.

One glance at the surrounding slopes revealed that some mining continued, however diminished it might be. Steam and smoke escaped the boilers and mills of a couple of functioning mines. To be sure, none of the mining going on in 1919 resembled the furious and frenetic quest to bring up the carbonate of silver in the seventies and eighties, but Leadville had not lost its flavor. And that discovery was so heartening that it drove my afflictions right out of my aging carcass. I was enjoying myself. And Emma was always a step ahead of me.

I found the site of the old, long-gone Texas House, 216 Harrison Avenue. I had bucked the tiger there in 1880, in the midst of the gaudiest decor I had ever seen in a gambling palace. Polished bars and a dozen gaming tables, well lit with gas jets, graced the street floor. Upstairs, which one reached through a separate entrance, the establishment catered to high rollers. There were three splendid apartments, a glittering gambling room, and a dining area that featured a fancy buffet available to any player at any time of day.

The upstairs operation was run by Con Featherly, one of the greatest of all card mechanics, although John Pentland, another great gambler, oversaw the whole layout. Legend had it that Pentland had earned the house eighty grand in its first few weeks. It was one of the few places in the country where a player could get into a no-limits game, and thousand-dollar bets were common.

They had wanted me to work there at a premium salary; I was well known to them as a former Ford County sheriff and sporting man, familiar with the green baize. But I didn't accept.

Now there was nothing but a dreary butcher shop on the lot. The Texas House had burned to the ground at the height of its glory, nearly incinerating the whole district.

But across the street stood the old Board of Trade Saloon, another great gambling parlor, saloon, restau-

rant, and showplace, not much different from what it
had been most of a lifetime ago. We peered in, and
Emma eyed me sharply, as if expecting something
from me. The gambling had vanished along with its
glory and now it catered to old miners with long memories and a tolerance for near beer. We checked out
the old Monarch, and then Manny Hyman's at 316
Harrison, next to the opera house. I had been in there
many times.

So had Doc Holliday, although he arrived in Leadville in 1882, and our paths never crossed there. His
consumption was no longer in remission then and he
was dying. He kept himself going with whiskey and
laudanum, which made him more unstable than ever.

Hyman's was where he put a bullet through the arm
of Billy Anderson, one of the old Tombstone crowd
arrayed against the Earps, after Anderson had threatened to kill him. It had been an act of self-defense.
Eventually, after months of delay, the case went to
trial and a jury swiftly acquitted Doc of the assault
charge. He walked away from the courthouse a free
man. But by then, Glenwood Springs and Lynwood
Cemetery were beckoning.

We prowled the area, blotting up memories.

After the scout of North Harrison, the heart of the
old sporting quarter, Emma beelined straight for the
opera house, which occupied the second and third
floors of the Tabor and Bush Building. The old place
had decayed, but not badly, though its street-level
rooms were vacant. Almost running now, Emma
dragged me around to the entrance and stairs that led
up to the legendary opera house itself.

I doubted that it would be open.

A fly-specked sign on the door said that the Benevolent and Protective Order of Elks met there Tuesdays. That's what it had come to.

I pushed. The grand old doors creaked and we found ourselves once again, as we had in our salad days, climbing the gilded stairs to the plush orchestra seats of the theater, all of it now shrouded in deep gloom and wrapped in frost.

It was all there, the frescoed ceiling, the seventy-two gas jets that lit the place, the gilded proscenium, the heavy and ornate curtain, the gilded boxes, especially number one, where the silver magnate Horace Tabor disrupted performances by popping champagne corks, the gallery one floor above, a saloon and parlors at the side, where theatergoers could drink and smoke during intermissions.

"Bat, I played here," she said. "I played here. Eight hundred and eighty seats!"

I detected a tone of voice so heartfelt and light and spirited that I knew this dismal barn touched her and she was remembering.

"I used to watch Horace and Baby Doe up there," she said. "I knew Baby Doe. Did you know that? We came here about the same time. That was before she met Horace Tabor. She was stage-struck and I was a variety-show girl, so we became friends. That was before this was built, of course. This opened in November eighteen-seventy-nine.

"She was a sweet blonde, half innocent, half vixen. She wanted to get into show business, but I discouraged her. It's a rough trade, not one for a sweet girl from Oshkosh who had a way with men."

"She sure did," I agreed. "And maybe Tabor had his way with her."

Emma found stairs leading to the stage and walked

to the center of the proscenium, in front of the painted fall. She peered about, wistfully.

"The first show was *The Rough Diamond*," she said. "Some company or other put it on. I saw it. The opera house was half empty because most of the town had gone to a lynching."

"A lynching?"

"They strung up two crooks that night. For lot-jumping."

I didn't recollect it.

"Oh, oh, oh," she said, steering toward a bank of light switches. She flipped them and the cavernous place bloomed into light. The old gas jets had been wired and each shed electric light except for seven or eight with dead bulbs.

"Oh!" she said.

I felt uneasy about our trespassing, but my old Emma had fled to memoryland, so I bided my time and thought up things I would say to some constable who might come to check out all the ruckus.

"I didn't play here until the next January," she said. "They booked a variety show. I did my own act and I was a free agent and did my own booking."

She gazed raptly over the empty seats, seeing things I could never see. Old Horace Tabor. Glittering people in evening dress. Diamonds and tiaras and pendant necklaces. Mining millionaires and their ladies.

Then she vanished behind the grand fall and when my old Emma returned, it was sans her woolen coat and flower-bedecked hat. She waited, poised, and then to the rhythm of some melody rising in her soul, she did a buck-and-wing, her movements as adept and graceful as when I had beheld her long before, and pirouetted across the apron of the stage, an invisible cane or baton in hand.

And then, amazingly, she began to sing in her smoky contralto one of the torch songs of the time, "Oh, lover boy, oh, lover boy, oh lover boy, come home . . ."

She began to tap-dance, the click of her street shoes muted and feathery as she fell into old routines. I wished I might hear the music, but whatever was flooding through her soul was for her ears alone.

She glowed.

For several more minutes she sang and danced, and wondrously I began to hear the orchestra in the pit, the trombones and violins, and then it all ended.

She was panting. She paused, bowed gracefully, acknowledged the waves of applause rising from the packed opera house, nodded toward Horace Tabor's box, and stepped into the nether regions behind that curtain. When I next saw her, trotting down that stair at the right, the sea of flowers was bobbing on her head, her coat was buttoned and her gloves had been restored.

We shut down the lights and the memories fled.

She smiled, and I knew why she had come to Leadville. But little did I then know there was another reason and that it lay in the Board of Trade Saloon.

CHAPTER 30

Emma dragged me into a building that once housed the California Concert Hall. An unfamiliar club occupied the site. Nothing looked the same, and I wondered whether the old cabaret and gambling hall even occupied the same quarters. My memory of those years gets a little hazy.

But it was all fine with her, and she steered me toward the rear, where an abandoned stage lay shrouded in gloom. I suspected it was where she had once worked and that proved to be correct.

"I danced here some. This is where I worked except when I booked the opera house," she said. "Does it look familiar?"

"No, not at all."

"Right there in that corner, does that mean anything to you?"

She was pointing toward a dark alcove in what had been a bistro. Maybe it was the gloom. Back in the gas-jet days the old place glowed all night and the party never stopped. I made nothing of it, and shook my head.

"William Barclay, that is where we met."

She looked disappointed, and I felt myself sliding into one of those black holes of embarrassment that afflict people caught in such circumstances.

"We did?"

"In May of eighteen-eighty. You watched my number and I saw you out there and liked the tilt of your bowler."

"I didn't take it off indoors?"

"When did you ever take it off, Bat?"

I remembered none of this. "Oh, yes, what a night," I said.

She squinted daggers at me. "You don't have the foggiest memory. That's because you had a dozen girls and I was just more baggage."

"If you say so, sweetheart."

"Don't you sweetheart me. I came all the way from California just so I could see this place again and remember where you and I first laid eyes on each other."

"Was that all we laid?"

"Yes." The little webs in the corners of her blue eyes were crinkling up again. I had this licked.

"And what did you think after you had met me?"

"I didn't. I stopped at that table when I was done and you winked, so we started talking, and I liked your looks."

"I must have liked yours."

"You saw enough of me," she said, purse-lipped.

"Ah, now we're getting somewhere."

" 'Want a drink?' That's what you said in eighteen-eighty, and I said I would after the last show, but you didn't stick around."

"How do you remember all this?"

"Because of you, Bat. I took one look and . . ." Her voice trailed away. She peered at me shyly.

"Then what?"

"Then you were gone. I saw you in Gunnison and Telluride. Trinidad one time, don't you even remember that? Once or twice in Cripple Creek. And once in Pueblo. Once in Fort Worth. And a few times in Kansas City. I worked KC a lot. And Denver."

Now, some of that I remembered. I smiled. Trinidad. That was when we began sharing a small apartment for a month or two. I had always dated my time with Emma back to Trinidad.

We settled onto bar stools. She settled for a cherry phosphate in propitiation of my faulty memory, and we examined the old saloon, finding bits and pieces of a great history on its walls.

"You're old-timers," said the gaunt soda jerk, if that's what he was, who had been listening in. This joint, like the others, probably did its real business out the back door.

"Eighteen-eighty."

He whistled. "This place was jumping then. Luke Short used to come in here, Doc Holliday. This side room here, through the double doors, was a big poker place in those days. The bar was jumping but that poker room was real quiet."

"I did my own dance act," Emma told him. "Right here, night after night except when the opera house booked me. Sometimes they had variety shows. I played the opera house a dozen times. I used to see Horace and Baby Doe up in the box popping Piper Heidseck."

"Yeah, she was something then, old Baby Doe, brass hair and a child's heart. Nothing much left for her now, I guess."

"She's alive?" I asked.

"She lives in a shack at the Matchless Mine up on Fryer Hill. She still owns it. Horace told her to hang on to it and she did. But she's a strange duck now. A recluse. She wanders through here sometimes."

"How is she strange?"

"She dresses in rags, almost, and she's got a big, you know, crucifix on her."

"She was my friend before she met Hod Tabor," Emma said.

"Well, she's up on Fryer Hill living in that shack on the mine property. She's got a lessee trying to put the old mine in shape but mostly they've been replacing timbers and pumping out water. I don't think much silver's left and what's down there isn't worth the cost of lifting it."

"Still alive," Emma said.

I suddenly knew exactly what was worming through her mind and decided to steer her away from that—if I could.

"Emma, let's get some air."

"Did I catch your name?" the keep asked.

"Masterson," I said.

"Yeah, well, if I see old Baby Doe, I'll tell her."

"She won't know the name and it won't be necessary," I said.

The December afternoon glowed but the sun was already brushing the bleak and hostile mountains. I had the feeling once again that something lay just beyond my consciousness. I wondered what good it was to revisit my past, stand in one place or another and try to dredge up memories even though everything had changed. Like this place.

Emma gulped her syrupy drink and seemed in a hurry to leave.

"I've got to visit her," she said.

"Baby Doe Tabor?"

"Elizabeth McCourt. She had divorced Doe, whatever his name was. Harvey, I guess. She used her maiden name when we lived in the same rooming house."

I resigned myself to it. When Emma set her cap, that ended the debate.

I had never set eyes upon Baby Doe Tabor though I certainly had heard about her. She was not visible in Leadville when I was there, although there were reports of a heavily veiled blond woman enjoying the bonanza king's hospitality in his opera house box. But as far as the world then knew, Horace Tabor, the former storekeep who had struck it rich, remained married to the tart-tongued and practical Augusta and lived a life of reasonable rectitude while enduring Augusta's withering contempt in peace.

Horace Tabor was not bright but he certainly was lucky. He had been a grocer. As the result of grubstaking local prospectors he found himself part owner of the first great Leadville mine, the Little Pittsburgh. Then, as the result of buying a barren twenty-foot-deep hole in the ground that was salted with Horace's own ore, he struck it rich again. Just eight feet below the bottom of that fraudulent hole lay rich carbonate silver ore.

Then he bought a worthless claim that was destined to become the Matchless Mine, which put eleven million clams in his pockets. In the briefest of times, Horace Tabor had emerged from an obscure shopkeeper to a man earning an incredible million dollars a year, and no matter where he threw his cash it sprouted still more wealth.

But he couldn't abide Augusta's sharp tongue and cutting remarks intended to whittle her dense husband down to size. And when he met a young divorcée, an Irish Catholic girl from Wisconsin with baby blue eyes, a pout, and a nature that mixed innocence with wantonness, he fell for her.

There were some messy goings-on, a vicious divorce, a dubious marriage by a Catholic priest who had not been informed of Baby's previous marriage, and a brief, blazing time of bittersweet glory, in which the Tabors rebuilt Denver in their image while Denver's elite rejected Horace and Baby Doe and wouldn't set foot in their gaudy mansion with its peacocks and nude statuary.

Then, suddenly, the crash and silver crisis of 'ninety-three destroyed Horace Tabor, along with numerous bad investments and stupid mistakes, and he lost almost everything. He and Baby lived in poverty.

After years of grinding misery, he wound up as postmaster of Denver when some politicians took pity on him. From then on, he lived in modest circumstances, his heart and soul broken, an obscure and forgotten man. Baby Doe had gone from fabulous riches to rags to petit bourgeois comfort. But Augusta, who had profited from the divorce and invested in Denver real estate, grew rich.

And here Baby was. I marveled that she was alive, but hell, I marveled that I was alive. But why shouldn't she be? She was more or less my age. Those legendary years of indescribable wealth, when she rode around town in liveried carriages that matched the dress she chose to wear that day, had consumed only a dozen or so years of her long life.

The Matchless wasn't far but I was finding the altitude troublesome and the trip had eroded my strength and health, so we hunted for a hack, which were few in modern Leadville. I finally corralled a passing motorist driving an Oldsmobile and offered him a buck to take us there.

"She don't see many people," he said. "You want me to wait?"

"We can manage the walk downslope," I said, wondering whether I could.

The Matchless sat upon some of the bleakest slopes I had ever seen, naked of vegetation and gloomy of prospect. Our driver dropped us before a drab tool house with a corrugated metal roof and board-and-batten siding, close to the shaft and hoist works of the old mine. In every direction grand but lonely vistas met the eye. How could Baby Doe Tabor, of all people, live in such a place, and so terribly alone?

Emma knocked.

After some time, during which the chill wind was eroding my comfort, the door finally creaked open a few inches. I could scarcely see the figure within.

"Elizabeth? I'm Emma Walters," my wife proclaimed.

"Who?"

"Emma. We had rooms on Poplar Street long ago."

"I remember."

"We've come to visit."

"Yes," Baby said.

She let us in and I beheld a neatly kept interior, furnished plainly, without a single item in it to remind Baby or the world of the opulent life she had once enjoyed.

Baby Doe Tabor no longer resembled the slightly fleshy brass-blond beauty of legend, but stood gaunt and solemn in severe old clothing that reminded me of a nun's habit.

"It is good to see you, Emma," she said.

"Oh, Elizabeth! After all these years. You didn't even know Hod when we knew each other."

Baby didn't reply.

"This is my husband, William," Emma said.

I shook Baby's hand and found the grip firm. She waved us to the battered wicker and wooden chairs.

"How are you, Elizabeth?" Emma asked.

"Fine."

"What do you do now?"

"I am making my peace with God. Maybe someday I will receive His grace."

"I hope you succeed," Emma said.

"I know I never will," Baby said, and sank into a silence that began to stretch tautly.

"I see you have some work being done on the Matchless," I said.

"Yes. The men are trying to make it go again. For a share of the profit."

"What are the prospects?"

"We won't know until we get the water pumped out. Hod told me there was lots of ore left."

"If it succeeds, you'll be able to live in comfort."

"No," she said.

I wondered what she meant.

It was not a good visit. The woman who once bubbled with ebullience had become taciturn. We left after half a dozen lame silences.

The downhill walk was sad.

CHAPTER 31

I hiked slowly to the railroad station, the thin atmosphere of Leadville wearying me. I wanted to examine a Denver and Rio Grande schedule.

The visit with Baby Doe Tabor had plunged us both into melancholy. Emma retreated to the Delaware to nap while I headed into the streets, restless.

We were relics, Emma and I, along with Wyatt and Josephine, and Baby Doe. This was another century, with its own commerce and war and technology and ideals. The failing Mr. Wilson was entrenched in the White House, talking of perpetual peace and a new League of Nations. Prohibition was drying up the country. The frontier had long since vanished. Aeroplanes delivered mail and telephones jangled in most homes and offices.

Even here, in mountain-girt Leadville, motorcar traffic was thick, and one rarely saw a horse and buggy or a horse-drawn dray. Who cared about the past?

I pitied Baby Doe. What had she done so wrong? Was a dozen years of indulgence deserving of a lifetime of penitence? Was a dubious marriage outside the canon of her church worth the mortification she had imposed on herself? Surely a loving God would forgive and forget such things and her church would too, but Elizabeth McCourt Doe Tabor wore her sorrows like a crown of thorns, year after year as the twentieth century spun along. And no one could heal her.

I plucked a schedule from a rack and studied it closely. As I suspected, Glenwood Springs was just down the line, two hours of coach travel on any of the four westbound passenger trains that reached Leadville each weekday. We could leave early in the morning, or mid-morning, and in both cases be settled at the Glenwood Hotel before noon.

I took the ornately printed schedule with me, walked slowly through a weary afternoon, and entered our room. Emma was staring at the ceiling.

"That was not the girl I knew," she said.

"The Irish dwell on shame," I said.

Emma nodded. "I've never seen anyone so alone," she said.

I sat down on the edge of the bed, catching my wind. "Would you mind if I change the plans a bit?"

I handed her the schedule. "I want to go to Glenwood Springs for a day. It's not far."

"Doc," she said.

I nodded.

"I'm glad you thought of it," she said. "We're on a trip that will take us wherever the wind blows."

"Let's get this nine o'clock one."

We laughed. The Mastersons were not early risers. We would be in Glenwood before lunch.

"The last time I saw Doc was in eighteen-eighty-two," I said. "I'd bailed him out of trouble in Denver and beat off the extradition to Arizona, but we had to cook up that charge in Pueblo to do it. I took him down there, and he thanked me. He said I had saved his life, which was true.

"Anyway, we shook hands there at the station in Pueblo and I saw something pretty close to tears in those pale blue eyes. I didn't know it, but that was our last hurrah."

"We'll go. I want to see his grave too. I never met him."

At five minutes past nine the next morning we boarded the Denver and Rio Grande coach. It seemed like a toy compared to standard-gauge coaches. A porter put all our luggage in the express car; we were getting too old to tote it around and Leadville's rarefied air, at ten thousand feet, was gravely afflicting my heart and lungs, making me dizzy and nauseous. I feared to stay longer.

We were soon snaking along the bottoms of the Grand River, now renamed the Colorado, and in very little time we pulled into the riverside station at Glenwood Springs, which proved to be bigger and busier than I had imagined. I could see at once that flat land scarcely existed in this resort town, wedged into an encompassing notch in the surrounding mountains.

We directed a hack driver to take us to the Glenwood Hotel, which proved to be just a hop away. I had reason to go there. That was where Doc died, faithfully cared for by the one woman who had always loved him, Big Nose Kate.

The hotel flaunted a certain grandeur, but maybe it was just pretentiousness. It was certainly rococo. We had no trouble engaging a room and were soon ensconced in comfortable quarters. Only a few weeks ago I would never have dreamed I would come here or that we would do what we were about to do.

We rested, ate a leisurely lunch—the hotel's kitchen left much to be desired—and asked directions to Lynwood Cemetery.

"Palmer Avenue and Twelfth Street," said the clerk.

"Should we catch a hack?"

"It's upslope some," he replied.

That was answer enough.

"You want to do this now?" I asked Emma.

She nodded. Her eyes told me many things. People who have lived together a long time communicate like that. This time her face was telling me how much she wanted us to go, how much she cared, and how curious she was about all this. For her, Doc Holliday had been only a shadowy legend and a few anecdotes narrated by her husband.

We captured the hack waiting at the hotel and told the driver of our destination.

"I expect you want to see Doc Holliday's grave," he said. "People trickle through here looking for it. I'll drive you to it. It's a pretty good-sized cemetery but there's a very old corner. You relatives?"

"No, but he was my friend."

"Yeah? Really? You someone I should know?"

"Masterson," I said.

He looked disappointed. "I know everyone that was in Tombstone at that fight," he said. "No Masterson."

I smiled.

He geared into double low and tackled the slope. The touring car protested but didn't stall, perhaps because our driver had to slip the clutch a couple of times. But shortly he deposited us in a wooded part of the cemetery and pointed toward a grave embraced by gnarled trees and guarded by a black iron fence.

I asked him to wait, and led Emma to Doc's grave.

There it was, with a massive marker burdened with a fresh bouquet of fall flowers, marigolds, and pine boughs. That surprised me.

Here was John Henry Holliday. I removed my hat. A warm wind ruffled my hair. Emma clutched my hand. Here, at last, was Doc. Here was another and darker American legend. It was all so long ago. The span of years since we had shaken hands for the last time in 1882 was thirty-seven, which was a year or so longer than Doc's entire life. He had been born in 1851, and had died November 8, 1887. They had buried him here the same day.

I was struck by something odd. This massive dark marker named the dead as "Doc Holliday," not John Henry Holliday. And something else: the dates were 1852 to 1887. I had understood that his prominent Georgia family had seen to his grave, but his family would have engraved John Henry Holliday in that stone, and would have gotten the date right. It was a mystery.

"I don't think that's the original stone," I said to Emma. "To his family he was John Henry Holliday, D.D.S. And the birth year's wrong. What the hell is that all about?"

"I don't know. The flowers are fresh, Bat."

And so they were. Scattered about were the brown remains of other bouquets.

"Maybe the cabbie will know."

I walked the twenty yards to the hack and asked the man.

The driver shrugged. "Sometimes Willis—that's the florist—sends me up here with them. She pays for a fresh bouquet once a month. Five dollars, too. Five dollars buys a lot of bouquet and pays a cabbie to bring them up here."

"You said *she*?"

. "Yeah, some woman in Arizona, Mary Cummings. That's what Willis told me. It's no secret. Some rich woman, I guess, five bucks a month. Dos Cabezas, Arizona."

The name was unfamiliar but the scent wasn't. I knew, suddenly, that yet another of us born to another century still lived, and the epiphany sent a shock straight through me.

"God bless you, Big Nose Kate," I muttered.

That was as close to tears as Bat Masterson had gotten in many decades of living. I returned to the grave, and Emma.

"I think I know," I said. "They come from the woman who loved Doc and always thought of herself as his wife."

"Kate," she said.

She saw the mist in my eyes and said no more.

"I never dreamed she's still alive. It has to be her."

Yes, Big Nose Kate, the occasional wife who had brawled and whored and drunk herself into a stupor, who had rescued Doc from a lynching with a clever ruse at Fort Griffin, who had separated from Doc and returned to him a dozen times, who had nursed Doc tenderly through his last days and hours and pain. It had to be her. It *had* to be.

I took one long look at the grave, the distant vistas, the slopes that cramped the city, the ambrosial pleasantness of the place. Doc lay in a good spot, with the fragrance of cedar on the air and the shelter of leaves overhead in the summer. I felt the deepest sort of loss.

Then we stepped into the hack and the driver shifted into gear and we coughed away.

CHAPTER 32

T he next morning Emma wanted to visit the spa. She had never stuck her pink toes into a hot springs before and pined for the experience. That stuff wasn't my idea of how to spend a morning, so I put her into a hack and agreed to meet her at the hotel for lunch. I had designs of my own.

There I was, in the very hotel where Doc had gasped his last, where Kate had cared for him. I wanted to see the room but there was something I wanted more, and that was to return to the grave and talk to Doc. There were some things to settle. I strolled until I found a florist, bought a good Christmas wreath, and found a hack to take me up there again. This time I dismissed the driver. I didn't fear a downhill walk back.

I couldn't find a way to climb over the black wrought-iron fence so I settled the wreath as best I could over Doc.

"Merry Christmas," I said.

I took my hat off again. It was another mild day.

"I wonder if you can hear me. I hope you can. Hell, Doc, in nineteen-aught-seven I wrote an article saying I didn't much like you and that seemed true enough at the time. But it was wrong. I like you; I liked you when I saw you at the Lady Gay or the Long Branch, or at the Oriental in Tombstone, or down in Texas when we ran into each other and in all the other places we crossed paths.

"What I didn't really understand was your desperation. You were fighting a death sentence. You could see the sunset on the horizon. I can see that now, too. The curtain is falling for me.

"I've learned a lot since then, from Wyatt mostly. About your good and honorable family, its struggles after the Civil War, your dental practice, your distaste for your gambling as a means to feed yourself, your desperation and anger, your wounded pride, your shame, the bad company you kept, the legend that grew up around you that you used, just as I used mine, to stay alive. About your faithful friendship with the Earps, a loyalty that extended even unto death.

"That's about all I have to say. You were my friend; you *are* my friend. God bless your troubled soul. I'd like to think that you're up there with Him."

He probably was laughing derisively at me somewhere.

I sat down and let the breezes toy with me. The pair of us didn't belong in this century but that was all right. People shouldn't be bound by history. The whole country was blooming with abundance and hope now that the Great War was over, and things looked good. Who cared about some old farts from dusty frontier camps?

Below me lay a bustling resort city. I could hear the horns of automobiles, the rumble of trucks. In every direction the arid slopes of the Rockies catapulted upward, cramping this town in their vise.

It was all right. Doc and I had become dark legends. This young nation was celebrating its march to civilization, and we were relics of a lawless time when a town or countryside wasn't safe and secure and comfortable.

Of course they exaggerated all that, ascribing piles

of corpses to each of us, if only to tell themselves how far they had come toward the safety and security of civilized life. The darker they made the frontier look, the better they liked it. And no figure had a darker reputation than the man whose frail bones lay a few feet from me.

This was the century of the fraternal brotherhoods devoted to good works: the Elks, Kiwanis, Rotary, Lions, Odd Fellows, Moose, Knights Templar, Masons, and all the rest. Many of those outfits had roots in previous times, but now they were all flourishing.

Most of those gents didn't know or care about men like Doc and me, but those few who did had heaped death and destruction upon our names, as if to prove to themselves how far the nation had come since those barbaric days. But I'll wager there were a few who, behind their secret handshakes and weird initiation rituals and white aprons, sneaked a little pleasure from the thought of old Doc or old Masterson burning black powder.

But the rest, if they cared at all, were congratulating themselves that the likes of Holliday and Masterson were no longer treading the earth. *Doc and I belonged to a different brotherhood, a solidarity of smoke and blood.*

As for modern women, they hadn't heard of us, which was a blessing. They had their own leagues and twentieth-century societies and clubs, made first-aid bandages during the war, and supported uplifting endeavors everywhere. Old Doc and I had escaped. I would not have enjoyed wedlock with Carry Nation or Frances Willard, to name a pair of nineteenth-century ladies who foreshadowed the clubwomen of this century.

Well, here we were, the survivors. I put Big Nose

Kate on the list and wondered what she was doing in rural Arizona. She was a heroic woman. I wouldn't have said that forty years ago; now, I would say it without reservation. And she knew love and how to give everything she had to her beloved.

She and Emma and I and the Earps. And maybe John Clum, friend of the Earps and the fearless editor of the *Tombstone Epitaph.* Last I knew, he was living in Los Angeles. And what about Tilghman? I had heard no report of his demise.

I thought of the dead. I watched life bleed out of my younger brother Ed, heedlessly shot by a drunken cowman in 1878. Jim died of consumption in 1895. Both gone so long I hardly remembered them. Why had I been given four more decades than Ed? Were the things that happened to us pure luck, pure happenstance?

Morgan Earp, shot from behind in 1882 by part of the old outlaw gang in Tombstone. Virgil, who was shot and survived, but with a bum arm, dead of pneumonia in Goldfield, Nevada, in 1906. At least he made it to this century. Warren Earp, shot by a drifter in 1900.

As for the Earps' enemies, who was left? Ike and Billy Clanton, Frank and Tom McLaury, Stilwell, Ringo, Brocius, Florentino Cruz, Pony Deal, gone, gone. Those and a dozen more.

Luke Short, my old friend, the elegant little card mechanic, dead in 1893. Ben Thompson, a dapper and dangerous man, murdered in 1884 in the Vaudeville Variety Theater in San Antonio. Wild Bill Hickok, shot while playing poker in Deadwood in 1876. Rowdy Joe Lowe died around the turn of the century.

Old Buffalo Bill Cody, the genuine article under a gaudy veneer, lived until recently. He died in 1917. I felt that one badly, not because we were close but because he had somehow captured within his person the whole period, and when he went, so did our memories of the frontier. He had helped me rescue Billy Thompson, Ben's miserable brother, from the clutches of the sheriff at Ogallala.

Sam Bass, Roy Bean, Billy the Kid, all long gone. Bill Dooley and Kid Curry, cold in their graves. Pat Garrett, shot in the back in 1908 while taking a leak. Geronimo, Doc Goodfellow, Blackjack Ketcham, all gone. John Wesley Hardin, shot in the Acme Saloon, El Paso, in 1895. Mysterious Dave Mather—no one knows where he cashed in. Buckey O'Neill, dead of a sniper's bullet near San Juan Hill in 1898.

Clay Allison, the cowman who had tried to tree Dodge and send me to ground, killed in 1887 when, dead drunk, he fell off a wagon and the wheel rolled over his neck. And the damned story was wrong. I wasn't even in Dodge when Allison supposedly treed it; I was off on Ford County sheriff business. And town-treers were the city marshal's business, not the sheriff's.

"Hell, Doc," I said. "Those are just a few. Not very many of those you knew lasted past the turn of the century. And why I'm still around I truly don't know."

Lynwood Cemetery seemed friendly that morning and I was glad to be among the dead. Old men aren't squeamish or frightened by such boneyards.

"Doc, there's something I want to know. Someone must have stolen your marker, the one your brother put here. This one here is a tourist item. It doesn't even supply your baptismal name. It's got your birthdate wrong. I'll bet this was the work of the local chamber of commerce, which knew how to rake in some tourist bucks. They didn't cut stone like this in eighteen-eighty-seven, before power equipment was around.

"I hate this thing, this advertisement. I hope to hell my gravestone doesn't say Bat. I was born Bartholomew but I want William Barclay carved on it. And I hope to hell no son of a bitch steals it. If I ever find out who stole yours, there's going to be one more time when I burn some powder."

The wind sighed through the gnarled limbs.

I sat there, feeling the bond. We of notorious reputation.

"Doc, it doesn't matter to the world who you really were. It doesn't matter to the world who I really am. They've got their cardboard cutouts of us, and that's all people want. That tombstone says it all. They've robbed you of your real name, and they'll rob me of mine. Now I know what this whole trip's about. They can stuff us into dime novels forever, but they'll never know who we were. And I'm not going to tell them."

I could have stayed there for hours but the wind was chilling me and this long trip had weakened me. It was time to go.

"Good-bye, Doc," I said. "You're one hell of a friend."

I tipped my hat.

I walked slowly downslope, through the cemetery gate, and back through quiet Colorado streets, all the while thinking that this trip was the most important thing I had ever done. Important for Emma, too. I had come home to something in Glenwood Springs, Colorado, and something was now fulfilled.

I found Emma in our room, looking pinker than usual.

"Well?" I asked.

"I had a soak. We could soak in a private room or

we could go into the public pool. They provide bathing dresses. Of course I chose the private room. It was very nice, all tile, and they leave you alone."

"You should have dipped with the public."

"I'm not that daring. Those are skimpy little skirts."

"You didn't seem to mind showing a lot more than that when you did the variety act."

She looked indignant. "I didn't have varicose veins then."

"Hell, Emma, you could have stepped into that pool in your little woolen skirts and you'd have twenty men buzzing around you in two minutes."

She pursed her lips but I could see she was not unhappy with the roundabout compliment. She winked. She had not forgotten our adventure on the Union Pacific Pullman.

"I had a visit with Doc," I said. "We talked about our notoriety. He gave me something from across the grave. I'm making some sense of my life now."

"Are you happy we came, Bat?"

"Babe, this is the best thing ever's happened to me."

CHAPTER 33

My bride and I had a little powwow over a lousy lunch. Glenwood Springs was competing with the Texas Panhandle for the bad-food crown. What is the most important historical aspect of the American West? Rotten food. That will never change.

"Where next?" I asked, over baked Alaska. "You name it."

"I've done what I wanted to do in Leadville."

"Not Gunnison? Not Central City?"

"Not unless you want to."

"You got your first billing in Central City, Babe."

"Yeah, but that theater's gone the way of the dodo."

"Then Gunnison?"

"One two-week run. Unless you want to."

There were lots of places I had been but somehow they meant nothing to me. We could drift to Gunnison or Pueblo, where I had spent time; dive down to Las Vegas, New Mexico, which was once one of the great camps on the circuit. Dive even farther south and try San Antonio, El Paso, or Dallas, where I played the odds for a living.

"Denver," I said, wiping runny merengue off my chin.

She smiled. "We have to go there."

"I once vowed I never would set foot in that dump again," I said. "But who is Bat Masterson to keep his word?"

She laughed, a trace of sadness in it. "I'll go dicker at the ticket window. Don't drift off, lover-boy."

She installed the narrow-brimmed bowl of fruit on her graying hair, wrapped the woolen coat around her and flung the mink collar about her throat like a boa constrictor at work, and sailed out of the hotel dining room. She had brought two hats, which I had named the Greengrocer and the Funeral Parlor. Today she wore the Greengrocer. I nursed some Turkish coffee, which scoured my innards.

So we were done with the frontier camps, the life as a peace officer, cop, sheriff, United States marshal. Done with the life of a gunman, a quick shot, a buffalo butcher, a jailkeeper, a cranium-banger, a star-wearer. The stuff of dime novels. We had looked at all that from Dodge to Los Angeles to here in Glenwood, and I had enjoyed the journey.

But now we would cross the divide; not just the physical one that split the continent, but the other ones that split my life into separate legends. Bat Masterson, frontier lawman, was about to vanish. The Masterson of pulp magazine legend consumed scarcely a dozen years of my long life. With minor exceptions, I was never a lawman again once I settled in Denver. But there were two other well-known legends dogging me: Bat Masterson the gambler and bon vivant, and Bat Masterson, the man who knew boxing better than anyone else alive.

And there was a third legend, known only to a few, and one I've never much talked about: Bat Masterson, womanizer. In Denver I would confront all three and see where they led me. I've always had women, more women than I knew what to do with. I lived with two or three in Dodge. I had a couple of sweethearts in Trinidad, including a Spanish beauty. In Denver I had my pick. Even in Leadville, in the few weeks I was there, I shared quarters with a grand serving gal.

I've never understood the men who say they can't find a woman. They don't look very hard. I lived in frontier camps where there were twenty men for every woman—like Dodge—and still had no trouble finding them. Some men are afraid of women, or mean, or hostile, or don't want to get involved, and so they're stuck. I never was stuck a day in my life.

My brothers never had any trouble finding women either. It must be something about the Mastersons. Hell, Emma figured that out long ago, bore with it, and outlasted my wandering ways. I was lucky. Women came and went but Emma stayed. I wondered what would happen in Denver, when we revisited a few of our contretemps. Maybe she'd just kiss me on the cheek. Or maybe not.

She returned and told me to pack up and check out swiftly; we would be on the three P.M. Denver and Rio Grande train to Pueblo, and catch a Denver and Rio Grande train up to Denver. I threw stuff into my bag, summoned a bellhop, and settled with the Glenwood Hotel. We beat the train by two or three minutes, and I was puffing harder than the locomotive. I was not yet accustomed to such altitude. It was hard to say good-bye to Doc, but I sure as hell was glad he and I had a visit.

I swiftly realized that the D & RG followed a twisting route along precipices and over spidery trestles, and I surrendered my life to Fate. I had yet to figure out how an aeroplane stayed in the sky but I doubted the locomotives could fly at all.

We got into Pueblo late at night and I sure as hell didn't feel like sitting up in a coach to Denver, and neither did Emma, so we got a hack and settled for the night in a downtown hotel, the old Victoria. I hardly recognized Pueblo. It had turned into a red brick industrial city with iron and steel works pumping smoke into the sky.

Was this the place where I had caught an escaped Kansas jailbird when I was Ford County sheriff? The place where I had organized a little army for the Santa Fe Railroad during its war with the Denver and Rio Grande? Was this the place where I talked my colleague, Sheriff Jamieson, whatever the hell his first name was, into issuing a warrant for Doc on a hokum bunco charge to keep Arizona from laying its murderous fingers on him?

It was dark when we landed at the venerable inn and I couldn't see much, but I guessed, come morning,

I'd be looking at another strange twentieth-century city through nineteenth-century eyes. I liked Pueblo. It was a warm, sunny, happy place on the mighty Arkansas River, looking eastward upon a vast and still-empty plain, looking westward into the broken and disconnected remains of the Rockies. The solid phalanx of the Front Range didn't exist there where the mountains broke into isolated ranges.

But all I could think of was the fiery furnaces of Colorado Fuel and Iron south of town, and Meyer Guggenheim's Philadelphia Smelter belching toxic gases. Soot and grit. After washing coal dust and railroad cinders and airborne crap out of my skin and hair, I fell asleep with the smell of sizzling slag in my nostrils.

I had some memories there, and I hoped I could refresh them and gild them and put them in mind. The Royal Gorge railroad war, for instance. Back in 1879 when Leadville was proving to be a bonanza town needing to ship out its rich silver ore and ship in the necessaries for several thousand inhabitants, both the newly formed Denver and Rio Grande and the Santa Fe lusted to run rails to it through the narrow, thousand-foot-deep canyon of the Arkansas River called the Royal Gorge, which was the only way in, and that was how the troubles began. Both railroads prepared to spill blood for it.

I was Ford County sheriff then and figured that any troubles afflicting the Atchison, Topeka and Santa Fe were troubles afflicting Dodge City, a town split by the rails of that road. So I gathered my army, bought and paid for by the Santa Fe. We had some pretty tough hombres in there, including Doc Holliday. Old Doc signed. He'd hired out, like the rest of us, as a Santa Fe gunslinger. So did Ben Thompson.

There were those among us who itched for a fight. I had a small problem because I was a sworn peace officer, but I figured with enough artillery showing we'd win the day against those Denver and Rio Grande gandy dancers without burning powder.

We had boarded a Santa Fe train for Pueblo on March 23, and then headed up to Cañon City at the mouth of the gorge. I had thirty-three tough bastards under me, every one of them a master of firearms. Men like Josh Webb and Kinch Riley, who had served on my posses. Jerry Converse, a Scotsman invented for war, was along. Doc had tried to enlist Eddie Foy, but he wisely figured he was better off pumping audiences than pumping lead.

In essence, we owned that town, and there wasn't much that General Palmer and his little Colorado railroad could do about it. He went to court and also went to the authorities. Palmer had been forced by insolvency to lease his road to the Santa Fe in 1878, but now he was claiming in court that the Santa Fe had violated the contract, and meanwhile he moved in gangs of toughs to defend his tracklayers. These were gathered into stone fortresses twenty miles upriver.

Then the court ruled that the Denver and Rio Grande had prior right to build, but not the exclusive right. If both roads could wedge track through the canyon the war would dissolve. It seemed to be over, and I took my army back to Dodge. But the Supreme Court still had to rule on the question of the lease, so I figured the war might heat up again.

It did heat up, and the next time, in June, I rounded up over sixty men and caught an express consisting of an engine and one coach bound for Pueblo. We were only a part of the Santa Fe's burgeoning army. Dick Wooten and forty-five "deputy sheriffs" arrived from

Trinidad, and Charles Hickey, sheriff over in Bent County, came in with eighteen. I was given charge of the Santa Fe railroad station and roundhouse in Pueblo, and there I set up my defenses. Pueblo was the key: it controlled the tracks to Denver and points in every other direction.

I had looked to my defenses, even appropriating the cannon from the state armory, and now its muzzle pointed outward from the roundhouse. Palmer won in court, as expected, and shrewdly tapped the telegraphs, learning that the Santa Fe intended to resist with armed might. Palmer lined up his own army, got writs and enlisted the sheriffs up and down the line, and then seized one Santa Fe depot after another, sometimes following a pitched battle, a railroad Genghis Khan riding out of the north. A pair of Santa Fe men were killed at Cuchara, and two more were hurt. So they stormed down on us, but the Pueblo roundhouse stood in the way of victory.

The only legal platform supporting me was my office as a U.S. marshal, and I could make use of that only if federal law was broken. We were being paid board and three bucks a day. But I was bound as a peace officer to prevent bloodshed, so I was, at bottom, in hopeless circumstances.

Colorado officials had gotten into the act. Governor Pitkin, Inspector General Sopris, and Pueblo's sheriff, Henley Price, were trying to figure out a way to drive us out of the roundhouse but they lost heart when staring down the muzzle of our cannon.

Finally they assembled before the Victoria Hotel, the very place where I now was staying, issued arms to fifty besiegers, and moved on us. They swiftly routed the Santa Fe men from the station house nearby, and then turned to face us. That's when their

commander, R. F. Weitbrec, actually treasurer of the
Denver and Rio Grande, asked to parley with me, so
I stepped out for a talk.

"You're the last holdout," he said. "Every other
Santa Fe station and property's surrendered. We've the
law with us, a legal writ to take this over, and the
support of the state government. The inspector general's out there and he's in wire contact with Governor
Pitkin. You'd better quit before there's more blood
spilled and every one of you is in big trouble. Here,
look at the writ." He handed it to me and I looked.

I quit. I had no way of confirming anything the man
said, no word from the Santa Fe, but I figured we'd
better pack up. The state got its cannon back and we
caught a Santa Fe coach bound for Dodge.

They criticized me back in Dodge for surrendering,
and maybe that's why I lost the next election so badly.
There were hotheads in Dodge who thought the national honor was at stake. But I had done the right
thing; the only thing a sworn peace officer could do.
One casualty was a broken tooth in the mouth of Josh
Webb after a scuffle with some Denver and Rio
Grande toughs, but John Henry Holliday, D.D.S., repaired the damage when we got back to Dodge.

The mythologists claimed I was bought off with a
ten-grand Denver and Rio Grande bribe, and that
didn't help the Masterson legend either. At that time
I didn't much care; now I do. I wasn't bought off.
Hell, even the offer of a bribe would have been enough
to keep us holding out for weeks.

I awakened early, the memories churning within me.
The Royal Gorge war occurred before Emma's time
and she had no interest in it or Pueblo, so she stayed
abed while I pulled on my suitcoat, clapped my fedora

over my gray hair, and descended to the street for a lookaround.

Right there, before the hotel, the Denver and Rio Grande army that ultimately defeated me had been assembled. I hiked over to the rails, found the old roundhouse intact and in use, and tried to remember how we had commandeered it and turned it into a fortress where we had bunked, eaten rotten food, built breast works, cut rifle ports, played poker, and boasted that no railroad gang in Colorado could break us.

I wandered freely; no one stayed me as I patrolled the interior, past giant black locomotives quick and dead, looking for a few relics of our occupation. I found a few: some rifle slits carved into massive plank doors.

That had been my longest stay in Pueblo and my sole experience as a generalissimo. This would be one of my shortest. We caught a decrepit passenger train to Denver just after lunch, riding the enemy railroad to the place I had called home for a decade, and despised now.

CHAPTER 34

Back in 1879, when I was commanding an army of skilled gunmen for the Santa Fe Railroad, I scarcely worried about whether I was on the wrong side of the law. What, after all, was a Kansas sheriff and sworn peace officer doing leading a private army in Colorado?

Perhaps the reason I didn't much care was that lawmen had gathered on both sides of that war, and most of them were Colorado peace officers. And a corporation did have the right to defend its property by whatever force was required.

Still, we were all at the edge, and with so much tinder around it was miraculous that we didn't start a small holocaust. I had always taken my duties seriously, unlike some lawmen who had, at one time or another, been on both sides.

I had, for years, insisted I had never broken the law apart from a few scrapes such as the war on the Dodge City plaza, for which I was fined eight dollars. But that was not really true, and I had been blinding myself to the one time when I did willfully and knowingly break the law.

That episode, in 1880, when I was out of office but floating around Dodge, was simply a favor to a friend, Ben Thompson. Now, Ben does not have a savory reputation. The dapper Englishman was first and foremost a gambler, and that was how I knew him. But he was also quick to use his revolver, an alcoholic, a bully, and an all-around rattlesnake.

He was one of those gun sharps who could be found occasionally on either side of the law. But Ben behaved himself in Dodge and I never had a bit of trouble with him. The trouble was that he had an even more ill-tempered and brutal younger brother, Billy.

When word came down from Ogallala, Nebraska, that Billy had gotten into a serious shooting scrape there, Ben asked me to help out. Ben himself was persona non grata in Ogallala and could do nothing on his own. Billy had gotten into a row with a local citizen, gotten shot up himself, and was in danger of being lynched.

So Ben asked me to rescue Billy and I agreed to do

so, leaving at once by rail and stage. Ogallala lay a formidable distance from Dodge. When I finally arrived there, via the Union Pacific, I found Billy at the Ogallala House, the only hotel around, with five shotgun pellets in his porky body.

The story Billy told me was that he had gone up there for the cattle shipping season and was running a monte game in Bill Tucker's Saloon, the Cowboy's Rest, and that he and Tucker had gotten into a spat over a local cyprian, Big Alice.

Billy got ginned up and then steered himself into the Cowboy's Rest and fired just as Tucker was passing a glass of whiskey to one of his customers. Billy's bullet shot off three of Tucker's fingers and the thumb as well. But that didn't slow Tucker, who grabbed his sawed-off ten-gauge shotgun and let fly as Billy fled down the street, putting five pellets into Billy's back.

When I got there, it was plain that Tucker would recover. Billy was under arrest and being guarded by a deputy sheriff at the hotel. I went to Tucker to see what could be done to settle the matter, and Tucker agreed to drop charges if Billy Thompson would fork over some massive sum—I don't remember the amount, but it was far beyond what squalid little Billy could pay.

So, I had a problem. I had to get Billy out of there. His young guard was armed with a Colt's forty-five-caliber revolver and looked entirely capable of using it. But I befriended the youth, we made lawman talk, and I discovered he wasn't exactly experienced in his trade. In fact, he had only recently arrived from the East.

I also took a good look at Billy's wounds, which were less serious or painful than he was letting on. He could travel, but certainly not by horseback, which

would have been our best option. And not by wagon,
which would leave a clear track across the prairie. We
had to take the train one way or another, and that
would leave us at the mercy of the telegraph.

Well, I found out a few things: Bill Cody was in
residence, for a change, at his ranch at North Platte,
fifty miles east. The eastbound UP flyer stopped in
Ogallala to take on water at midnight, and then went
on to North Platte.

I also knew that just about the whole town was
watching Bat Masterson, friend of Billy Thompson.
They were waiting for me to make my play and licking
their chops. It was going to be a tough snatch, and I
didn't know how to do it.

But then I heard that there would be some Sunday
night fiddling in a little schoolhouse just outside of
town, and the sheriff happened to be the town's fid-
dler. He'd be fiddling up on the hill but he would
prime his deputy not to get too friendly with Bat Masterson. That was the only chance that came my way.

I enlisted an old bartending friend of mine, Jim
Dunn, and we hatched a plan. He got the chloral hy-
drate and I was in business. During the fiddling I wandered in, started gabbing with the wary kid guarding
Billy, and lamented that I couldn't be up there at the
schoolhouse enjoying the fun. The deputy was of the
same mind, and pretty soon I ordered a couple of whiskey sours from Dunn, and he delivered them.

The Mickey Finn swiftly did its work, and when the
deputy was soundly asleep and filled with innocent
dreams, I got Billy up and dressed, carried him down
to the station, and manhandled him aboard the flyer,
which was just coming to a stop when we arrived.

We got off at North Platte and I carried Billy over
to Perry's Saloon, which was still open, and Master-

son's famous luck was with me. There, before my eyes, was Colonel Cody himself, surrounded by cronies, or toadies if you prefer, and of course we were instantly welcomed. I explained our dilemma to him and he pitched in with all the gusto of a born conspirator. Leave it to old Cody to do it grand opera style.

The colonel swiftly hid us in a safe house in North Platte where we could lay low while he outfitted us for a trip down to Dodge. He was enjoying every minute of it and so were his toadies. We slept soundly.

The next day, Cody offered us a big dray horse and a new phaeton he'd just purchased for his wife, but he suggested we stay there in North Platte for a couple of days; he was expecting distinguished foreign guests sent to him by General Sheridan, and planned to take them to a ranch south of town for some western hospitality. We did wait, and eventually traveled south in the company of twenty more or less inebriated dukes and duchesses.

I drove the mess wagon with poor old Billy in it. I considered him spare lard and drove cheerfully along with Moldavian barons and Rhineland counts and lesser Italian princes. We enjoyed a grand fandango down there at the ranch, and the next day took off for Dodge in Louisa Maude Cody's phaeton, making it safely through some rough weather that had poor old Billy's teeth rattling.

Cody later told me he had a devil of a time explaining the missing phaeton to his wife. But plausible explanations were not beyond the rhetorical skills of the showman, and that was how it ended. In Dodge, Billy telegraphed the Ogallala sheriff and invited the sheriff to come get him if he wanted to. He didn't. It was all

over. Ben pronounced himself a lifelong friend of Bat
Masterson. Billy was less grateful.

Well, hell, that wasn't just bending the law. That
was jailbreak. It took me years to admit I did it. I
ruminated over all that as the Denver and Rio Grande
train huffed its way north, along the Front Range,
heading for Denver.

I wondered whether I would despise the town as
much in 1919 as when we left a quarter of a century
earlier. At that time I'd vowed I would never set foot
in that burg again, but my various travels, mostly following the fight game, had taken me all over the country and I had passed through Denver often. I even
stopped briefly in Dodge when the Santa Fe pulled in
there; long enough for my boxing cronies and me to
stand still for a photo on the station platform. But that
was a thirty-minute Harvey House layover. I'd spent
similar moments in Denver.

We were running through snow, which swept into
the coach window and turned liquid. I wished we had
ventured West a few months earlier. Emma stared into
the whirl of white, saying nothing, but I knew Denver
was on her mind. Important things had happened there,
not the least of them moving in with Bat Masterson
for good.

The thick overcast hid Pike's Peak from us, and the
rest of the Front Range, but I am not an outdoorsman
and one mountain is as fine as another. There were
people living in Denver for whom the mountain view
was everything. For me, the green cloth of a gaming
table meant more, and I had spent a dozen years in
Denver scarcely aware of the Rockies. To tell you the
truth, I hate the damned West. I don't know what I
ever saw in it.

The train slowed and we found ourselves rocking

past apartments, warehouses, grimy factories, back-
yards, and lines of boxcars.

"Where are we staying?" I asked.

"Brown Palace."

"There goes the retirement income."

"This is more fun."

I had to agree with that.

The cold wet wind hit us hard when we stepped out
of the coach and onto the slippery conductor's stool.
But a strong blue-uniformed arm settled us safely on
the platform and we headed into cavernous Union Station, where everything echoed. Hacks were going to
be hard to find, especially for those of us who had
checked our luggage. It took the better part of an hour
before we were reunited with our bags and I had
grown weary of the stinking room by then. I was getting too old to travel.

I hunted down a redcap and he conjured up a taxi
on Wynkoop, employing a mighty whistle and some
sort of authority not given to ordinary mortals. He got
four bits for his effort. In short order, we were pushing
through the Denver blizzard for the Brown Palace, the
wipers clanking and thumping, speeding up when we
were running, barely moving while we idled in traffic,
and lifting thick gobs of snow from the glass whenever
the spirit moved them to.

We pulled up before the dark canvas marquee of
the Brown Palace on Tremont and the driver unloaded
us with indecent speed. Snow was good for business.
I gave him a dime tip and thought that was pretty
damned generous. Wet cold snow smacked us.

Emma pushed in while I dickered with a bellboy.
She had never seen the hotel. We had left Denver before it was built. She gaped at the height of the huge
central well and the layered balconies surrounding it.

I wasn't interested in wells, or decor, or marble lobby ornaments. I studied the place for a good restaurant and checked in at the desk. They had female clerks, which was a pleasant novelty. I was ready for a double whiskey sour in our room.

I signed us as Bartholomew Masterson and wife, wanting to keep the bloodhounds at bay. Plenty of people knew me here, and very few of them did I wish to see.

But it did little good. Ten minutes after we closed the door of our room on the bellhop, the telephone jangled.

"Is this Bat Masterson?" asked a voice.

"I imagine so," I replied, thinking of whiskey sours.

"That's what I thought. This is the *Denver Post.*"

That was fat Harry Tammen and slippery Freddy Bonfils's yellow rag, sitting about two blocks away, and the last newspaper I wanted to talk to. As a sideline they owned the Sells-Floto Circus, which specialized in freaks. And it was the lair of my nemesis, Otto Floto, the reason I hated Denver.

"I'm not available," I said.

"You don't have to be," said the male voice. "Long as we know you're in town."

"Go to hell," I said, and hung up.

CHAPTER 35

regretted my rudeness, but for no more than two seconds. I winked at Emma and steered her to the elevator, and moments later we

were enjoying double whiskey sours in the well of the
Brown Palace, surrounded by potted palms.

Colorado had been dry since 1916, but we got set-
ups and added the booze from our flasks. The hell with
hotel dicks, cops, and feds. No one in a flossy joint
would be offended anyway. They sure as hell knew
what I wanted when I ordered ice and bitters. We intended to get a little potted too at this oasis in the
Rocky Mountain wilderness, a reward richly earned
after days of grimy rail travel.

That's when a gent of indeterminate age descended
on us. I knew at once he was a veteran reporter. The
fedora, nose hair, grimy collar, spectacles, bad teeth,
worn-out shoes, tobacco-stained fingers, and dirty fin-
gernails gave him away.

"Ah, there you are. I knew I would find you here,"
he said. "You don't look like your photographs anymore."

I stood, retrieving some manners from wherever I
had banished them. "Masterson," I said. "And you?"

"I'm with the *Post*."

"Yes, and your name?"

"Oh, Leonard Deutsch. I just want to pop a few
questions, okay?"

I shrugged.

"How come you registered as Bartholomew?"

"It is my name."

"Maybe it's because you wished to escape detec-
tion."

"Mr. Deutsch, do you want me to answer questions
or not?"

"Sure, Masterson."

I sat down but did not invite him to join us. I sensed
what was coming. In New York I was fairly well in-
sulated from celebrity hounds and predatory journal-

ists. That was not because the *Telegraph* staff protected me, but because of the circumstances. New York was a bustling, towering, cosmopolitan city; and if a few determined people did track me down, they didn't find what they had come for: the man they met wore dark business suits, white shirts, and cravats instead of cowboy boots, and my messy, paper-strewn cubicle was at such a remove from my frontier life that they wondered whether I had ever been a frontier lawman.

Deutsch pulled out a wad of newsprint and a stubby copyediting pencil and settled himself in the overstuffed couch next to my chair. He had bad breath and I wished to distance myself, but there was no escape. The double sour helped.

"You're good copy. I'm gonna make a great item out of you. Everybody in the country knows who you are. Like the bellboy that gave me the tip. You're a notorious man. It's not often I get to interview a famous gunman. You and Earp are about all's left. How many did you kill?"

I debated whether to say a word, but the sours were mellowing me. Whiskey is the avenue to my tongue.

"I had some tough fights with Indians."

"You killed more than twenty."

"I am unaware of it."

"And probably lots more, known only to you."

"I suggest you check the record."

"That wouldn't prove a thing. Records are mostly crap. How did it feel to gun someone down?"

"Mr. Deutsch, if you want an interview, you'd better take my answers."

"Hey, Masterson. I just want to write a good yarn. How long's it been since you snuffed someone out?"

"That's a little like the old lawyer's question, 'When

did you stop beating your wife?', isn't it?"

"Masterson, it's all in the *Post*'s morgue. You can gimme some good quotes and the story will go easy, or I can pull everything I want out of the clips. Fat bunch of them, too."

I smiled.

He lit a Turkish cigarette that smelled like camel dung.

"Who's this lady?" he asked.

She winked. "I'm not a lady; I'm his wife."

"You're Emma. Come on now, when and where did you get hitched?"

This joker had been tracking me a long time.

"She's more married than you ever will be, Deutsch."

He didn't like that. "You're not giving me a good interview, Masterson."

I smiled again.

"Were you as fast on the draw as Holliday? Earp?"

"I wouldn't know."

"How many you kill beating them to the draw?"

"I have never been in such circumstances. I'd be dead if I tried."

"You ran a cathouse in Denver before it got shut down."

"No."

"The Palace. That was a theater, cathouse, gambling parlor, and saloon."

"It was a variety theater and gambling hall and restaurant and saloon."

"That ain't the way it was, Masterson. You had girls for sale all over the joint."

"I wonder where you got that misinformation." It was time to go. I nodded to Emma.

"I got my sources. Lots of old-timers remember

you. I can talk to any old-timer from Blake Street and he'll remember plenty, especially after I slide him a buck or two. I know more about you than you can hide, Masterson. You got kicked out of town after almost getting into a shootout. You got on the four o'clock Burlington because you had to."

"I don't recollect the specifics."

He smirked. "The more you deny, the better my story, Masterson. Now, why are you here?"

"Mrs. Masterson and I are on a little holiday."

"Naw, you're doing something like maybe setting up an illegal fight. Boxing exhibitions, that's okay; prizefights, you got the law coming down on you. That it?"

"You seem to know my mind better than I do." I stood, and Emma stood too.

"That's what I'm paid for. You're a boxing writer, but that's a front. Who ever heard of a gunman writing newspaper columns? Who writes them for you?"

I handed him my card, which announced that I was a secretary of the *New York Morning Telegraph*.

"How much schooling you have?"

"Not enough."

"I seen your stuff. There's a pile of it, from when you wrote all them screeds here. We got everything you ever wrote in Denver."

Deutsch was scribbling some canard on his pad. "You carrying?" he asked. "Earp carries. He got nailed for carrying a few years ago when he was refereeing a boxing match."

"You don't say."

"All you big-time killers carry."

I unbuttoned my gray suit coat. He peered.

"You got you a hideout gun somewheres."

"Your grammar and diction could stand some polishing, Deutsch." I took Emma's elbow and steered her toward the dining room, but Deutsch followed.

"Hey! Stay put. I just want to ask a couple more."

"No."

I had tried civility with no effect. This bird had flown straight out of Joe Pulitzer's *World* and I knew the type. His object was to make a splash, the bigger the better. His questions didn't rise from curiosity about me or any desire to elicit truth, but only as snares.

He would write his gunman story without reference to anything I had told him, other than to rebut me. This, unfortunately, was how legends were made, including the one hung on me. I could have told him, item by item, how things were and it wouldn't have altered his preconceived story an iota. Well, the hell with him.

"That's it, Deutsch. I'm taking Mrs. Masterson to dinner."

"All right, Masterson, I tried to give you a good shot."

That was an odd figure of speech. I steered Emma across the lobby toward the hotel's restaurant. Just as we entered, I saw Deutsch picking up our glasses in the lobby and sniffing them. He added something to his notes.

I smiled at Emma. She had slid into her usual silence around that bird, but she'd soon come out of it.

"I can't remember. Did we ever get married?" I asked.

"Tell me after you get me pregnant," she replied.

The standing rib roast was better than any I had sampled in New York. We went to bed early, weary from weeks of travel.

"You look damned nice for an unmarried woman,"

I said when she appeared in the Mother Hubbard sleeping gown she favored.

"You should say that I look damned nice for a married woman."

I woke late the next morning, wondering what Tammen and Bonfils's yellow rag had to say about me. I called the desk and asked a bellboy to bring me a *Post* and two coffees.

They all arrived while I was shaving, and I accepted them half lathered, half scraped, and gave the kid two bits.

They had it on page one, under Leonard Deutsch's byline.

NOTORIOUS GUNMAN IN CITY;
CONNECTED WITH FIGHT GAME

Pretty good head, I thought.

William B. Masterson, frontier gunslinger, lawman, and legendary killer, arrived in Denver yesterday and registered under false colors at the Brown Palace. Masterson, no stranger to Denver, once owned the Palace Theater on Blake Street, a notorious dive that purveyed all the vices, from salacious girlie shows to gambling to booze to women of easy morals.

He was run out of town by the city fathers in 1902. It is known that the Palace Theater was a gambling hell that cleaned out the wallets and bank accounts of Denver's vulnerable citizens.

It went downhill from there:

Masterson is associated with prizefighting and once ran a gymnasium here that staged illegal

fights while calling them boxing exhibitions. He
has been spotted from coast to coast following
the fight game.

Masterson was a frontier lawman and sheriff
in the seventies and eighties in such wild towns
as Dodge City, Trinidad, and Tombstone. He has
been closely associated with such gunmen as Wyatt Earp, Doc Holliday, and Luke Short. But his
principal profession is gambling, and he ran
games of chance in every town where he wore a
star.

It is commonly believed by those who keep
track of such matters that he has killed more men
than he has fingers and toes, and that's only the
known murders. Many of the deaths reputedly involved gambling. He is an accomplished and
slick high-stakes gambler.

Out on the lonely prairies there may well be
scores of others sent to their lonely graves but
their number is known only to Masterson. Most
of the shootings happened under the thin color of
law while he was a peace officer, which con-
cealed his private motives from public view. He
and his notorious brothers were known to own
games of chance or saloons on the south side of
Dodge City, and any cowboy bucking a Masterson faro or monte game was likely to be out of
luck.

He is in town with the woman he calls his wife,
though there is no local record of any marriage.
Emma Walters was one of his "showgirls" at the
Palace. When asked by the *Post,* they declined to
say where or how they were married.

He operates as a newspaperman, and even
proffers a card announcing that he is the vice

president of a large New York paper. We are not saying that Masterson is a bunco artist. He apparently does write a column for a New York paper, but of a caliber so low that it invites mirth.

Masterson has an arrest record as long as one's arm. He was arrested and fined in Dodge City for assault with deadly intent, arrested in New York on bunco charges, and was infamously involved in the fraud that allowed Holliday to escape justice in Arizona, among other items. The sources of his income are unknown. When asked what he was doing in Denver, he replied guardedly that he and his wife were on a little holiday. He declined to answer most questions put to him by the *Post* reporter.

There was more in this vein. When they are determined to turn you into a legend, light or dark, good or evil, you may as well sit back and enjoy the ride because there's no way to get off the train.

CHAPTER 36

Emma wanted to go home. She had read the story with darkening spirits and when she had finished she fell into one of those deep silences I had come to know over many years.

"Let's go, Bat," she said.

"Soon, babe. We came for the memories. Let's take the bad with the good. Some good things happened here."

Among them, we had at last settled into a married state. We had been living together off and on for many years but her variety act took her one place and another, and I wasn't ready to call one woman my own. She was calling me her husband before I was calling her my wife. Whenever she was booked in town, she moved in with me; then she'd be off again and I'd find some other temporary sweetheart to share my bed.

We were going to visit the old places, Blake Street, our little apartment, the saloon I owned briefly, shut now because the state had gone dry in a moment of lunacy. Not that anything would be the same after three decades, but we would take our little stroll through the past. That was what this trip had come to. Ever since she had taken off her coat and done her little buck-and-wing at the Tabor Opera House in Leadville, this trip had been delicious for her. There is nothing so sweet as a good memory. It can't be stolen or diminished.

"Forget that piece," I said. "It's mostly bunk. A few grains of truth to give it some plausibility. It doesn't affect you or me. It doesn't erode our happiness."

"Let's go," she said, almost plaintively.

"We'll cut it short but I want to do a few things first. Give me a couple of days. We'll be out of booze by then anyway."

"I don't know what I'll do. Stay here, I guess."

She would get over that. Emma, in her own way, was more the adventurer than I.

We dressed and ate breakfast, eggs benedict, orange juice, apple slices, Melba toast and marmalade, and plenty of coffee, without being molested. Our presence was now a front-page matter.

"I'm going over to the *Rocky Mountain News*. You want to come?"

"Why?"

"To fight back if I can."

She looked doubtful, then nodded. "If the weather's good."

The *News* was Denver's oldest paper but no match for that obstreperous *Post,* even though the owners of the *News* had recently consolidated it with a couple of other papers all being whipped by the nefarious and gaudy yellow rag that dominated Denver journalism.

I hoped to find a conscientious reporter there. I was ready to punch back. I've never been one to take things lying down and was just as good with words as weapons as with firearms. Was there just one newsman in Denver who wanted to get it right?

Emma changed her mind and said she would do some last-minute Christmas shopping. I knew she didn't want to deal with reporters and legends and lies. I hiked over to the old *News* building and found my way to the newsroom, which was familiar turf for me. There was the green-eyeshade crowd, the ancient golden oak desks scalloped with cigarette burns, the spittoons, and gents with black garters on their sleeves. I steered toward a likely-looking suspect, a gaunt fellow with a homburg and wire-rimmed glasses.

"Masterson here. I'd like to talk to a reporter."

The gent eyed me longer than necessary. "The notorious Masterson?" He had a copy of the *Post.*

"That's what I'm here for. I want to reply to that crap."

"We don't normally lend our columns to exchanges of that sort. Is there a newsworthy aspect of your visit to Denver?"

"No, just a visit for old time's sake."

He nodded me to a wooden chair. "I'm Wayne Ambrose. I cover city hall. You're not my beat but let's talk."

We shook. I told him that nearly everything in the story he had before him was bunk and I was damned tired of that sort of stuff being printed about me.

"I can't promise you a story, and I can't promise you a story you'd *like* if we do run one," he said. "Maybe I'll write one and the editors won't run it. But let's examine these allegations."

He began perusing the story. "You get run out of town?"

"Cops invited me to leave, once. That was nineteen hundered and two, and some broad at a polling booth had whacked me with an umbrella, and I'd gotten mad, hit a few gin joints, said a few things I shouldn't have about crooked officials and elections, and next thing I knew the cops decided it was time for me to vamoose."

"You own the Palace?"

"Yes, for a while."

"Variety shows, gambling, booze. Did it sell women?"

"Never."

"You legally married?"

"Common law. Long time. Legal in most places."

"You kill all these people?"

"No."

"You have proof?"

"Yes, it'd be in old papers in Dodge City and elsewhere. What you'll see is a lot of nothing. Contact the editor of the *Globe* in Dodge City, Jess Dennis. He's got the old copies of several early papers."

Ambrose sighed. "Negatives never make a case. The absence of information doesn't mean that something won't show up. I believe you, but I have no way to dig out stuff all over the West: How come you're listed as a big-time killer, then?"

"Yellowback novelists mostly. Quack writers. Fantasy. Maybe the country wants killer lawmen. Who knows?"

"Something's wrong there. Where there's smoke there's fire."

"I'll pay you one hundred dollars for every killing laid to me as a peace officer that you find in contemporary court records or the current issues of papers in the towns when and where I worked. Dodge, Trinidad, briefly Tombstone as a posseman. Go ahead. Get rich."

"Maybe you'll owe me a few hundred. You a gambler by profession?"

"I was. Not now. I'm a newsman like you, and secretary of the *New York Morning Telegraph*."

"You get fined in Dodge City for discharging a firearm at someone?"

"Yes, but—"

"Yeah, well, a lot of this story is true. You get indicted in New York on a bunco charge?"

"It was dropped. I was in bad company by accident. I sued the bastard that accused me and he skipped out."

"You seem to hang around bad company. Prizefighters, saloon men, petty crooks, gamblers, horse race touts."

I was learning once again the virtue of silence.

He eyed me through those thick glasses. He struck me as a pretty serious man. "I tell you what. I'm going to dig up what I can in our morgue. Maybe I'll do a story. Unlike the bunch at the *Post,* I get at facts, try to state them accurately, and try to run stories that are inherently honest."

"That's all I ask."

"If I do a story with damaging material, I'll let you respond to it."

"Mr. Ambrose, I would not have become a sheriff, a city marshal or police officer, or a United States marshal unless I met certain standards. I would not have been appointed U.S. marshal for the Southern District of New York by Theodore Roosevelt if I had a record."

"Maybe that's debatable."

"Go ask. And try to understand how it was on the frontier. Most peace officers had other businesses on the side, usually running a monte or faro game. You can't live on fifty a month."

He nodded. "You'll be at the Brown Palace?"

"For two days."

"Not enough to do any serious checking. Anyone I should talk to?"

"Wyatt Earp, in Los Angeles." I dug up his address and wrote it out.

"One thing more. You know the *News* campaigned for years to shut down the sporting district. We succeeded. In nineteen-thirteen the Market Street red-light district was shuttered. Blake Street saloons and joints are long gone, including your Palace. This state's dry."

"So I noticed."

Ambrose grinned for the first time. "That doesn't stop the intrepid," he said. "One last question. Why, really, are you here? Give me a real reason."

I told him how it started. Louella Parsons, Damon Runyon, a wish rising from old age to put the record right, a trip that ended up a walk through a lifetime. Hell, I even told him about Emma at the Tabor Opera House, dancing there just for me and her memories.

Ambrose brightened up. "Now there's a good story.

A living legend ransacking his past. A man fighting his legend."

We shook on that.

I plunged into a wintry world. Christmas was close but there would be no Tom and Jerrys here, no punchbowls, no wine at Christmas dinners.

I cussed the prohibitionists. That was all I did these days. Yes, they saw the ruin that booze could inflict on a man and his family, or a woman and her children, but they missed the rest: the quiet companionship at the corner pub, the peaceful evenings with friends, the good company. A little whiskey lubricated friendships, opened lovers' hearts, primed a marriage, washed the blues away.

They had gone berserk, these people, thinking they could elevate mankind into—what?

As long as I was a block or two away, I hiked over to the Blake Street sporting district, which had decayed into an empty, lonely avenue of dreary shops and boarded windows, its vitality dead, its very reason for existence lost. The closest thing to a saloon now was a tired place peddling near beer and boasting a soda fountain. A faded sign said that medicinal prescriptions might be had there. But the fanatics had plugged that loophole in 1914. I suspect it did a different trade through its alley door because soda fountains didn't earn a living.

I tried to find the Palace, and stared at a building sawed into small mean shops that sold items like galoshes and kimonos and lawnmowers. Was that it? The Palace, with its gas-jet chandeliers, mirrored backbar, gilded-trim, green-topped gaming tables, big velvet-draped theater? Where the hell had it gone?

I walked a block over to Market and surveyed the old bawdy district, what was left of it. I could find not a trace of the old bordellos. I patrolled the residential areas that once housed the sporting gentry. I saw nothing familiar, nothing to take me back to the days of my youth. Gone.

Denver had turned its face away from the life I knew and enjoyed. Empty of heart, I started toward the Brown Palace, thinking that maybe this miserable city deserved its fate.

But did I deserve mine?

CHAPTER 37

I passed the corner of Curtis and Eighteenth Street and paused there. Emma and I had lived in an apartment at 1825 Curtis for many years. I kept up the rent even though I was often away. The place was convenient to everything, including the sporting district a few blocks north.

I always voted. I am a twice-dyed, true-blue Republican and have been active in Republican politics ever since I was old enough to cast a ballot. In the old days when I was out on the circuit I often traveled back to Dodge City just to vote, or rally the party.

In 1902, just before I left town for good, I went to vote in a school board election at the precinct polling place on Larimer. But a cabal of reformist women, determined to put females on the board, had anointed themselves poll watchers, and when I presented myself one of them proclaimed me ineligible.

Now, mind you, I had been voting there for years and had my residence there for nine years, and had been voting in Denver for fifteen. I explained all that.

The lady upped from her chair and began whacking me with her umbrella and there was nothing for me to do but take it, the rules of chivalry preventing me from defending myself. She didn't even know who I was but correctly surmised that I had come to vote against her cabal, and her approach to reform was to deny me my civil liberties.

That was the crystallizing moment: I knew then it was time to abandon Denver. I went on a two-day drunk, cussed and threatened the whole city and its lousy politicians, and the cops decided I was right: it was time for Bat Masterson to ditch Denver. They weren't going to let Masterson tree Denver the way the cowboys tried to tree Dodge. They invited me to catch the Burlington east.

Now I stood on the corner, remembering that. There was little I recognized. Denver had transformed itself since then and not even my apartment house stood. I had made Denver my home for more or less two decades, with brief stays at first while I followed the gambling circuit, but then, from the mid-eighties, more or less permanently. There were gaps, of course, such as the period when I managed the Denver Exchange in Creede during the last great gold rush in Colorado. But I kept that apartment.

It has been my fate in life to be dogged by reformers. No sooner did I settle in one place or another to engage in my vocation, which was gambling and managing saloons, than one or another damned reform movement was busily putting me out of business. It has never stopped. Even now, with national Prohibition threatening to turn the nation into a living hell, it never ceases.

All this has happened because women were given

suffrage, which was the worst mistake in American history. They are at the root of all this reform. Colorado went downhill the instant women entered the polls. And the reason the whole nation is now on the brink of Prohibition is simply because so many states allow women to vote. If women should be enfranchised nationally, it's all over. I'll move to Timbuktu.

I do not understand reformers. If, say, they are opposed to liquor, what right does that give them to enact laws making liquor illegal? They are, after all, perfectly free not to enter a saloon. Free to proselytize for temperance. Free even to limit the hours a saloon may do business, though I oppose such infringements on my liberty.

But that is not enough. They have in their heads to deprive other people—whom they regard as benighted—of their liberty to take a drink or enjoy the good company of their neighbors in a saloon. In short, their notion of reform is to impose their will upon everyone, employing the police power of the government. Thus do they reduce the liberty of everyone else.

It has come to such a pass that I now am forced to take my spirits with me, hidden in flasks in a picnic valise, and even that is illegal in most of the states we have visited. I am forced to replenish by contacting a bootlegger, and that offends me.

This is madness. Next thing you know, they'll be banning cigars in public places on the ground that they are no good for you or they are noxious to others.

Now in a perfectly free society, these things work themselves out naturally. A person who despises cigars is free to remove himself from their presence. He can go to restaurants or tea gardens where the proprietor forbids smoking. Likewise the cigar-smoking man can puff away where he is welcomed and avoid those places where he isn't, all in perfect liberty and harmony, without the infringement of anyone's rights.

The railroads figured out how to do it: smokers repair to the smoking compartment; nonsmokers enjoy perfect protection elsewhere in each coach. That's freedom. You would think that would be the model in a free nation. But reformers don't think that way.

Freedom isn't on their minds. They are tyrants at heart, wanting to forbid us all to indulge in anything they have condemned, no matter how we feel about it. For our own sake, of course. Hell, they'll never ban cigars or cigarettes. People would string up the first politician who proposed it.

If I was sour on Denver in 1902 when we left it for good, I found myself even more sour now. My morning tour of downtown Denver had awakened memories of better times. I found Emma in our room at the Brown Palace, admiring a new chapeau she'd bought herself for Christmas. This one was as plain as a Salvation Army girl's bonnet.

"This is your Christmas gift to me," she said.

I felt guilty. I hadn't given much thought to Christmas, even though the season was manifest on every street in Denver, and its citizens were hustling through the winds burdened with packages wrapped in kraft paper.

We had been on the road a long while and I wanted nothing more than to get back to civilization and our own hearth, belch out more columns for the paper—I had some blistering things to say about reformers—and spend happy hours with my pals at the Metropole's bar, where whiskey sours were still legal for a few more weeks. But as long as I was on a journey spanning my life, I wanted to see it through. We would be home by New Year's Eve, at any rate.

"You look great in it, Emma. Actually, I have another gift in mind, but I'll have to find a bootlegger."

She laughed. "Yes, and who's going to drink most of that gift?"

She was right.

"I walked over to Blake Street. Nothing there. Remember the Palace, how it was when you were booked there? The gilded theater, people like Eddie Foy, Lottie Rogers, Cora Vane, the Holland sisters. Remember that? Remember your act?"

The piquant smile on her face was something to behold. I was stirring memories. I had bought the place in 1888 from Ed Chase and Ed Gaylord, paying cash for it from a good bankroll I had built up over the years from poker, faro, and monte in one border town after another. The two Eds had been square gamblers and ran a reputable house or I wouldn't have touched it.

It was undoubtedly the finest club between the two coasts. A sixty-foot mirror graced its back bar, shooting light from the gas chandeliers into the saloon and onto the gaming tables. It was the Mecca for every sport in the Rockies, and through my doors came them all.

I had no trouble running it. I knew gambling as well as anyone alive. The theater stuff was all new to me, especially the grumbling of performers, and I got tough with some of them. Quit bitching or get out. A few left in a huff. But the rest of it, the feed we put on for players every night, the tables, the dealers, all those I dealt with easily, mostly just sticking to what Chase and Gaylord had done, and for a while the Palace was the center of the world, there in the mile-high city.

But the two Eds had seen something I had missed:

the reformers gathering like a thundercloud over the Rockies, ready to hail on the Palace and every other sporting establishment in Denver. The women were behind it, and the women voted, and the women ruled the roost in the homes of every ward heeler in town.

Blake Street was doomed. And Market Street would last only a few years longer, fading out by 1913.

Emma lifted me out of my reveries with a question: "Did you find the California Hall?"

Something passed between us in that moment. The California Hall was one of Denver's great theaters in the 1880s, and I headed there to watch almost every new show. In 1886, one of my evenings at that place made the *Rocky Mountain News*. There was a minstrel show that night, featuring the blackface comedian Lou Spencer. I went to every performance, but not because I thought that highly of Spencer. The reason was his wife. We met, hit it off, and ere long she was joining me each evening in a box in the wings. Her name was Nellie McMahon, and she was a singer, and a lead performer with the Kate Castleton Opera Company.

Trouble was, Spencer discovered Nellie sitting on my knee one Saturday night, and showed up at the box. The exchange got pretty heated and I buffaloed him with my revolver and he lashed back with his fist. The cops nabbed us and took us to the station, and the paper got wind of it.

She was remorseful at first, but a couple of days later filed for divorce, charging him with brutality, nonsupport, and habitual drunkenness, and then took off with me for a little trip to Dodge, where we were cheerfully greeted. Nellie was one hell of a beautiful woman, and I have a way with women, and that's how it happened. I'm a sucker for breathtaking women and always have been.

The thing didn't last long. I went on these tears once in a while until I got older and my pants cooled down. Emma waited me out that time but she was plenty hurt. She had waited me out more times than I ever wanted to admit.

The moment passed, but I realized that Emma's remembrances of life in Denver were laced with pain. Our sentimental journey wasn't always very sentimental. Denver seemed to heighten everything: the legend, the joy, the pain, the memories. But I felt glad we came. We had to face Denver before going home.

CHAPTER 38

We headed back for lunch in the Brown Palace. Where better to eat in all of bad-food Denver? I stopped at the desk to pick up messages and the clerk handed me a fistful. Well, after a front-page story in a scandal-monger rag, that was to be expected.

I stuffed them in my suit coat pocket until later. They seated us beside a window looking out on Broadway and hurrying Christmas shoppers. We ordered seafood platters and I silently ordered phantom goblets of ghostly white wine.

Emma dove into a copy of the *Rocky Mountain News* while I retrieved my wad of notes and envelopes. Some old and familiar names cropped up, mostly from my days operating the Olympic Club and promoting boxing. Old-timers in Denver hadn't forgotten Bat Masterson. Some messages contained unfamiliar names with a phone number. One was from a woman who professed to be a reporter doing a story. She wanted an interview and please call. Another was a business envelope with a law firm's return address.

But there were seven or eight other items I examined with mounting dread. Three of these messages were simply a woman's name and phone number. One of the names was vaguely familiar. The rest were sealed envelopes, obviously hand-delivered to the hotel, addressed to me in a feminine hand, and splashed with lilac or spice cologne. I pretty much knew what I would discover in those.

"Dammit all to hell," I said.

Emma peered at me over her little reading glasses.

I gathered my courage and showed her the envelopes. She studied each one calmly, sighed, and gazed benignly at me. I wondered if it was a pose.

"Read the damn things. I can't," I said. That was an understatement. I had faced the bores of loaded revolvers with less dread.

"Maybe you should just tear them up," she said.

"I will leave it to you, and damn this state for keeping me bone dry in a time of need."

She smiled. "Are you sure? Should I read them?"

"How much alimony do you want?"

Something mischievous began building in her face. She set down her paper and gently severed an envelope with a fingernail while I watched like a condemned man.

"Um, lilac," she said, sniffing the blue paper as she extracted it. She read while I itched and scratched.

"It's from your old friend Claire," she said.

"Claire who?"

"Claire in your bed after the show at the Palace."

"That's clarifying. Oh, hell, read it to me."

She read, smiled, and eyed me cheerfully. "My dear

Bat. How pleased I am to learn you are in town. I haven't forgotten our evenings long ago, and your promises. All these years I have kept mementos of my life as a serving girl at the Palace. I've married and divorced, but now live alone. I thought perhaps you would enjoy an evening with me just to talk about old times. I know where we can get something to drink. Remembering you fondly, Claire."

"Alone," I muttered.

"Alone, she says. You're not a man to be alone, Bat."

Her lips were slightly pursed, the way a sheriff's are when he nods to the hangman.

"Damn Colorado," I muttered.

Emma laughed. "Let's see now. This one, in a fine female hand, smells of cloves. Lilac and cloves so far."

She tore the cream-colored envelope open, hummed as she read it, smiled, and tucked it back into its envelope. She set it on the white linen tablecloth, where it lay accusingly. She began to hum while she slit the next one, this on parchment stationery, and sighed softly. That, too, went back into its envelope.

"Women are still mad for you," she said.

The waiter arrived, relieving me from my execution for the moment. He set down plates full of shrimp, crab meat, filets of some fish or another, parsley, and a sharp tomato sauce.

Emma ate daintily, the little twist of her lips never fading from sight. I tried to enjoy the lunch but condemned men don't particularly enjoy their last meal, no matter how delectable.

"Read this thing," I said, thrusting the business envelope from the Denver law firm at her.

"Oh, my," she said, slitting it open.

"This is from a counselor named Elmer Hotchkiss, who represents a certain William Barclay Lipscomb."

"Oh, God," I said.

"Maybe you're a father."

"Let's get out of here. Colorado's writ doesn't run in New York. How much does he want? Who is his mother?"

My Emma, my own sweet Emma, was laughing at me with wicked intent.

"Nora Lipscomb."

"I never knew a Nora in my life. There have never been Noras in my clubs, on my stage, or in my bed."

Emma perused the letter. "Well, you see, this Nora was known as Fifi LaTour, and was a comedienne and singer. I gather you and she were friends."

"Friends!"

"Very, very, very close friends. You never brought her over to our apartment, though."

I pronged some white crab meat and plunged it into red sauce and wolfed it.

"And what does this mountebank want?"

"The attorney doesn't say. He does mention that William Barclay has a few mementos he inherited from his deceased mother."

"Such as?"

"A double-sided gold locket, with handsome tinted pictures of you and Fifi. What a nice gift you gave her, Bat."

"What does the attorney want?"

"A meeting."

"Let me see the letter."

I read the brief note. It made no demands, did not threaten, didn't talk money, did not allege that this gent was my son, and requested nothing more than a meeting. There was one way to deal with it and that was to go there, fast, and if this was a bunco game they would see what Bat Masterson was made of.

"I'm going over there. You don't have to come. I don't remember any Fifi or Nora and that's what they're going to find out from me."

"What if this man looks like you?"

"What does that prove?"

Emma shrugged. Her face was crumpling. All this was too much for her, and for me. Denver was dealing jokers. Mother Nature had not seen fit to give us children and I knew what a hole that left in Emma's life. We weren't young when we finally did settle down together.

She was soldiering across the table, picking at her crab meat, but I knew that all her years of stoic resignation about my wandering had not prepared her for this, and that our adventure had suddenly gone bad for her. I reached across and caught her hand and squeezed it.

"Over the years, I hurt you, and I'm sorry. You're the only one, have been for decades, and I love you. I'll deal with this. No two-bit bunco artist is going to clean us out or embarrass us."

She squeezed back.

I took a hack over to the Tabor Opera House, where the law firm was located, and stormed in. The receptionist was demure and so buttoned up that her hands looked naked.

"I'd like to speak to Mr. Hotchkiss."

"He's with a client."

"Please tell him it's Masterson and I want to talk."

She eyed me as one would an alley cat, and retreated.

She returned with the news that Elmer Hotchkiss would see me in a moment, and she ushered me into a dark conference room. The lawyer appeared at once, bearing a manila envelope.

"Mr. Masterson. Please be seated. I'm with a client but this will take only a moment."

I let myself sink into a plush leather chair, ready to hear him out.

"This is simply a favor I'm doing for a friend, actually my rector, William Lipscomb. He told me he would be uncomfortable meeting a man of your notoriety, but he wished to give you this."

The attorney slid a locket onto the burnished walnut table.

"Open it," he said.

It looked to be a cheap locket, gold-plated filigree, but within were tinted photos, one indisputably of me, and the other of a raven-haired girl I had never seen in my life.

"I don't know who this woman is," I said.

Hotchkiss smiled thinly. "Actually, you've met her. The story, passed along to me, which I will convey to you, is that you discovered her begging coins in front of the Palace in its heyday, and when you tried to chase her off she replied she had nowhere to go; she had run away and was hungry.

"She was too young to be in the saloon or gambling hall, so you took her into the theater and arranged for some of the performers in the variety show to work up a simple little act. They took over and within a few days this girl was performing as Fifi LaTour between acts while the curtain was down, little comic numbers and songs, and rather, ah, lightly clad.

"Within a few days a stage-door johnny showed up, and his name was Lipscomb. Within a fortnight they were married. He turned out to be a man of means and business acumen. For as long as Mrs. Lipscomb lived, she had a crush on you, put your image in one side of the locket and hers in the other.

"She never forgot what you did for her when she was shivering, hungry, and a runaway from eastern Colorado someplace. She believed you had rescued her from a fate—well, from the hellholes of Market Street, where she was about to go in despair if you hadn't intervened. . . ."

He let that sink in a moment, and then continued.

"When the Lipscombs had a son, she named him after you. Eventually, when that boy became an adult, she told the story to him. It was hard for her to do because the Lipscombs were respectable people, and William Barclay Lipscomb never dreamed his mother had a brief career on the stage of the notorious Palace. And thus did our rector learn he is named after . . . a western legend, of sorts."

I stood there, amazed. I had expected quite another ending to the yarn.

"And what is wanted of me?"

Hotchkiss smiled. "Nothing. The Reverend wanted you to hear the story of what your charity wrought, and keep the locket. He apologizes for not coming himself."

I studied the cheap locket, the picture, remembering nothing.

"Now, if you'll excuse me, Mr. Masterson . . ."

We shook. I slid the locket into my greatcoat, ill at ease. I am embarrassed whenever I am caught in charity. I rarely commit it, and when I do, it's never first-degree premeditated charity, but a low crime of passion, a moment when I have taken leave of my senses. I always think I'm being suckered by some con artist or other.

Whenever I'm caught, it's like having flashlights shining on me in the middle of a burglary I'm committing. I have never in my life admitted to giving anyone so much as a dime. I wondered whether I should confess to Emma.

I clapped my fedora on my thinning hair, caught a hack back to the Brown Palace, and girded myself to face my distraught wife. I didn't have a son after all, at least not by blood. But in an odd way, I did have a son. Maybe Emma and I could celebrate.

CHAPTER 39

Old Emma was ready for me. She had broken out our last pint of good Tennessee, and had some ice delivered to the room. She was a soldier.

When I walked in, she began mixing drinks, adding bitters from our wicker picnic case, and silently handed me my glass. Her face was a mask.

"It's okay, Emma," I said.

She sipped suspiciously while I described the events of the last hour. I dropped the locket in her hands. She opened it and studied the twin portraits.

"Beautiful girl," she said.

"They all look beautiful to me now. The older I get, the prettier all girls look. It's a phenomenon that happens to old men."

Emma squinted at me skeptically.

"Nora was a little underage," I said. "That's the only reason why I was so virtuous."

"Don't joke. So is this minister your son? What do they want? How much?"

"No, and nothing. The minister wanted me to hear the story about his mother and give me the locket. That's it."

Emma didn't brighten up, and I realized Denver had bared old hurts that had been sealed away over the decades. Now they were back, before us and between us.

She sipped the whiskey and stared out the fourth-floor window toward the Christmas crowds below. "What was wrong with me, Bat? Why wasn't I enough?"

I was acutely uncomfortable. "You were always enough, but I was too young to know it."

"No soft soap. Not now. You weren't so young. Didn't you like my figure? Wasn't I much of a lover? Was I just a dumb song-and-dance girl? Were you just randy? Did any one woman belong in your life? Or was it all your male pals, and gambling, and sports, and wearing a badge? And no place in it for a woman? I mean, a mate, not just sex."

"Emma—it wasn't you. It was . . . I was always looking. Men do that."

"Women do it too. But I only had eyes for you. I changed my bookings to be with you. I gave up the act to live with you."

I wished this would stop; wished we'd drink up and go Christmas shopping. But it was here, and Denver had coughed this up and forced me to see it.

"We were apart a lot. I was traveling the circuit; you had some bookings."

"Not very much in Denver. Not when you owned the Palace. There were so many," she said. "So many nights you never came home."

I nodded. I didn't like this, but this was a boil in our marriage, scarred over but hot and swollen under the surface, and now Denver was lancing it. Or, rather, Emma was. I wondered whether we would go back to New York separately.

She downed the whiskey and poured another and refused to look at me because she was crying and she thought I didn't see. Hell, I didn't know what to do. I felt lousy. The funny thing was, I never touched that girl, Nora, and couldn't even remember her, and this wasn't about some son showing up I had never heard of.

Other women have told me over the years I fathered their child and I always told them to beat it; I don't buy that racket. Emma knew of one or two of those. But this time it wasn't about a son, wasn't about a woman I'd bedded, wasn't about someone black-mailing me. It was about charity for a girl and that was what broke Emma's heart.

Because I hadn't ever been very charitable to her.

I felt about as bad as I get. I wished Louella Parsons had never started probing around in my past. I wished to hell we weren't in dry Denver, Colorado, tearing each other apart while downing illegal whiskeys.

This Denver, this damned Denver. It was sitting on its haunches, waiting for me to return, licking its chops.

My old Emma had come along for the ride for nearly forty years. I hadn't given her what she deserved but she had stayed with me, shared a life with me, been faithful to me in all the ways she could. I didn't deserve it.

"When's Christmas?" I asked.

"This is the twenty-third."

"Already?" An inspiration was climbing up my

mind. "Emma, you go buy yourself the best dress you can find."

"For Christmas or for saying you're sorry?" That wry, comic look had stolen across her face.

"Neither," I said.

"I don't know if one can be fitted in time for Christmas."

"Make them do it. Pay extra."

"I should feed you more whiskey sours."

She was pleased; I could see that. "I'm going to run on an errand or two," I said.

"Don't buy me another hat."

"It never crossed my mind."

We went down the elevator together. I distrusted the damned things but emerged alive and sound at the lobby and was tempted to kiss the floor. Emma braved the sharp wind and vanished down the street while I flagged down a hack and had the driver take me over to the opera house.

A few minutes later I was in Hotchkiss's office, asking to see the man, and in five minutes I was granted my request. The bald, bespectacled attorney seemed slightly annoyed but it didn't matter.

"Mr. Masterson?"

"I have a request. First of all, what denomination is the Reverend Mr. Lipscomb?"

"Why, Episcopalian, sir."

"Good. I'd like to talk to him about something as fast as possible."

Hotchkiss was hesitant. "I believe he would rather not see you, Mr. Masterson."

"All right, would you call him and tell him what I want?"

Hotchkiss stared. "Is this going to upset him? He is deep in Advent and Christmas preparations."

"No, it would make him happy, I think. I want to ask a favor of him."

Hotchkiss didn't like it, but I told him what I wanted. It took some explaining. The attorney's expression gradually softened. He even smiled when I had finished.

"All right, I'll ring him up. When you get back from City Hall, I should have an answer for you."

This time, Hotchkiss warmed to me and shook my hand heartily.

Episcopalian. Well, all right. Times go by. It had been the Very Reverend Henry Martyn Hart, dean of the Episcopal Cathedral of St. John in the Fields, who had led the charge against Blake Street in general, and my Palace Variety Theater and Gambling Hall in particular. He said my place was "a death trap to young men, a foul den of vice and corruption." He and his allies, the suffragettes, the umbrella-wielding biddies, the WCTU, the church congregations from one end of Denver to the other, were going to triumph, and I had seen that my establishment was doomed and along with it my bankroll.

I had sold out to Billy DeVere, who kept it going by lavishly wining and dining city and county officials, with assorted chorus girls always on hand. Possum parties, he called them. But he could only delay the steamroller a little while, and not even possum parties were enough to save the joint.

Eventually the Palace Variety Theater was padlocked and Blake Street swiftly became an anonymous urban hinterland. I had barely escaped with my bankroll intact.

And now I needed an Episcopalian, and that was all right. I had never rejected the Christian faith, but neither had I practiced it. I knew it well, thanks to the

Gideon Bibles in a hundred hotel rooms.

Ugly old City Hall, on Fourteenth and Larimer, was just a hop away. I sailed over there and found the city-county clerks getting ready to close up shop. But I did some fast talking, got the paper I wanted, and retreated to the opera house. Masterson's Luck was with me.

This time, Hotchkiss was all smiles. "You know," he said, with a lemon-twist of a smile building at the corners of his lawyerly lips, "Father William Barclay Lipscomb began a highland jig on the other end of the line. At least that was my general impression. He said your request is a chance to return the favor you did for his mother. Would one o'clock, here, suffice? We close early on Christmas Eve. My staff works to noon."

"That would be perfect," I assured him. "Now, I've taken some of your time. What do I owe?"

"Mr. Masterson, nothing at all. Not a thing. This is the sacred season and you are engaged in sacred business."

I agreed with him. A sacred business. Something I should have done long ago.

Emma had beaten me back to the hotel.

"I tried Denver Dry Goods, the Golden Eagle, and Daniels and Fisher, and finally found something at Daniels."

"Will they have it ready for you tonight?"

"No, tomorrow noon. That's a nice Christmas present, Bat."

"Noon? Are you sure they'll have it done by then?"

"Bat, it's Christmas. Everyone wants alterations. Why do we need it so fast?"

"Emma, you just tell me who to talk to and I'll make sure it gets done."

Emma stared at me as if I had gone daft. But finally

she dug up the name of the clerk on the receipt, and I headed out into Denver winter again. The store would stay open late and I had time.

It took some doing but I found my way to the right department and the right saleslady, Ruth Plumb; made my case, and offered to grease the necessary palms.

"Oh, no, Mr. Masterson, we wouldn't accept money for that. Your . . . fiancée didn't tell us what it was for. In fact, if you'd care to wait . . . it wouldn't take much. One tuck in the waist."

I settled down in a barrel-backed chair amid corsets and chemises and nightgowns, and assorted wives eyed me suspiciously. If they had known I was the notorious Masterson they would have attacked me with umbrellas. My only defense was old age. Silver hair gets a man through life's difficult moments.

It took longer than a few moments. It took an hour. But I walked out of Daniels and Fisher with a pasteboard clothing box under my arm, braved the wind, dodged last-minute shoppers, and found my way back to the Brown Palace, which glowed brightly in the evening darkness.

I presented the box to Emma, who opened it, pulled aside the tissue, and lifted a handsome navy dress with white trim and ebony buttons.

"But why the rush?" She seemed truly bewildered.

"Because we have a date at one tomorrow," I said.

CHAPTER 40

I should have known that an old showgirl like Emma would do a tap dance on the conference table, or something like that. I had expected a tear or two, which seldom sprang from her gleaming eyes.

That morning was hectic. I summoned the hotel valet and sent my spare suit off to be pressed. I wired New York for more funds, and felt dizzy when I calculated my balance. But what the hell.

I plunged into a brisk morning, bought a plain gold ring even though she wore one, and headed for a florist, where I arranged to have a raft of poinsettias sent to the law office of attorney Hotchkiss.

Through the morning Emma studied me curiously, never dreaming what I had on the platter.

"A Christmas dinner! Dressed to the nines! That's a nice treat, Bat," she said, all innocence, and fishing for answers. She knew me well but this time she was unable to conjure my intent.

Actually, I hoped the wedding would heal ancient hurts, many of them stemming back to our life over on Eighteenth and Curtis. We were indubitably married, and had been for decades, but it had never been solemnized; no vows, no pledges, no blessings.

I thought a bit about rousting up a few old friends still around from the sporting days to witness all this, and decided against it. The marriage would be our private affair.

I hoped I could finally heal the hurt inside of her.
There was another good reason. Now she would in-
herit my estate, what little there was. It would not go
to my Masterson family nor would it be disputed. I
had been too long reaching this point, and knew I must
draft a will even though the legal marriage would secure her.

At the last moment I realized we were scheduled to
depart for New York that evening, Christmas, on the
Burlington to Kansas City and Chicago, and I hastily
talked Emma into juggling the tickets once again. We
would stay in Denver a couple of days. The Brown
Palace was mostly empty anyway.

We were ready by twelve-thirty.

"You look gorgeous," I said. "Never better in your
whole life. Flo Ziegfeld ought to put you on as his
featured act."

She surveyed me as if I were a reptile. "Dammit,
Bat, what's going on? Why are you wearing that car-
nation? Have you gone crazy?"

"Oh, just so a couple of high-stepping New Yorkers
can show this rube town a thing or two. They're all
hicks around here."

"You are behaving very—you're nuts, that's what."

We had to wait for a hack, which irritated me. I was
doing God's work and He failed to arrange for our
transportation.

"What are you so upset for?" she asked.

"I'm not upset."

She squinted. "Where are we going? Tell me that?"

"Tabor Opera House."

She beamed. "Oh, we're going to see *Nutcracker*.
That's what's on. I was thinking about asking you. No
wonder we're all gussied up."

I smiled blandly, and a divinely guided hack pulled

up just when I was about to abandon my faith.

We unloaded at the opera house all right, but Emma was peering at me again when I steered her to stairs that would take us far from the great theater and into the business warrens of the ornate red brick and white limestone building.

I escorted my doll down a long corridor metered by frosted glass transoms, and then into the office of Hotchkiss and Thornton, Esquires, attorneys at law.

Emma was studying me again.

There Hotchkiss greeted us and took us back to the conference room, where the table groaned under poinsettias. A sandy-haired, ruddy gentleman with a clerical collar and a white satin stole around his neck awaited us.

"Well, now, we're gathered together," said the attorney. "Reverend, may I introduce you to Bat Masterson and his lovely Emma. And this is Father Lipscomb."

"Ah, Mr. Masterson, truly you're a legend, and you, Mrs. Masterson, how pleased I am to meet you. How happy I am to do this, not only for your sake, and our Lord's sake, but in simple gratitude for your kindness to my mother in a time of peril."

Emma looked bewildered, and it was time to enlighten her.

"Now, Emma," I said, "Father Lipscomb is going to ask some questions, and all you have to say is, 'I will.'"

She nodded. "All right, Mr. Ziegfeld, it's your show," she said.

The remark sailed past the others.

I had never rehearsed that particular tap dance before, but I knew the lines and cues, and whenever I needed advice, there was the choreographer, guiding us. He had in hand a white leather-bound Book of Common Prayer, opened to the Solemnization of Matrimony, and proceeded to run up the curtain and throw on the spots.

My showgirl was crying.

We put the "I wills" behind us, and I pulled out the gold band and recited, "With this ring I thee wed, and with all my worldly goods I thee endow: In the Name of the Father, and of the Son, and of the Holy Ghost. Amen."

I wiggled the ring on her already beringed finger.

Father Lipscomb offered a prayer and then bade us hold hands.

"Those whom God hath joined together let no man put asunder."

I supposed that was aimed my way.

"Forasmuch as Bartholomew and Emma have consented together in holy wedlock, and have witnessed the same before God and this company, and thereto have given and pledged their troth, each to the other, and have declared the same by giving and receiving a Ring, and by joining hands; I pronounce that they are Man and Wife, in the Name of the Father and of the Son and of the Holy Ghost. Amen."

Emma wept. Father Lipscomb added the benediction and a smile.

We shook hands. I tried to slip the man some bills in a hotel envelope but he refused them, saying the rite was the best Christmas gift he'd received.

I thanked them both; Emma hugged each, and we proceeded into an empty corridor.

"How'd you like *Nutcracker*?" I asked.

She drew me to her, arm in arm, so fiercely that I thought my song-and-dance gal was going to topple us.

"Where are we honeymooning?" she asked.

"Brown Palace, I guess."

"You utterly surprised me."

"I surprised myself."

"Emma Walters Masterson," she whispered as if it were a prayer. "Emma Walters Masterson."

We reached Sixteenth Street and hunted a hack to no avail, so we let the wind harry us toward the Brown Palace, past hurrying shoppers, their breath steaming in the chill air, past wreaths on shop doors, and daring, short-skirted mannequins in windows.

We reached the Brown Palace breathless, and panted our way to our room. We peeled off coats and hats.

"Just hold me, Bat," she said.

I did.

When the sun crossed the yardarm, I ordered some ice, and we mixed some whiskeys. I'm not very good at toasts, especially the nuptial variety, so I just dinged her glass with mine.

"Oh, hell, Emma," I said.

"Flo Ziegfeld would do a better toast."

"But you're stuck with me."

We drank to that, and then again, and then descended that dangerous cage down to the dining room for a roast goose Christmas dinner. There was no wine on the table and I consigned every miserable prohibitionist to the bottom layer of hell.

I sat there nursing coffee, listening idly to carolers out in the lobby sing "Adeste Fidelis" while Emma was nursing Earl Grey and tears, when we were visited by one of those things that occur only in great hotels. Our waiter appeared bearing two copies of the *Rocky Mountain News* and laid them before us.

"Your Christmas dinner is compliments of the

Brown Palace, Mr. and Mrs. Masterson," he said.

"Why, thank you," I said, wondering how the gent had gotten my name.

"And congratulations to you and Mrs. Masterson."

Emma squinted. "For what?"

"This is your wedding day, is it not?"

"How'd you know?"

"Fine hotels, Mrs. Masterson, know *everything*." He collected dessert plates, sherbet cups, and retreated.

Puzzled, I examined the newspaper, seeing nothing but expecting that maybe Wayne Ambrose had done something about me.

"Rear of the front section," Emma said.

There it was. An image of myself in younger days, wearing my bowler and looking the dandy I was back then. And a story bylined Wayne Ambrose, with a discreet headline: LEGENDARY FRONTIER LAWMAN IN DENVER.

I couldn't argue with that.

Ambrose had penned a careful, well-grounded story about our odyssey through the places where we had spun out our lives. He described our long-ago sojourn in Denver, the demise of the Palace, my effort to build the finest gymnasium and athletic club in Denver, the Olympic Club, and hold boxing exhibitions there, and my ultimate defeat by rival groups connected to the *Post,* especially Otto Floto, the paper's sports editor and Masterson-baiter.

Then he turned to the gunman legend, the bane of my existence. He had, he said, gotten in touch with numerous sources by wire and telephone. He had talked with editor Jess Dennis in Dodge and learned that none of the early papers recorded any death at my hands; likewise, he had enlisted the Ford County clerk of court to do a quick search of the records during my

brief peace officer career, and the clerks had come up
with nothing. He had talked to people in Trinidad and
Pueblo and Leadville.

He did describe the Melvin King affair in Texas, in
which I had apparently killed the army sergeant in
self-defense after he had killed my girl and gravely
wounded me. The verdict then, and valid in Ambrose's
view, was justifiable homicide. He went into the Doc
Holliday affair and faulted me for my legal maneuvering to save Doc's life.

"Masterson agrees that he's shot at plenty of crim-
inals but there is no conclusive proof that any died at
his hand while he was a peace officer. In one case, an
escaping prisoner died of gunshot wounds after being
fired upon by Masterson and a deputy, but whose bullet found the mark is not known.

"What is certain is that Masterson was so accurate
and deadly with a revolver that he didn't need to kill;
he knew how to shoot a gun out of an outlaw's hand
or drop a man with a nonfatal shot to a limb. He actually spared lives.

"In short, the legend about Masterson the killer of
two dozen men is bunk. And so is the idea that Masterson has ever been anything other than a reputable
boxing and gymnasium entrepreneur, lawman, saloonman, and newspaperman. His bylined column is ea-
gerly read in the sporting world clear across the
country, and his acumen about boxing and horse racing is unparalleled."

There was more along those lines, and an explora-
tion of my reputation as a gambler and owner of faro
and monte games, all to my benefit. He went into the
sole case in which I had gotten into trouble, fairly
recently in New York, and noted that it had been dismissed.

"In France, they would call Masterson's sporting world the demimonde, perhaps not quite respectable in some circles but far from disreputable or evil. He was one of the greatest of frontier lawmen, fearless and capable. He honors Denver with his presence."

The piece was more than I had hoped for. Ambrose had done his homework and had come through.

"Oh, Bat," Emma said as she put down the paper. "What a Christmas."

CHAPTER 41

We stepped off the train at Grand Central Station the morning of December 29, 1919. I was half-sick, weary of travel, and glad to be home. I wondered if I would do much more traveling. Bad diet had worsened my health and the diabetes was undermining me. We got a hack and in a few minutes we were home. It had been one hell of a trip and I had no regrets.

What Emma wanted most was to get back to Flo Ziegfeld's show and her chorus girl pals, and what I wanted most was to get back to my office and knock out some columns. I had plenty of new material, most of it on the forthcoming Big Dry.

Christmas at the Brown Palace had proved to be pretty slow, with only a handful of guests and all of us parched. Who ever heard of a Christmas without a drink or two?

I had taken a walk Christmas afternoon, mostly to get away from the hotel, strolling up to Sixteenth and

Market, where in 1899 some colleagues and I had converted an old theater into the Olympic Club, a gymnastic outfit with some seating in it for spectators. I had enlisted the help of a local weekly to publicize the place, and we had a good trade at first.

That had been my last attempt to make a life in Denver but I had hardly opened my doors before I ran into trouble from rivals connected with the *Post* in league with sleazy city officials. I won't go into all that. The Olympic didn't last long, and by then I was sick of Denver and all its pious frauds and reformers bent upon making life as miserable as possible for ordinary citizens.

My feud with Otto Floto didn't end when I left. Even though we were fifteen hundred miles apart he regularly jeered at my New York column, and I made light of his cranial capacity. I discovered one time that a horse named Otto Floto was running at some track or another, and when the nag lost I had a good time in print. Then the sonofabitch began to win, and I never printed a word about all that.

But Floto got even. Another horseman named his gelding Bat Masterson, which was an insult. A gelding! And then the damned nag dropped dead on the backstretch, and Floto got busy and I never heard the end of it. Floto announced that not even an elephant could bear the burden of a jockey and a bad name.

That fat fraud still rankles me.

The trip across the nation was pleasant enough, although we had run out of booze and the observation car's bar remained shuttered throughout the West. By the time I reached Chicago I was testy. Fortunately we were able to replenish in Illinois by asking a few questions of old friends, which made the trip to New York, across the parched wastes of Indiana, Ohio, and Pennsylvania, bearable.

I don't know what the hell has come over the United States of America. In one month, January 29, 1920, the whole country will go dry when the Eighteenth Amendment takes effect. I will have to do enough drinking between now and then to last the rest of my life. That, or move to Tierra del Fuego.

I had no conclusions at all about our long trip. It had stirred old memories sometimes, changed my life very little, and cut deep into my retirement savings. I hardly knew my old haunts. Dodge City had become a peaceful and prosperous farming center, supporting vast fields of grain. Trinidad and Pueblo had become industrial and mining centers. None of what I saw there had any relationship to me or my past.

"Was it worth it?" I asked after we had unpacked, bought booze, and looked at bills.

"Yes," she said. "I got to dance in Leadville and you got to adjust your legend. And now I have a spare wedding ring, just in case." Her eyes were gleaming. I knew that before the afternoon was over she would be backstage repairing costumes, digging up gossip, and checking on the greasepaint.

"That it?"

"I got to see some scenery . . . and we got married. You're not a bad catch, Masterson, even if you don't know how to tap-dance."

She was alluding to our honeymoon in the luxurious bed of the Brown Palace, which consisted of gentle hugs. Once youth flees, it doesn't return. But hell, who needs it? I'm not much good for anything anymore except indignation, which I have in plentiful supply.

"One more thing," she said. "What I got out of this jaunt was a love affair with New York. If I ever leave town again, shoot me."

I grinned. "I agree," I said. "I never knew I'd get homesick for New York until it happened."

"You were looking for the perfect interview and Wayne Ambrose gave you one."

"I don't much care anymore. If they want to make me a mankiller, I don't give a damn."

"I think you care," she said.

But I no longer did. That's what the trip accomplished. Let Earp wallow in that gunman and marshal stuff. He doted on it. I never would again. I could never understand what he did with his life. He was spending the rest of it living on his reputation, always looking around for people who might recognize his name.

I reported for work, glad to set foot in the old car barn that had been transformed into the *Morning Telegraph.* I was back among the living.

I would have about two days to catch up with my mail and do a column, and then the new year would be upon us, the year when the whole damned country would go dry. I knew what I was going to say even if it wouldn't make a difference: to hell with Prohibition. If they want to make a mankiller out of me, they're pushing in the right direction by shutting off the booze.

After greeting a few cronies and reporting to my publisher, Bill Lewis, I settled down to the serious business of slitting open envelopes. I turned first to a pair of letters postmarked Denver, because I figured they were responses to Ambrose's piece.

The first one tickled me.

Dear Mr. Masterson,

I had occasion to read the story about you in the Rocky Mountain News. *I never read such a pack of lies in my life. That reporter, Ambrose, was obviously out to wreck you, and destroy the admiration that people from one end of the country to the other hold for you.*

Your skill with short and long firearms, and your courage in dangerous circumstances, are well known, and no two-bit newsman can pull you down. I have been saving clippings about you for years. I have the New York Sun *article with Dr. Cockrell's estimation that you killed 26 men, seven on one occasion, and that you cut off the heads of several and brought them back to Dodge in a sack.*

I also have the Kansas City Journal *article about you that said you had killed your man. That one pointed out that you had been tried and acquitted for first-degree murder four times. That story, of course, confirms the* Sun *story that you killed seven men at the time your brother was murdered, and shot Peacock and Updegraff as well.*

I also have the story that says you have killed a man for every birthday you've had, and added thirty-seven graves to Boot Hill. Of course, in court that time, you admitted to killing thirty-eight.

So along comes this quack reporter named Ambrose who says maybe you didn't kill anyone. Who am I supposed to believe? Of course the preponderance of evidence is that you've killed somewhere between twenty-six and thirty-eight men. That is the mark of a brave and courageous lawman, and also a man skilled with weapons. Or if you didn't kill them people as a peace officer, then you are the greatest badman of all time. Just so long as you killed a mess of gunslingers, that's all I ask.

Tell me this new article by Ambrose isn't so, Mr. Masterson. If it's so, you aren't no one's hero but just another fraud letting people believe that you were the best gunman on the frontier. Please reply to the address on the envelope, and tell me plain and honest how many men you killed, so I can put this Ambrose article in the stove where it belongs.

It was signed by some fellow named Ash Benziger. I started in on another letter from Denver, this one taking Ambrose to task for not mentioning my long criminal record as a stagecoach and train robber, rustler, horse thief, whoremonger, and badman, and I had obviously pulled the wool over the reporter's eyes. If I had any decency I'd set the record straight, because everyone knows that Bat Masterson was the worst man on the frontier.

That's when Louella discovered I was back.

"Bat!" she exclaimed. "Tell me everything."

"Hell, doll, what's to tell you? Here I am."

"I got a long wire from Bill Hart yesterday. You're a movie star."

"Emma's a movie star. She did the acting."

"Bill Hart says you're a natural. He saw the rushes and thinks you ought to move out there and star in films."

"I hope never to venture west of the Hudson River again. It's *dry* out there."

"Is that all you have to say about your trip?"

"That's all that's important. We are about to plunge into a national dark ages."

"What did you do in Dodge?"

"Tried to find one memento, just one, of my times there. They don't think highly of the early years. They've torn out anything that looks like history. I did meet a newspaper editor, Jess Dennis, and he let me look through his old papers. Dodge is a nice farmers' town now, with Thanksgiving parades and grain elevators. That's the future. Bat Masterson's the past."

She was grinning. "Okay, I'm going to do a story about you and Bill Hart making a film. So tell me everything."

Actually, I didn't mind. I told her how the script was altered slightly, and how I had bumped off one villain against all odds. I couldn't bump off all four because some had to remain alive for Hart, the hero, to bump off, but at least they let me wipe out one and give the others a few licks before I got tied up, which amused me because Masterson never loses.

She was scribbling on her pad, and I supposed I would soon be a Parsons Exclusive.

"Look, Louella, I'm supposed to have wiped out thirty-seven or eight, or maybe twenty-six, so a few more bodies, Hollywood style, should improve the quota. Here—" I thrust the letters at her. "A good newsman named Ambrose with the Denver paper tried to get it right and that sounded like nonsense to these gents."

She read them, her agate eyes agleam.

"How do you feel about being a legendary mank-iller?"

"Before I started the trip, I wanted to set the record straight. Now . . . I'm not sure it matters."

"Are you going to write an account of the trip? Are you going to set the record straight?"

"I'm going to attack Prohibition, is what I'm going to do."

She laughed, but I wagged a finger. "In one month you and I won't be able to walk into the Metropole's bar and order whiskey sours. That's the end of the world. *My* world."

She quit scribbling. "I've got a great story about you and Bill Hart doing a film," she said.

"Go write it up. And give me a copy for Emma. She's the one who'll enjoy the limelight. See ya, babe."

I turned to my legal pad and began scratching it with my fountain pen:

The fanatical reformers, aided and abetted by the sordid and hypocritical politicians, have succeeded in swarming all over the country in the last few years, and like the boll weevil in the cotton fields of the South, left nothing but sorrow and destruction in their wake.

Maybe this would be my last battle. My weapons would be words and ideas, not bullets. But I knew an old man could still shoot,

CHAPTER 42

ell, the trip was great. But it took a few days of thinking about it to understand that. Emma and I don't rub well together; we need some elbow room, and when we're together too long we start bickering. Now that she's back doing her stuff at the Follies and I'm chained to my desk, things are just fine between us.

That trip settled more things than I realized at first. When I got off the train I was exhausted and half-sick, and that affected my frame of mind. In fact, the trip was a tonic for my spirits. I saw myself at last for what I am. I grasped the nature of my foolishness and also my strengths and courage. I saw what good I did in life, and also the harm I'd done.

The same was true of Emma. The more we reminisced about what we had done on our lark, where we had gone, the more she brightened. And even though she didn't say much about getting hitched, she had acquired a new little tic: now she twisted the new ring around and around on her finger, like it was some sort of omen or talisman or good luck charm. Once in a while she winked at me.

Emma had always been a winker, but now she was a wry and smiling winker, the way an old pal is. She even winked at me at breakfast the other day when I started muttering about Prohibition. She just needed to do a buck-and-wing on the cold stage in Leadville, or maybe say some "I do's" to put her life right.

I thought about those letters written after Ambrose's piece about me appeared in the Denver paper, and I sat down and penned a reply to each. Hell, it wasn't a reply; it was a fusillade. Here's how I responded to that first gink:

Sir:

I am in receipt of your December 24th letter. My response is that you are one twisted son of a bitch. If you admire a man for the number of corpses he is responsible for, the number of mortal lives he has snuffed forever, then you had better crawl back under the rock where you live.

For the record, I doubt that I killed any white man, with the possible exception of an Army sergeant, in self-defense, after he killed my girl and wounded me. I have fought Indians in some bad scrapes, and probably killed some, and I regret every life taken. They were simply fighting for their homeland and food, and if it had not been a case of them or me, I would not have shot at all. I do not glory in war or death, and those scrapes sadden me.

I never cut off the head of a single man, much less put such heads in a bag and bring them to Dodge. I never got into a scrape where I killed seven cowboys, as alleged by the pulp press. If you admire a man for doing such things, then you have got everything in your skull twisted around.

I will take credit where I rightfully can. Dodge was a wild town when the cowboys were in it, and I had to tame them, and it. I did so. I have stared into the barrel of a loaded six-gun. I dealt with crowds ready to gun me down.

When I used my revolver, it usually was to buffalo my man with a blow of the barrel to his cranium, not to pump bullets into him. It was never my purpose to take lives. When I was forced to shoot, I shot to wound, not kill. My goal was to be a good peace officer, not to be the biggest killer in the Old West.

If that makes me less a legend to you, then that is exactly the way I want it.

Sincerely,
William B. Masterson

I stuck that in an envelope and laid it in the Out box, feeling just fine. I knew what I was going to do about the Masterson legend. I was going to correct it whenever anyone wrote me about it. I got letters every little while and I intended to set things straight in my replies.

In truth, I had no stomach for writing an autobiography. Masterson on Masterson would be just too damned much Masterson for the twentieth-century world. The best thing to do with old centuries is to jettison them and get on with the future.

I credit my trip with that insight. From the train windows I marveled at the changes I saw. Where nothing but prairie grasses once grew, now there were wheat fields and orchards. Where once there was only buffalo and antelope, now there were fat cattle, hogs, poultry, hamlets, and county seats. That was progress, making use of the land the Indians never used, and I believed in progress right down to my bones.

But the West was no longer home. For me, living on one of those farms, plowing fields and raising wheat and brats, would be pure hell. I can admire progress, but that doesn't mean I want anything to do with the West. It's a damnable dry place and if they sawed it off and floated it into the Pacific, that would suit me fine. One thing I learned on that trip. The West be damned. Everything between California and New York City is alien turf. If I never see another damned cowboy or farmer, if I never see another mining camp or stagecoach or wild Indian, that would suit me just fine.

There's no place on earth like New York City, where I am rich in friends, where every species of entertainment and good food and nightlife and theater is at hand. There isn't one place in the entire West where a man could enjoy what I have right here.

That's what the trip taught me. I found my home, and to hell with every Bisbee and Tombstone and Dodge and Butte and Virginia City ever stuck on a map. Emma's with me on that. If she never sees the country west of the Mississippi River, she'll count it a blessing.

I fell into my old routine as soon as I got back, and that meant dinner at Shanley's after a day hammering out a column, and the gathering of old friends at the Metropole. But now those routines were numbered, and life at the Metropole is hung with black crepe. As January ticked by, the Big Dry loomed over us like a guillotine blade.

You would have thought everyone was attending a funeral, which in a way we were. All the sports were there drinking as fast as they could so the drunk would last a few days beyond January 29, 1920. The only sport I knew who was enjoying himself was Runyon, who was penning one great yarn after another about these wet birds facing dry times. He came in every night, settled down next to some old wreck trying to beat Prohibition by drinking himself to death, and got the story.

Sometimes he joined Tex Rickard and me in a banquette, and told us how the sports were dealing with the inevitable.

"Now you take Slow-Horse Harry," he said. "Slow-Horse figures if he can store enough stuff in his closet, he'll be in the sauce for two, three, four years. But he ain't got the dough to buy that much stuff, so he's at the track trying for a lucky hit so he can buy a dozen kegs of good Kentucky, as if the stuff's available. He ain't alone, you know, and it's harder than hell to get a case of booze, much less a barrel."

I had been hearing such stories for days. Everyone was laying up booze. The prices had climbed.

"Now you take Nicky Rico," Damon continued. "He's buying pure grain alcohol and he figures he can hide a lot of drunks in one gallon. Or take Willy, the wine man. He's bricked off a chunk of his cellar over on Waverly Place, figures no federal cop's gonna figure out he's got a whole vintage collection racked in there."

"Hell, what good does that do. It just delays the day when we all go dry," I said. "We've got to stop the feds, and that takes political muscle."

Rickard laughed. He laughs like that when someone lays a big bet on a hundred-to-one longshot. He was right.

The Metropole was preternaturally quiet, as if New York's sports were watching the ticking clock rather than enjoying themselves. It wasn't just the booze. It was the clubhouse that was going under. I'd walk in there and know maybe three-quarters of that crowd, everyone from pickpockets to kept broads or second-story burglars. Some of the best of New York's detectives dropped in, too. They loved that bar.

I knew them from my days when I was a United States marshal for the Southern District of New York. I had gotten that through my friend Teddy Roosevelt. He'd offered me a marshal's job in Oklahoma, big deal, twenty-two deputies, and I wrote the White House and said I was permanently glued to New York.

Next I knew, I was a marshal here for two grand a year, and it hardly interfered with writing my column. When fat Taft came along, he decided the U.S. marshal corps didn't need an old Kansas gunman, and that was that. What a joke. If I still had my federal badge, I'd soon be hunting down my friends and busting up their bottles.

I figured when the Big Dry came along about half of those NYPD detectives I knew would have their own cache of booze in some walled-off alcove somewhere. But now, in January of 1920, I was already seeing how it would play.

We had all crawled inside of ourselves. We still came to the old clubhouse, the Metropole's bar, but it was different. Men sat on the stools or stood at the rail all alone. If they brought their dolls, they would perch gloomily in a corner and hardly look at each other, just waiting, waiting. The lubricant was gone and every friendship in the city squeaked.

I suppose in an ideal world, friendships wouldn't depend on drinking, but in my world they did. Give a man a couple of shots of Kentucky and the world was better, and those guys were pretty good to talk to. Put a few whiskey sours into me, and I'd tell them all they wanted to know about old Bat, the Dodge City lawman, and the more booze, the more fanciful my yarns.

Now it was dying, and my way of life was dying too. It was the revenge of the twentieth century for all the fun we had when the nation was a whelp.

CHAPTER 43

or anyone without the cash to become an expatriate, there was no escape. I had no place to run. Rickard talked of moving to Canada.

I knew guys talking about Paris, or Argentina, or the Solomon Islands. There was wild talk of setting up floating saloons and gambling parlors just beyond the line out in the ocean. But it was all just yakking. We were trapped.

I spent those January days fulminating in my column. There wasn't anything I could do other than to rail at the reformers and divines and female liberationists who had conspired to ruin the republic. The *Telegraph* didn't mind: the only thing the paper was against was reform.

I debated whether to stock up on booze, like the rest, and decided not to. Having a year's supply would only prolong the agony. Maybe in a century or so, the country would come to its senses and repeal the Eighteenth Amendment, but I saw no hope for it.

Dodge City was the wave of the future. If I had not gone on that trip, seen what life was like in old Dodge and what those midwestern American burghers were proposing for the rest of the world, and seen what life was like in dry Colorado, I would have some hope that the American people would come to their senses. But that trip instilled reality in me, and that's what I told my pals in Shanley's and the Metropole.

"Hell, pal, those farmers and divines and suffrage broads control the country; they have the votes and they're going to go right ahead and wipe out the world we know."

"You're exaggerating," Tex Rickard protested.

"Go drop off the train at Dodge. Go talk to the sheriff and the politicians and then tell me what you've learned."

Tex turned quiet that night. It wasn't just booze and gambling being driven underground; boxing was being chased out of one state after another. And other states were enacting blue laws making it illegal to do anything but breathe on Sundays. And that went double for theatrical performances.

Not that Broadway shows would have much of a chance when Prohibition arrived. I figured people would arrive, sit on their hands, and ache for a drink. I figured everything in a six-block radius from Forty-second and Broadway would become a depressed area when the curtain rolled down on the saloons.

For once I didn't mind being so old or so sick. I could scarcely imagine living another ten or twenty years in a world without a bar rail to put a foot on. My world was vanishing and I had outlived it.

We were all condemned men, awaiting the noose.

Runyon became my consultant on matters spiritous. He, more than any other reporter in New York, knew what was going on at subterranean depths far below the cyclops eye of the coppers.

"Don't worry, Bat, there'll be booze. Plenty of blind tigers starting up. You just knock, and if they know you they'll let you in. Good stuff, coming down from Canada."

"Hell, what good is that? Running around knocking on locked doors? Look at this place here. Big, happy saloon, doing an open and legal business. Anyone of age can buy a drink. Those guys in the white aprons know their customers, call them by their right names. They're good listeners, even father-confessors. Don't tell me that some rathole in the basement of a dry-goods store is gonna make life good again."

"It's the best anyone can do. Big guys, plenty of capital to invest, see this as an opportunity. You'll pay a stiff price for a drink and a little saloon society, but you'll get it. I know. Guys like Rico and Lucci are dipping in, setting up. Here, I'll write you an address, pal."

He started to scribble something on a page but I stayed him. I saw what was coming. Stool pigeons, blabbers, trouble, Bat Masterson, former U.S. marshal and Ford County sheriff, cop in Trinidad and Dodge, gets nabbed for downing some hooch in one of those joints. No, I wouldn't do that. I just preferred to hate. I was becoming a good hater, and the damned female do-gooders envious of good male companionship topped my list.

Louella slipped me news, too.

"You wouldn't believe how those Hollywood people are treating this. Salting away whole warehouses of whiskey and wine and beer. They've got the money. They aren't going to let some law get in the way of a good time."

"That'll be something. Fatty Arbuckle arrested for drunken driving a year after Prohibition starts."

She smiled. "Great copy. Hollywood doesn't intend to comply, and that is going to make some delicious gossip. My readers will eat it up."

"Louella, you're incorrigible. How much booze have you put by?"

"Not a drop. I can take it or leave it, and I believe in being law-abiding."

I laughed so derisively she got miffed.

"Have a double before the curtain descends," I said. "Now, who's going to get in trouble first?"

"John Barrymore. He'll probably walk into the nearest police station, down half a drink, and toss the other half into the desk sergeant's face."

"At which point the sergeant will lap it up before arresting him."

"Well, don't count out Tom Mix," she said. "He's a man who likes a party." ·

"Lousy parties, Louella. They'll hold a bash and next thing, the cops will be busting in with their whistles blowing. Hollywood's doomed."

"My readers'll love it," she retorted. "This is good for Hollywood. Now everyone'll go see films because there's nothing else to do. Prohibition will make Sam Goldwyn rich."

"And make you a celebrity if you can dig up enough dirt."

She pouted. I laughed. "Help me shut down the Metropole," I said.

"Can't. I'm going to be on the long-distance telephone getting stories from Los Angeles that night. Wouldn't it be great if I got an item on America's Sweetheart, Mary Pickford, drunk as a skunk?"

I sighed. Louella was a peculiar woman.

The clock kept on ticking. And I fell into a depression, which is a rare thing for old Bat.

One evening I asked Emma about it. "What does Flo Ziegfeld say?"

"Oh, he's worried. He's putting in more comic stuff to loosen people up, and baring a little more female skin to take people's minds off Prohibition. But he's worried. Everyone is worried."

"The shows'll survive," I said. "Maybe even prosper. What else will there be to do but go to the theater every night?"

"Read," she said.

"Since when has any novel equaled the pleasure of a good whiskey sour?"

"Never ever," she said.

Then the day arrived. Wednesday, January 28, 1920, would be the last any citizen could purchase a legal drink. We were planning a big hurrah at the Metropole, which made the Considines nervous. They finally agreed, but said they were quitting at eleven-thirty. They would sell off any booze that remained and shut the sonofabitch down at five minutes to midnight.

I thought about buying some of that booze. Under the Eighteenth Amendment, possession was not a crime. Manufacturing, selling, transporting, and importing were the federal crimes, all enforced by the Volstead Act, which Congress managed to enact over President Wilson's veto. When that professorial Princeton snob vetoed that bill, I revised my opinion of him a notch or two upward, even though he was one of the looniest of the reformers and do-gooders and a damned Democrat. Woodrow Wilson made me proud to be a lifelong Republican.

When the damned Wednesday arrived, the Metropole was only half full. Most of the sports couldn't bear it. I walked over there after my usual dinner at Shanley's with Damon Runyon and Tex Rickard and a couple of others. I don't know what we expected, but not the hollow silence that we encountered there. Was this furtive downing of booze a last hurrah? No, it was a burial, not just of whiskey but of friendship, happiness, good times.

We were done with the cussing of the enemies of civilization and liberty. Done cussing those whose object in life was imposing rules and regulations on others. Done cussing busybodies, finger-waggers, holier-than-thou churchmen, and zealots. I had done all of that in my columns.

Instead, we were either thinking of the future, or burying the life we knew and loved. It turned out to be the quietest evening at the Metropole in memory.

The end came not with a bang, but a whine.

Billy Cox, one of the mixologists, said simply, "Time's up, gents. Drink up, buy what's on the counter, and then we'll turn out the lights."

Just like that.

Sighing, Runyon and Rickard anted up some cash, plucked some bottles, and vanished into the night. New York seemed damned quiet that night, especially right there along Broadway. The shows were done, theaters dark, and sure as hell no one was going to Sardi's for a nightcap.

I walked home and found Emma sitting up, drinking a whiskey sour with a wry grin on her puss.

"One for the road," she said.

"Hell of a long road, this time," I said. She had mine ready for me, and I polished it off.

"I don't belong in this country anymore," I said. "How'd the show go?"

"All right. We took people's minds off of doomsday. And Billie Burke had 'em howling tonight."

"But will they howl tomorrow? Will there be a tomorrow for Broadway?"

"Flo thinks so."

We sat in companionable silence, sipping our executioner's drink.

I knew that my world had ended, and that I would be a stranger in a strange land henceforth. Thursday would last forever.

CHAPTER 44

A nd so, at the stroke of midnight, my world passed away. I was little more than a beached relic on the shores of the new one. I minded less than I had earlier supposed. My world had been driven underground, and I could still find it if I wanted to patronize speakeasies or head for backroom crap games.

This had been coming since the nineties and I had seen it and knew it portended the end of my chosen life. A few states permitted boxing. A few states permitted wagering on horse racing. I probably could quietly enjoy a mint julep and some friendly low-stakes draw poker and lay a bet on some thoroughbred horseflesh in Kentucky. But Emma and I were veteran New Yorkers, and we had no plans to hunt for the shards of a lost era like a pair of archaeologists.

I was so old all of a sudden.

I had plunged into our great western adventure wanting to know what was true about me and what was legend. The papers in Dodge and Trinidad, Pueblo and Denver, Tombstone and Creede, would refresh my memories. Along the way I discovered there were several legends, each catering to one or another species of the human beast.

For some I was the great western hero who fought the wicked with six-guns and raw courage, in a lofty league populated only by Wyatt Earp, Wild Bill Hickok, and a few others.

To others I was the ultimate or penultimate gunman and fast-draw artiste and mankiller, a peer of Ben Thompson, Billy the Kid, John Wesley Hardin, or Doc Holliday, who allegedly had put twenty or thirty or more souls in their graves.

To others I was an immoral rake, running games of chance, selling booze, booking wicked productions in my theater, and driving innocent men and women to perdition in my houses of sin.

I was all and none of that, and as I patrolled the precincts of my youth, or read the clippings, or hunted for old-timers who recollected me, I began to realize I was asking the wrong question. Whether the legends about me were true or false didn't much matter. What counted was what I had done with my life and what I intended to do with the remainder of it.

If my life was important enough to attract future historians of the frontier West, they would sort out the details. I did not need to. They would deflate the myths, reduce the death toll, cut me down to size. I didn't need to defend myself.

What I needed from that long train trip to my old haunts was to discover myself, and discover Emma. Not the ones I thought I knew, but the other Bats and Emmas. And the trip did not disappoint me in that respect. The Kansas farm boy who began his adult life skinning buffalo hides off dead meat for Billy Dixon on the plains west of Dodge had come a long way, most of it a good and honorable way.

About a month after Prohibition started, New York seemed to turn brown. About then, people were drinking up the last of the booze in their cabinets and pulling into themselves. My pals and I met for dinner at Shanley's as usual but the talk faltered and wasn't any good. After that, people drifted apart, torn from one another by the police power of the government. The city had lost its color, its vivid hues. Some joints had sprung up to cater to the sports, but I scorned them.

I turned to my work. I was a veteran newsman and everywhere I turned there was a good story. If this was the way the people of this century wanted to live, let them. I think that each generation should set its own rules, with due respect for what went before. I thought my health improved slightly now that the booze wasn't aggravating my diabetes. But life was brown and getting browner.

Some good things had come of that epic journey, and one of them was the rediscovery of Emma. She must have felt it too, because she hurried home after the show closed to spend time with me rather than sit in some tea parlor with the chorus girls and listen to them bitch. We were food and spirits to each other at last.

I can date it to a precise moment, when she doffed her cloth coat and climbed to the boards of the Tabor Opera House in Leadville, where it was cold as hell, and did her routine for me; just for me. The old gal bowed, tapped, whirled, smiled, helloed the balcony, and sang a love song for me. She was telling me then and there that her life was grand, that we'd share the rest of our time on earth closer than we were, and that everything that had come between us was forgiven.

When she stepped down off that stage and wrestled her coat back on, panting slightly, there was something in her eye that spoke to me of lifetimes. That was weeks before the Denver marriage, too. That wedding was my gesture, my way of saying the same thing. When I pulled that one on her, she saw in my eye what I had seen in hers: a sense of lifetimes.

That's how it has been since we returned. Even

when the booze still flowed at the Metropole, I ducked out earlier to greet Emma after the show; and she, in turn, packed up her knitting and caught a hack to our apartment just to be with me for a last sweet hour of our day. We didn't say much. Some of the best companionship is the silent kind.

My pals are still my pals. Runyon, Rickard, Bill Pinkerton of the detective agency, Wyatt and Josie; my publisher, William Lewis; Val O'Farrell, my favorite cop; Tom O'Rourke and Bill Muldoon, my pals in the fight game; Irvin Cobb, and a bunch more. I see less of them since the saloons closed. I hear from Bill Tilghman now and then, even if he is a Democrat, and kept in touch with Theodore Roosevelt until he died a few months ago.

But I have outlived most everyone else. Save for Wyatt, the Earp brothers are gone. Doc Holliday's a distant memory. Nearly all the Dodge City people are gone. About a hundred women I once knew have vanished, and most are gone. Hickok, Cody, Ben Thompson are dust, just as the wild old frontier days are dust.

I tell myself this is not regrettable. If I were given the magical power to reinstate the frontier, the wild towns, the aching wilderness, the men living at the border of civilization, the cowboys and Indians, the drunks and miners, I would not do it. I'm mostly for the future, except when the whole country goes nuts and abolishes booze and forbids good times and stamps on personal liberty.

I have nothing very profound to say about the world. I don't regret running saloons and games of chance. An adult makes his choices and lives by the result. A free man, living in a free country, shouldn't have some nanny government telling him he can't have a drink or buck the tiger. Adults govern their appetites; children don't. You don't become an adult by being denied choices.

I figure what the prohibitionists and their kind are really doing is making children of American citizens. But this is a nation that periodically throws off its busybodies and nannies, and someday, long after I'm gone, I guess, it'll tell the prohibitionists to go to hell. I'll be on the other side of the River Styx, but wherever I am, I'll cheer them on.

Does this mean, then, that I approve of immorality? Not at all. I've tried to live honorably all my life, and I hope others will too. But you see, out there on the edge of civilization, where law and order were thin and the chances of getting away with any sort of crime were good, we all had plenty of motive to go bad. And most of us didn't. That's the whole point. What I favor is the freedom to make our own lives and pay the consequences and reap the rewards.

I've bought a lot out at Woodlawn, and some day Emma and I will lie there. We've lived a damned good life.

B at Masterson died on October 25, 1921, a few weeks before his sixty-eighth birthday. He was at his desk, writing a column, when he keeled over. He had been fighting a bad cold.

The column was classic Masterson, savvy and contentious. He had contrasted the twelve grand a fighter had just gotten for an hour in the ring with the poor farmer who was lucky to see twelve grand come to him over a lifetime of brutal toil.

"Yet there are those who argue that everything breaks even in this old dump of a world of ours.

"I suppose these ginks who argue that way hold that because the rich man gets ice in the summer and the poor man gets it in the winter things are breaking even for them both. Maybe so. But I'll swear I can't see it that way. . . ."

That was all.

The funeral service was conducted by the Reverend Nathan A. Seagle of St. Stephen's Episcopal Church. The honorary pallbearers included Bat's closest friends, among them Tex Rickard, Tom O'Rourke, Damon Runyon, Val O'Farrell, and William Muldoon.

In a eulogy, William Muldoon, New York's boxing commissioner, said he had never known Bat Masterson to do a dishonorable deed, never to betray a friend, never to connive at dishonor, and never to fear an enemy. Which summed it all up.

Tributes to Bat from all over the country deluged the paper. The nation had not forgotten.

Emma died in her New York room at the Hotel Stratford on or before July 12, 1932.

AUTHOR'S NOTE

Bat and Emma's great adventure in search of their past is fiction. But it is drawn from reality as much as possible. For instance, the people of Dodge City did, at that time, try to extirpate their past. William S. Hart did try to talk Bat into making some films. And no marriage license has ever been found for Bat and Emma. The traditional wedding date given for Bat and Emma is November 21, 1891, a date supplied by Bat's brother, but there is no supporting evidence.

There is abundant material about Bat, but almost nothing about Emma. She is believed to have been reared in Philadelphia, and to have lost her father early in the Civil War. She became a variety show song-and-dance performer, and she appeared at Bat's Palace Theater, but the rest is murky, so I have invented an Emma who fits what is known of her, especially her reticence. Few of Bat's friends had ever met her.

It is not known where she and Bat met, or what their relationship was through the early and mid-1880s. There are various tantalizing references to "Bat Masterson's wife" going back to the early 1880s, but it is not known whether the woman was Emma, or whether the term was a euphemism for one of his many female companions. In a letter written by Bat in 1890 he said he had been married eight years. Josephine Earp recalled being given a canary in the winter of 1883–84 by "Bat Masterson's wife."

The fictional Dodge City editor, Jess Dennis, is loosely based on a real editor named Jess C. Denious, and the story about his being discouraged from distributing a booklet about Dodge's wild past is true. As late as World War II, many residents refused to discuss or acknowledge the town's early history.

Bat evolved from an unschooled farm boy into a shrewd, well-read, and sophisticated New York executive and newspaper columnist. Wyatt Earp never grew beyond what he was from the beginning: a courageous lawman who was barely literate and untrained in any other field. While Earp was spinning out his life as a saloon operator, gambler, and junkyard dog, Masterson was learning how to write, educating himself, acquiring administrative skills, gambling, and operating fairly large enterprises such as the Olympic Club in Denver, a major saloon and casino in Creede, and even his own weekly newspaper.

Eventually he became a renowned expert on boxing and horse racing, and a gifted columnist whose writings ranged widely from the narrow world of sports. Masterson made a comfortable living; Earp had some high and low moments financially, but he remained impoverished and probably dependent in the end on Josephine's family. Masterson's was the larger and better life.

Damon Runyon was so taken with Bat and his yarns about the wild life on the frontier gambling circuit that he created the character Sky Masterson, a high roller from the West, in a short story called "The Idyll of Miss Sarah Brown." That story, in turn, became the successful Broadway and film musical *Guys and Dolls*. And in the movie version, the one Hollywood actor who actually resembled Bat, the young Marlon Brando, played the role of Sky Masterson.

It is known that Bat enjoyed the company of many women, but who they were and what they meant to him are things the world will never know. He apparently was unfaithful to Emma—if in fact he had any serious connection with her through the 1880s.

This novel rests heavily upon the splendid biography of Bat written by Robert DeArment, *Bat Masterson.* The author assiduously separates fact from myth by working with primary sources, and gives us the truest and most penetrating portrait of an amazing and likeable frontier peace officer, gambler, and entrepreneur. DeArment's companion book, *Knights of the Green Cloth,* gives us a vivid portrait of the most important frontier gamblers and the circuit they traveled.

While my interpretation of Masterson's interior life and belief is largely my own, I acknowledge my debt to the gifted biographer, and I have hewn to the structure of Bat's life as depicted by DeArment.

Doc Holliday: A Family Portrait is a remarkable new biography by Karen Holliday Tanner, and the first written by one of the Holliday family. It presents a radically different picture of Doc, based on family correspondence and tradition, from what one finds elsewhere, and I have incorporated the new material, portraying Doc as a gentle, fragile, disease-haunted man in this novel.

Great Gunfighters of the Kansas Cowtowns, 1867–1886, by Nyle H. Miller and Joseph W. Snell, is a mistitled but valuable compendium of contemporary newspaper stories dealing with frontier peace officers and gamblers, bridged by explanatory material by the authors. The vast array of primary source material about Bat Masterson does not include reports of any killings by him.

Dodge City: Queen of the Cowtowns, by Stanley

Vestal, has been the traditional source of information about the old cowtown. But it has largely been superseded, especially by the valuable *Dodge City: Up Through a Century in Story and Pictures,* by Fredric Young, a book that enabled me to portray the Dodge City of 1919, and to indicate which of the early residents were still alive.

Some other books that supplied extensive material for this novel include *The Great Rascal: The Exploits of the Amazing Ned Buntline,* by Jay Monahan; *American Silent Film,* by William K. Everson; *The Longhorns,* by J. Frank Dobie; *Doc Holliday,* by John Myers Myers; *Denver: Mining Camp to Metropolis,* by Stephen J. Leonard and Thomas J. Noel; *The Cattlemen,* by Mari Sandoz; and *Historical Atlas of Colorado,* by Thomas J. Noel, Paul F. Mahoney, and Richard E. Stephens.

I am grateful, as always, for the inspiration and encouragement given me by my editor, Dale L. Walker.

—Richard S. Wheeler

Get caught reading.

Jake Lloyd reading *ENDER'S GAME.*

A Message from the
Association of American Publishers